RECKLESS LOVE

THE SINGLE DAD PLAYBOOK
BOOK 3

WILLOW ASTER

All rights reserved.
No part of this book may be reproduced in any form or by any electronic or mechanical means, including information storage and retrieval systems, without written permission from the author, except for the use of brief quotations in a book review.

Willow Aster
www.willowaster.com

Copyright © 2025 by Willow Aster
ISBN-13: 978-1-964527-03-1

Cover by Emily Wittig Designs
Cover artwork by Kira Sabin
Map by Kess Fennell
Editing by Christine Estevez

NOTE TO READERS

A list of content warnings are on the next page, so skip that page if you'd rather not see them.

CONTENT WARNINGS

The content warnings for *Reckless Love* are sexual content and profanity.

PROLOGUE
THE NIGHT WE MET

RHODES

Then

I HEARD her laugh before I ever saw her. A wild, carefree burst of sound that managed to still be delicate. I turned to find the face to that laugh and when I did, I tried not to gawk. She was beautiful with long, black hair, dark brown eyes, and cherry red lips...dressed in an oversized dress that went all the way down to her ankles.

Somehow she still made that dress look sexy.

I was about to go introduce myself, when a guy walked up to her and handed her a red Solo cup. I frowned when she took it without hesitation, and I moved in closer when she looked disgusted after a sip.

Doesn't she know you don't take a drink from someone without seeing where it came from?

But the next second, I relaxed, laughing to myself when she handed the cup back to the guy and shook her head like it wasn't for her. He downed it in three huge gulps and then burped loudly. A slight flicker of distaste crossed her face before he took her hand and led her through the crowd to dance.

I found myself looking for her throughout the night, but people kept coming up to say hi, and every time I saw her, she was still with that dude. He was getting sloppier by the second, and the later it got, the more she looked like she wanted to escape. A bunch of us were out by the bonfire and the guy sat on the ground next to her chair as she stared into the fire. Next thing I knew, he tried to pull her out of the chair, his voice rising to an obnoxious whine.

"Come on, I'll take you home," he said.

"I'll get another ride," she said.

"Come on, I'm fine, Elle. Let's go."

"No."

I stood up and was there to block his path when he tried to walk away with her.

"Hey, man, can I give you a lift home?" I put my hand on his shoulder and he swayed into me.

He held onto my arm to keep himself standing. "Nah, I got it."

"Well, why don't you stay longer? The party's just getting started. Here, why don't you stretch out on this chair?" I led him to an open lounge chair and helped him sit.

He stretched out his legs and leaned his head back. "Thanks, man. I'll stay a little bit longer."

Within seconds, his eyes closed and his mouth gaped open as he fell asleep.

"You're good," the girl said as we looked down at him. "I've been trying to hide his keys from him for the past half hour, but he was onto me."

"Looks like he'll be out for a while. You okay?"

She turned and looked at me directly for the first time, and damn, I liked her smile.

"Much better now, thank you. I was trying to step out of my comfort zone...go to my first college party, say yes to Logan since he's asked me out every day for two weeks straight...but I have horrible luck with guys. Next time I think I'll just stay in my dorm room." She laughed that tinkley laugh and it made me feel warm all over.

"Aw, now, let's not make rash decisions like that," I said. "Come on, let's turn this around. Why do you have horrible luck with guys?"

"Uh...because they either cheat on me...or put me down...or get drunk and pass out on the first date." She laughed.

"Damn. Guys are assholes, what can I say?" I crinkled my nose. "How about you tell me what would make your first college party experience better? It's my first college party too, by the way." I leaned in conspiratorially. "Did you try the Jell-O shots?"

She laughed again and I wanted to keep them coming.

"So Jell-O shots aren't just a college myth?" she asked.

"Nope. They're very real. Come on. I'll show you. There are even different flavors."

"Well, anything has got to be better than the beer I tried earlier."

I laughed at the face she made. "You don't like beer?"

"Turns out, not at all. I didn't know that until tonight either, but—" She lifted a shoulder.

"You tried it for the first time to have the full college experience," I finished for her.

"Exactly." She grinned. "It's not like I'm new to *everything*...but a lot of things." She made another face, and I couldn't stop smiling.

"I'm Rhodes, by the way." We walked into the house and into the kitchen.

"I'm Elle. Nice to meet you."

"You too."

"Do you know who lives here?" she asked. "Logan told me who was throwing the party, but I forgot the name..."

I paused and gave her a sheepish smile. "I actually live here with a few guys, but Shep is the one throwing the party."

"Wow, it's a really nice place."

A few girls walked up and I could tell what was coming next by the way one girl's mouth parted when she saw me.

"Oh. My. *God*. You're Troy Archer's son, aren't you?" she asked.

"I am," I said, glancing at Elle.

Elle's eyes widened. Fuck. I wanted a little more time to get to know her before she found out who I was. It inevitably made people weird around me.

"And isn't Amara your mother?" the other girl asked. "She's so beautiful. And your dad is *so* hot."

My eyes narrowed when she reached up and touched

my hair. I'd been growing the curls out for a while, but that didn't mean I wanted just anyone touching them.

"I can't get over your eyes. So *unusual*," she said, moving even closer.

I took a step back and her hand dropped from my hair.

In my opinion, my hazel eyes weren't that unusual with a blond-haired, blue-eyed dad who was white, and a black-haired, brown-eyed mom who was Black, but I didn't bother saying that. I looked at Elle and lifted two Jell-O shots.

"Red or blue?" I asked.

"Red, please," she said.

"Excuse us, ladies," I said to the girls.

They still stared at me like I was an exhibit as I motioned for Elle to follow me.

I leaned in toward Elle's ear. "Want to see a fun part of the house?"

"Where is it?"

"The roof."

Her eyes widened and I hedged.

"It's safe, I promise. And it's not the highest part of the roof...it's just outside my bedroom window. We can sit out there and pretend to be gargoyles, checking out the party from up above."

She snorted but looked hesitant for a moment.

"We can tell your friends where you're going in case you're worried about going to the roof with me."

"Maybe if I had any friends." She giggled. "I don't really know anyone but Logan and look how that turned out. I'm not worried about going with you. I'm just not the best with heights. I mean, I probably *should* tell someone where I'm going, but you feel safe."

I lifted my eyebrows. "Not what everyone would think when they see me coming."

She giggled again and it was so fucking cute. "You *are* ginormous. But have you seen your dimples? I could be wrong, but I think I read somewhere that guys with dimples are harmless."

I smirked. She was adorable, and I liked how she seemed exactly the same as she did before she heard about my famous parents. Don't get me wrong, I'd benefited from having a movie star father and a supermodel mother my entire life, growing up in a mansion in LA and going on fancy trips all over the world, never lacking for anything.

Except anonymity.

But people knowing who I am wasn't the worst thing, I guessed.

I just never knew for sure who wanted to get close to me for *me* and not my parents.

I started walking toward my room and she stayed close.

"I hadn't read that about dimples before, but you're safe with me," I said over my shoulder.

When we got to my door, we walked in and I went straight to the window, opening it. I turned, and Elle was looking around my room and then paused near my bookshelves. She rubbed her arms as she shivered.

"Do you need a sweatshirt?"

"Yes, please. I'm from Colorado, so I'm used to colder weather than this, but Palo Alto at night is chilly to me, for some reason."

"I grew up in Southern California, so it's chilly here for me too."

I grabbed one of my Stanford sweatshirts and handed it to her.

She pulled it over her head and beamed up at me. "Much better."

"I don't believe you don't have any friends. You're so nice and smart and cute."

Her cheeks flushed. "I'm pretty sure my roommate thinks I'm the biggest nerd she's ever met, and she's not wrong," she said.

I grinned and climbed out the window, stepping aside to make sure she got out safely.

"Can nerds dance like you do? I don't think so," I told her.

She looked at me in confusion. "You saw me dance?"

"Uh, is it creepy to admit that? Earlier...with Logan. You're good."

"Thanks. I love to dance. *Love* it. That's what got me to this party...I wanted to dance."

"You could be a cheerleader. Stanford's cheer team is pretty great." I motioned for her to sit on the ledge next to me and she did, both of our feet dangling from the roof. The sounds of the party drifted up there, but it was slightly muted. "I guess you've already missed the cutoff for this year. But you should try out in the spring."

She looked at me with an odd expression and my eyebrows lifted.

"What?" I asked.

"I'm actually on the team. I guess I look quite a bit different when I'm off the field."

I grinned. "You don't wear your crop top everywhere you go?"

She laughed and shook her head. "I'm still trying to get used to that." She scrunched up her nose. "Wait...you're on the football team, aren't you?"

"Yep. Sure am."

"Oh, gosh. I totally should have known that."

I chuckled. I hadn't heard anyone say *gosh* in a long time.

"I've been so nervous about doing all the right steps that I'm not paying close enough attention to the game yet," she said. "But I know you're a big deal!"

"I do all right." I shrugged.

I just signed another NIL deal this morning. I was doing more than all right.

She laughed at my cocky grin.

"Tight end's my thing." I tilted my head in a slight bow.

"It totally makes sense, now that I think about it. You're so tall and you have muscles on top of muscles." She smirked when I laughed but didn't seem embarrassed. I liked how she said what she thought. "You're nicer than most jocks I've met. Well, I guess I haven't met that many, but...you're definitely nicer."

"I'm not that nice. It's you bringing it out in me," I admitted.

She let out a derisive sound. "Right. And why would I bring that out in you?"

"You haven't acted any different since finding out who my parents are," I said, ticking off my fingers. "You seem very genuine and down-to-earth."

Her shoulder bumped mine. "That's such a kind thing to say. See? You can't tell me you're not that nice." She sighed contentedly and looked over at me, her eyes crinkling with her smile. "I didn't know I was going to make a friend tonight."

My heart both warmed and cracked a little. I didn't think I'd ever had such an easy conversation with a girl and I'd certainly never been friend-zoned before. But the thought of having her as a friend suddenly seemed like the best possible option. I didn't just want a hookup with this girl and then never see her again, and the thought of starting out our freshmen year of college in some sort of relationship didn't seem smart or realistic.

I bumped her shoulder back. "I've really needed a friend," I told her.

Her face softened and she gave me that smile that felt like it was shining from the inside out. "Me too." Her lips puckered and her eyes narrowed as an idea formed. "We should make a pact."

"Okay," I drew the word out. "What would this pact be?"

"That this will be a legit friendship...we'll talk like this always."

"Okay." I nodded.

She had me intrigued. *Talking like this always* sounded pretty damn nice.

She snapped her fingers and pointed at me. "Oh, and we won't let anything come between us...not other guys or other girls or love. Just pure friendship for the rest of our days." She laughed. "Or at least throughout our four years at Stanford...and we won't even let ourselves get in the way. Friends, no matter what."

I nodded. "I can agree to all that. Should we shake on it?"

"I think we should."

She held out her hand and I took it, shaking it firmly.

"That settles it. Friends forever," I said.

Now, if I could just lose this crush on my newfound best friend.

CHAPTER ONE

OFF-KILTER

RHODES

Now

I LOOK in the rearview mirror and smile at Levi. We're on our way to the coffee shop to meet the guys and Levi is bopping his head to "Training Season" by Dua Lipa. I blame Weston Shaw for getting my son hooked on this...as my fingers tap to the beat on the steering wheel.

"We see Elle?" Levi asks.

And damn. My soon-to-be four-year-old isn't the only one missing Elle. I can't stop thinking about her.

Last night, before I ran off of Clarity Field, my eyes scanned the crowd for Elle Benton, my best friend in all the world. She was still on the sidelines, looking better than any cheerleader had a right to look, and her dark brown eyes burned into mine.

The anger was still there, glaring back, and it's killing me.

I thought there was nothing I hated more than losing.

Okay, there are other things that suck too.

Like it's the worst when Levi is sick. He's a happy little guy and it takes a lot to get him down, but when he's sick, those sad eyes make me want to cry.

Or it's rough when his mother, Carrie, tries to use a new angle of manipulation on me yet again.

When I'm benched with an injury sucks too.

I intensely dislike all those things.

Being on a losing streak after being the first team to ever win three consecutive Super Bowls in a row doesn't help.

It has me feeling more off-kilter than I have in a long time.

Not fucking good. But *especially* not good when everything else is also going wrong.

Henley, another best friend and the most incredible wide receiver I've ever had the honor of playing with, was injured this season and most likely won't be playing again.

We've been practicing so hard trying to make up for Henley being out, there's not even time to get laid.

Well...if we're going for full disclosure here, I was off my game *long* before Henley's accident.

Normally, I'm the chillest guy I know. I like to have fun,

not take anything too seriously, and enjoy life with my son, my guys from the team, and Elle.

But things being weird with Elle...now *that* is more than I can take.

I honestly didn't know we were capable of a fight anymore. We became best friends during our freshmen year of college and that bond has only gotten stronger over the years.

I wish we could talk all night right now, like we did that very first night.

I barely get a spare minute with her these days.

Clara, my favorite barista and owner of Luminary Coffeehouse, holds up my matcha latte when I walk in, and I kiss her cheek.

"And here's a chocolate milk for Mr. Levi Archer!" she says, leaning down to give him his drink in a sippy cup.

"You're the best, Clara. Thank you." I glance down at Levi and tilt my head toward Clara.

"Thank you, Miss Clara," Levi says, leaning in to hug her legs.

I grin at Levi and he takes such a long swig of his chocolate milk, he has to take a gasping breath when he's done.

"Oh, you are so welcome, sweet little man." Clara beams at my little boy.

"Are we the last ones to get here?" I ask.

"I haven't seen Henley yet," she says. She takes another look at me and frowns. "You doing okay? You don't seem yourself this morning."

"When are you guys gonna get it together?" Marv calls across the coffee shop.

Marv and Walter are the two grouchos who are at Luminary whenever the doors are open. They love football and they love complaining about everything we do wrong, even when we're doing everything right.

During a dismal 5-8 season, we're giving them plenty of material.

I wince and look at Clara. "Not my best day, no."

"No trash-talking in my shop," Clara tells Marv, her hand on her hip.

Marv grumbles to Walter but listens to Clara. Everyone loves Clara, even Walter and Marv.

"Hopefully we'll get it together by Sunday," I tell Marv.

I lift my matcha, thanking Clara again, and Levi and I head back to the room where my guys are waiting. My teammates, Bowie, Henley, and I started meeting regularly to talk about dad life, and it sort of grew into hanging out with my best friends and talking about *everything*.

Bowie has a daughter and Henley has three, so we had plenty to cover. Weston and Penn started showing up because they wanted to hang out with us, but then Weston became a dad and Penn started mentoring a kid, so the Single Dad Players now consists of five of us. We write shit in The Single Dad Playbook, and hanging out with these men has become some of my most treasured times, outside of the football field.

There are fist bumps all around. Levi goes around the table, saying hi to everyone, and stops when he gets in front of Caleb, Weston's son. Levi plops down in front of Caleb with his toys and hands him a toy he knows Caleb likes.

"Good job, Levi. I love it when you share." He hasn't always been the best at sharing, so I make sure to praise him a little bit for it.

"What have I missed?" I ask.

"Not much," Bowie says, leaning his elbows on the table.

I'm saying, "We look old this morning," when Henley limps in. He's still recovering from ACL surgery, and he turns and acts like he's going to walk back out of the room when he hears me.

I jump up and tug him in, laughing when he pretends to hit me in the gut.

"If I can't talk about how old I feel, you can't either. And only one of us can be depressed at a time. Last time I checked, that was me," he says.

He's grinning as he says it, but he's right. I wouldn't want to be dealing with what he is for anything.

"I thought you were feeling better," Penn says, eyebrows puckering in concern.

"I am, but it's not a joyfest overnight or anything. And that game last night..." He looks around at us and sits down, stretching his bad leg out to the side.

We all groan.

"I need to drink this tasty beverage before I go there yet," I grumble.

"How are negotiations going for you?" Weston asks.

"Pretty good." I nod. "Sounds like they're trying to get everything I wanted."

"That's awesome, man," Henley says.

"Okay, then let's talk about what's going on with you and Elle and the way she looked at you after the game last night," Bowie says.

"Elle?" Levi echoes, standing up to see if she came into the room. He goes back and sits down when he realizes she's not here.

I give Bowie a pointed glare and he returns it with a contrite one.

"You noticed that, huh?" I say under my breath.

Bowie lifts his shoulder as if to say, *Who didn't?*

"Hard to ignore those daggers," Weston says.

If these guys noticed, who else did?

"You think anyone else noticed?" I look around at each one of them.

"I doubt it," Penn says. "It's just because we know you guys. So what's going on? You were weird at Friendsgiving too...and at the dance recital."

"Are we really saying Friendsgiving when the girls aren't around? It's just so..." I sigh.

"We do Friendsgiving now and we own it," Weston says, laughing.

"I love doing it, it's the *word* that I never thought I'd be saying..."

They all laugh.

Weston elbows me. "Out with it. If it were one of us not talking about our mess by now, you'd be all over us. Spill."

I groan and pick up a napkin, twisting it. "I don't know where to begin, I guess. When she told me she wanted to be a cheerleader for the Mustangs, I was all for it. She loves to dance...she was the best cheerleader on our college team. She has that IT factor that makes everyone want to get another look at her. I mean, you've all seen her. She's *fucking* gorgeous," I whisper the F-word since Levi and Caleb are here. "She belongs out there, and she needed something to boost her confidence. She's spent her whole life trying to fit into the box her parents wanted her to be in...she deserves this time. But she's busier than she's ever been. And you guys know we're skirting the rules even hanging out at all, with the no-fraternization policy between us and the cheerleaders. But it's *me and Elle*. Everyone knows we've been best friends forever."

Thirteen years is a *long* time.

"Can't the rules be bent a little?" Penn asks.

I tilt my head and make a face. "I thought so. But since she got on the team, we've hardly seen each other. We've hung out at Henley's and at each other's houses a couple of times, which is technically prohibited, but come on! It's ridiculous to think that we'd cut off ties with each other just because she's a cheerleader on the team."

I scowl at the floor.

"Elle doesn't think it's so ridiculous," I add. "She's been adamant that we can't be seen together, ever, and she came *this* close to not showing up at Friendsgiving. She'd come over the night before upset, and we drank a little...and..." I pause, still unable to meet them in the eye because again, it's *me and Elle*.

"The anticipation is killing me," Bowie says.

"Same, bro. What happened?" Penn pounds on the table.

I clear my throat. "Well, one thing led to another, and..."

The room is silent. I look up at them and they're staring at me in shock before they all start speaking at once, demanding to know what happened.

"We kissed," I admit, wincing. *And a little more than that*, I think but don't say.

"Why are you making that face? Was it bad? Did it feel wrong?" Henley leans in, disbelief on his face.

"No, not even a little bit. I thought it was all kinds of right...but apparently she didn't, because she's been pissed at me ever since."

CHAPTER TWO

DETERMINED

ELLE

Now

WE FINISH practice and I'm on that high I get after I've danced my heart out, but it's laced with more fatigue than usual. Being a cheerleader is so much harder at thirty-one than it was at eighteen, and the hours I've been keeping haven't been helping.

Our director, Lisa, is in a mood today. She rode us hard during practice and has followed us into the dressing room, which doesn't bode well for me getting out as soon as I'd hoped. I need to shower and meet my girlfriends at Starlight Cafe in an hour and a half, and it takes a while to drive to Silver Hills.

"I want to talk about something. Can we all take a seat?" Lisa calls out.

I can tell by the look on her face that we're not going to enjoy whatever she's about to say.

We drop to the floor and she faces us.

"I just want to reiterate some of the rules we have to uphold when we're part of this organization. I've noticed some of you have not been wearing a full face when you go out, and that's just not acceptable. Brynn, I also want to mention that your tanner is a little too orange-y this week, while I'm thinking about it." She sighs and Brynn nods, her orange-y cheeks darkening in embarrassment.

"I'll work on that," Brynn says.

"And I need to remind everyone that there is a strict no-fraternization policy that we all have to follow. If you go to a restaurant and see a player there, you turn around and walk out. If you're attending the same event and it's not a Colorado Mustangs event that you're both required to attend, you're the one who has to leave." She looks at me and I wait, heart in my throat, for her to call me out, but she doesn't.

I'm pretty sure everyone knows she's talking about me anyway. Several of the girls have asked me about my friendship with Rhodes because they used to see me on his Instagram feed before I became a cheerleader, but I've downplayed how close we are. Everyone has always assumed that we've dated, but we never have.

"It's cause for immediate removal, so it bears repeating. But that goes for all the rules. If you don't respect them, we can always find someone else to fill your spot."

Lisa pulled me aside at Henley's daughters' recital last week and told me all of this there. I hadn't expected to see her that night. She lives in Denver, and the small town of Silver Hills where I live can feel like another planet sometimes, with just enough distance from the city. Turns out, she has a niece who is a dancer at Wiggles & Whimsy and Lisa attends her dance recitals whenever she can.

I told her I'd been friends with several of the Mustangs players for years through Rhodes, my friend since college, and she said it was no excuse, that I needed to follow the rules. I've had good intentions about avoiding seeing Rhodes in public, but I admit, I haven't followed those intentions like I should have. I've seen him in places I knew we could keep it on the down-low, like our houses or our friends' houses...who are also on the team.

But I didn't think I'd be barred from going to Cassidy and Audrey's dance recital. Yes, they're Henley's daughters, and he's our wide receiver, but he's recovering from ACL surgery and isn't even playing right now. His girlfriend Tru has become a really close friend, and she's the girls' dance teacher, so I wanted to be supportive of her too. All loopholes I thought could be worked around, but Lisa only saw them as excuses.

She warned me it couldn't happen again, and her way of calling me out today is just highlighting the fact that I'm on her radar.

As I drive back to Silver Hills, I'm mad and embarrassed...and disappointed.

I hate being in this position. I'm having the time of my life out on the field, the girls I've met from the team are wonderful, and it's filling a void in me that I didn't even know was missing.

But Rhodes' little boy Levi is my godson, the light of my life, and he already looks bigger every time I see him. I don't want to miss a second of him growing up.

Rhodes, on the other hand...it's possible that a break from seeing him is exactly what I need to get my head screwed on straight. I'm still reeling about our kiss—scratch that—our little *make-out* session.

It was...something I need to stop thinking about every minute of every day.

I've gotten a little too good at hiding things...it's shameful really.

And I'm hit with that stark reminder when I walk into Starlight Cafe and see a paperback copy of *It Was Always You* by Zoey Archer sitting on the table with my friends. My hands instantly go clammy and sweat beads form along my forehead even though I'm walking inside from a cold winter wonderland. Sadie spots me first and stands to hug me. Calista's next and then Tru and her mom, Stephanie. I take the empty seat between Stephanie and Calista.

"I'm sorry I'm running a little late. Our practice went over a bit today."

"It's totally fine," Sadie says.

"We've been passing the time by talking about this book!" Tru holds it up. "Mom couldn't stop talking about it after she finished, so I asked her to bring it for me so I can start it today."

Calista shakes her head. "You'd think I would've read it by now, and I *will*, but I've been on a romantasy kick." She picks up the book and waves it. "I cannot keep this book on the shelves!"

Calista has taken over Twinkle Tales from her aunt and

turned the already thriving bookstore into even more of a book lover's sanctuary.

"Have you read it yet?" She looks at me, and I swallow hard, frowning slightly as I look it over.

"I think I've heard about it." I nod.

"You've got to read it," Stephanie says. "The love story is just so poignant. It's funny and angsty and heartwarming..." Stephanie leans in. "And is it ever steamy." We all laugh and I fan my face with my napkin.

"Sold. I'll stop by the shop and get a copy on my way home," Sadie says.

"I'm starving," I say.

It's true. I'm *not* just saying it to change the subject.

But the last thing I need to get into with these girls is my familiarity with *It Was Always You*.

Our favorite waitress, Abi, comes and takes our order, and it's just the diversion we need.

"How was practice today?" Tru asks.

"A little bit humiliating. I'm still paying for coming to that dance recital. Totally worth it though," I add, when Tru's face falls. "I just need to watch myself." I crinkle my nose. "I'll have to stay home or call you guys when I want to go hang out with Levi."

Sadie's head tilts. "Is Rhodes okay with that?"

"I...don't know," I say finally.

"What's going on there? The two of you were very icy at the recital," Tru says.

Calista looks at me and nods, her eyebrows raised high. "Mm-hmm. I've been wanting to ask that very same question."

"Let's just say we crossed some boundaries we put in place way back when we first became friends."

"You had *sex*?" Sadie whisper-shouts.

"*No.*" I look around to see if anyone heard her, and the coast is clear. "But we—"

Our drinks are brought out and when they look at me expectantly after our waitress leaves, I lean in.

"We got a little too close for comfort and it's never happening again."

"What? Why?" Sadie pouts.

"You're so close. I love the thought of you and Rhodes together," Tru says.

"You and me both, honey," Calista adds.

"Why can't...whatever happened...not happen again?" Tru asks.

The food comes then and I think I'm saved from answering, but no. They want all the gritty details.

"We made a pact to never let anyone or anything get in the way of our friendship, including ourselves."

Well, at least *one* of us was determined to stick to the pact the last time I checked.

CHAPTER THREE

MORE THAN LOSING

RHODES

Now

A FEW DAYS later when we get in the car and Levi asks about Elle, I skip the park plan and drive to Elle's house. We worked our asses off at practice this week, but now I have the afternoon off, and I can't leave things hanging with Elle like this for another second.

I park in her driveway and get Levi out of his car seat, carrying him to her front door so he doesn't get tempted to explore. Elle's eyes widen when she opens the door and sees us.

"Elle!" Levi cries.

"Hi!" She yanks me in the door, as she frantically scans outside.

"Did anyone see you?" she asks, shutting the door.

I was hoping I'd exaggerated the weirdness between us in my head, but it's still off as all hell. With me. With Levi, she beams when he holds out his arms for her to take him. Once she's holding him, he lays his head on her shoulder and her eyes close as if she's soaking it in.

When she looks at me, I realize she's still waiting for me to answer.

"No, no one saw me."

"Don't be so sure of yourself. Brock, next door, is watching my every move and he would love nothing more than to pal up to the Mustangs' tight end."

My face curls up in annoyance just hearing her neighbor's name. The dude kept coming over when I was trying to move Elle in and could barely keep his eyeballs in his head for staring at Elle's ass.

I have a hard time tearing my eyes away from her myself. Beyond her gorgeous face, she also has a body that just won't quit. She's always been the most beautiful girl in the world to me.

And I'm not the only one who thinks so. But there's something about the way her neighbor ogles her that makes my blood boil.

"Is he bothering you? Do I need to go over there and make my presence known?"

She rolls her eyes and stalks into the living room. "No. I can handle Brock."

I can read her expression because I know her so damn well. It says: *You're the one who's driving me crazy.*

"I like my job and I want to keep it," she says instead.

"Levi asked about seeing you, and I couldn't resist. He asks about you all the time."

She deflates and her eyes are sorrowful. "That kills me. I got to see him at Sadie's the other day, but it wasn't long enough. He hardly even played with Caleb because he didn't want to leave my side."

Since she became a cheerleader, we've still snuck in ways for her to see Levi, but it's not as often as they're used to seeing each other.

"Lisa's not messing around though. I don't want to be on the cheerleader director's bad side, Rhodes. The other day after practice, she lectured us about fraternization. She's *hot* about me being at that dance recital. Now that I'm on her radar, she's not going to let up about it. We cannot be seen together."

I stare up at the ceiling to gain my composure because I really don't want to be at odds with her.

"I hate this," I say out loud and then cringe.

Normally I can say anything to Elle, but we're on shaky ground right now.

"I don't want things to be weird between us," I add. "That's why I'm here, to make sure we're good. I miss you. I'm worried about you. I'm worried about us. You're my best friend, and I don't like hiding our friendship, but I want to be supportive of you being on the team. You look amazing out there..."

She shoots me a nervous smile, which is not like her

either. We're so off our footing, this tension, the skating around each other.

"Are we ever going to talk about it?" I ask quietly.

She glances away, setting Levi in front of the little basket of toys she keeps for him, and then walks into the kitchen. "Would you like something to drink? Water? Gatorade?"

"Elle." I follow her into the kitchen, and Levi glances at us from across the room before plopping down on the floor to read his book.

He's happy just being able to look across the room at Elle.

So am I.

But the need to fix this between us is overriding everything else.

"Why talk about it?" she says, finally leveling her gaze on mine. "We already said plenty."

"I've regretted the things I said that night...and wish I'd said more. But I don't regret kissing you."

She holds up her hand and shakes her head. "Don't do this," she says quietly. "We made a pact, remember?"

"Maybe it's time we rethink the pact."

CHAPTER FOUR

COLLEGE LIFE

ELLE

Then

"GO, GO, L-E-T-S-G-O!" I did a high kick and tried not to think too much about my parents being out in the crowd, watching me cheer.

I wasn't proud of it, but in high school, I let my parents think I was working for the school newspaper instead of being on the cheer team and taking all the dance classes at the rec center for free. The truth came out when they saw my yearbook senior year, and they were still not over it.

They weren't happy about me doing it in college either, but I hoped they'd let it go. I was far from home and our time together was limited, so I didn't want to spend it arguing with them.

After our win, I ran off of the field and showered quickly. It had been a good game, so I hoped my dad had been a little distracted by that. I didn't have much hope that my mom hadn't been watching my every move.

"Don't you have something a little more...fun to wear than that, Elle?" Delaney eyed my long, baggy flannel dress. "If I didn't see you in your cheer outfit all the time, I'd never know the body you have underneath."

"I'd prefer not to show that side of me all the time," I told her.

She snorted. "Little Miss Innocent only brings it out on the field," she sang.

I rolled my eyes but laughed. I wasn't as innocent as she thought I was, but I wasn't going to bother correcting that. She lifted her eyebrows and looked me over, her nose crinkling slightly. Geez. I knew I needed to update my wardrobe, but I couldn't afford to yet. Even with a good scholarship, it was still pricy to be there. I'd chosen to go to Stanford instead of taking the full ride at Denver U, so my parents were only willing to pay for the remainder of my tuition. I had to pay for everything else on my own.

Worth it.

But not something my fashion-forward roommate could relate to, I didn't think. She only slept in Eberjey pajamas... which was fine by me. If I could afford Eberjey pajamas, maybe I'd splurge on them too because they looked cute and super soft. But that was unlikely for me, and either way, I didn't want to ever be the kind of person who cared so much about the labels I did or didn't wear.

"My parents are here, and they're already not happy about me being on the team," I said. "I'm going out to eat with them and...maybe meeting Rhodes' mom too."

I grabbed my jean jacket and put it on over my dress.

She tilted her head and nodded. "That's a little better," she said. "But no. Here—borrow something of mine. You can't meet your boyfriend's fashion icon mom wearing that!"

"He's *not* my boyfriend," I repeated for the jillionth time.

Ever since Rhodes and I had met at the party, we'd been mostly inseparable...at least when I wasn't hanging out with girls from the team and he wasn't playing or surrounded by girls who couldn't get enough of him. He wanted to hang out even more, and so did I, but it scared me because I didn't want to get too attached to Rhodes Archer.

"Aw, you think I don't see how the two of you look at each other. That's so cute," Delaney teased.

Delaney was a combination of sarcasm and sweetness, and I loved her. I'd been so excited to come to school, ready to spread my wings and be free for a while, but I thought I'd miss having the peace and quiet of having a bedroom to myself. Living with Delaney had been so fun though. Never a dull moment.

"We look at each other like two friends who love hanging out together and don't want the societal constructs of having to be romantic just because we're close to get in the way and destroy us." I glanced in the mirror one more time and paused when I caught Delaney staring at me. "What?"

"I don't know what that nonsense was you just spouted, but call it whatever you want," Delaney said, waving me off. "You like each other."

"Yes, we like each other!" I agreed. "Platonically."

"I think it's great that you're calling it that...but I don't know how you do it. He is the hottest guy I've ever seen."

He was. I'd give her that. Rhodes Archer just got better every time I looked at him.

All the more reason for me to keep things in the friend zone.

Tristan Johnson had taught me the hard way not to trust the pitter-pattering of my heart. I'd thought he was the guy for me since he came into our youth group that first time three years ago. He claimed we were meant to be, and I believed him. So much so that he managed to take my virginity while I had a pretty purity ring on my finger. I hadn't fully agreed with my parents' beliefs about purity culture, which entailed strict rules on dating and dress and abstinence not only from sex but kissing and any other things you might want to fill in the blank with...but I also hadn't expected to cave so easily with Tristan.

Turned out that hormones and excessive words of love had been hard for me to resist.

But lesson learned.

Tristan had gone through multiple purity rings in the youth group by the time I left for school, and I had a less-than-healthy view of guys and dating and sex.

I wouldn't make the same mistake twice.

WHEN I FINALLY REACHED MY parents in the

courtyard outside my building, their relief was evident. My mom visibly relaxed as she looked over my outfit.

"Thank God you're out of that ridiculous costume," she said.

"Good to see you too, Mom," I said, laughing as I hugged her.

She groaned. "I'm happy to see you, but you know I don't approve of you displaying your body like that for the whole world to see."

"I know, but it's so fun to be on the team. And it's not like I dress that way all the time, right?" I hugged my dad and his expression made me tense.

"I don't know what possessed you to do this, but I guess you're going through your wild phase, right? It had to happen sometime?" He frowned and patted my shoulders when we pulled apart. "I guess it's been going on longer than we knew, right?"

"If cheerleading for my school team is a wild phase, then I guess I'm in the thick of it," I said, lifting my shoulders.

I hated any kind of tension with my parents, but I didn't know what else to do. It wasn't like I could hide this from them. I hid plenty of things when I lived at home—how far things got with Tristan being a huge one, all while being thoroughly covered in public, I might add. I thought college could be a time when I didn't have to hide things anymore, but the way they were acting made me wish I had kept the fact that I was a cheerleader to myself.

I heard my name being called and turned to see Rhodes walking toward me with the most beautiful woman I'd ever seen. I recognized his mom, Amara, from commercials and magazine covers, but seeing her in person was even more incredible. She was *staggeringly* beautiful. Her skin was a deeper brown than Rhodes', and her full, shoulder-length corkscrew curls were magnificent. Her cream cashmere sweater with matching pants were elegant and understated, yet on her, it looked like a *Vogue* photo spread.

Rhodes walked up to us and grinned, hugging me quickly before acknowledging my parents. Every time he hugged me or even brushed his finger against mine, I reminded myself of our pact...because touching Rhodes affected me way too much.

I could *feel* my parents practically holding their breath as they watched the whole interaction.

"I'm Rhodes Archer," he said, holding his hand out to my dad and then my mom. "I've been really excited for all of us to meet." He sounded more energetic than his typical laidback tone, and I wondered briefly if he was nervous.

His mom held out her hand to me and smiled. "I'm Amara, Rhodes' mother, and Elle, you are as beautiful as he described you. It's wonderful to meet you." Her South African accent sounded like music, and the things she was saying!—I couldn't believe she was so nice.

"Oh my goodness. I can't believe I'm meeting you. You're even more gorgeous than I imagined," I gushed.

She thanked me quietly and introduced herself to my parents, who thankfully, were back to being their charismatic, friendly selves. Once the introductions were made, there was an awkward lull.

"We talked about going out to eat. Does that still work for everyone?" I asked.

I was completely thrown when my dad said, "Unfortunately, we have to get to the airport."

"What? You can't hang out for a while?"

"Our flight is leaving earlier than I thought," he said. "Next time we'll stay longer. We just wanted to be here for family weekend and get the hugs we've been missing so much."

"You're really leaving right now?" I said, still shocked.

"You know I have to be back tonight to be ready for church in the morning," he said. "I hope you'll be attending your new church tomorrow too?"

"I'm still looking for a place," I told him.

It was true. I knew my parents wouldn't rest until I found a church, but I had yet to find one where I felt comfortable.

"You'll find the right one. Take care of yourself, okay? Stay out of trouble." He held my arms and looked at me firmly.

I nodded. "I will. You know me."

Everyone laughed and said their goodbyes. We watched as they walked away.

"That's too bad," Rhodes' mom said. "But we still get to keep you, right?" She looped her arm through mine.

"Yes, please...if you don't mind me tagging along."

"We're happy to see our boy, but we really came to see you," she said.

My eyes widened. *So this is where Rhodes got his charm*, I thought.

She leaned in and whispered, "We have a little surprise...if we can keep it under wraps. Rhodes' dad really wants to meet you too. Shall we head to the restaurant? He's waiting there."

"Oh my God," I whispered. "I'm meeting Troy Archer tonight too?"

She laughed. "Yes, and he's going to love you," she said.

Rhodes flanked her on the other side, and the next thing I knew, we were climbing into an Escalade and driving to a fancy seafood restaurant in San Francisco. As we walked inside, Rhodes leaned down and whispered in my ear, "You sure you're okay? You're not as chatty as usual."

"Freaking out a little bit over meeting your parents." I leaned back and made a face. "Pretty sure you didn't know this, but...they're famous," I whispered.

He chuckled that low, gruff chuckle that always hit me in the stomach and then worked its magic throughout my body like a chakra overload.

"I had a pretty good idea," he said. "But they're easy to be around, you'll see."

"Sorry my parents couldn't hang out. I had no idea they weren't staying tonight."

"You think they were okay with me?"

The tone of his voice stopped me and I turned to face him. "What do you mean?"

"Not sure they approved of us...being friends."

"I think their weirdness came from seeing me in so little clothing earlier, but...I'm sorry if they acted anything other than wonderful to you." I frowned. "Were they rude? I was so enthralled by your mom, I didn't really hear what was being said."

He laughed. "They were fine. No one was rude."

We turned the corner and were ushered into a private room overlooking the water. Troy Archer stood up and held his arms out, hugging Rhodes and kissing him on each cheek. He was blond with blue eyes, but I still saw so much of Rhodes in him.

Rhodes laughed and glanced at me shyly over his dad's shoulders. "My dad's a hugger," he said in a British accent.

"I most certainly am," Troy said in the same accent. He turned to look at me and I giggled...and did my best to remain in an upright position.

I fanned my face, looking at the three of them. "Whew. Beauty overload is going on right now," I said.

Their eyes widened and then there was a burst of laughter. Troy walked over to me and held his hands out.

"May I?" he asked.

"Yes," I answered, not even sure what he was asking, but the answer was yes.

He kissed each of my cheeks and beamed at me. "Hello, Elle Benton," he said. "No wonder you're Rhodes' best friend. You are beautiful and funny and a breath of fresh air."

"You think so?" I squeaked.

Troy nodded and Rhodes stood next to him, smiling at me fondly.

"Told ya," Rhodes said.

I wasn't sure if he was saying that to me or his dad, but it just further highlighted that I needed to remember the *best friend* part. Because there was no way that someone like Rhodes Archer would ever be interested in me as anything more.

CHAPTER FIVE

IF YOU ONLY KNEW

ELLE

Now

I SHAKE MY HEAD, trying my best to yank myself out of the past. All this talk about pacts is messing with me.

"That's the thing about pacts. You don't go back on them."

Rhodes fights back a smile and levels me with those

eyes. I've been a sucker for those eyes since the night we met.

And the dimples. We can't forget the dimples.

His lips demand attention, the fullness so alluring I have a hard time not staring at them.

His skin is like topaz kissed by the sun, and his eyes, they're the prettiest hazel, constantly changing from a light amber to touches of green. The best part is how they're always smiling at me, even when his lips haven't gotten there yet.

His curls can be unruly at times, and I love it.

His shoulders are so broad, absolutely perfect for the best hugs.

It should be illegal to be as hot as he is.

But I'm not the only woman in the world who feels that way about Rhodes Archer. He was a hot commodity in college, but that's nothing compared to now.

"Elle," he says softly, his raspy voice reminding me of the things he said the night we kissed. His voice oozed sex and made my body feel like I was trying to run underwater. "We can't pretend it didn't happen. You felt something too. I didn't dream that up."

I shiver and smile big at Levi when he walks over and wraps his arms around my legs. "Hey, little man. Do you need a snack?"

He nods, and I pick him up, taking him to my pantry and opening the door wide. The snacks I've always kept for him are on a shelf that he can reach and I set him down, smiling as he hurries toward them.

"You still have his snacks even though we're not supposed to be here right now?" Rhodes asks.

I turn and he's *right there*, so close my chest brushes

against his. He looks amused when I back into the pantry, away from him.

"I keep them in my purse too, just in case I get to see him somewhere. The blessing and curse of living in a small town...I run into you guys everywhere and I'm supposed to be staying far, far away." I sound way too breathless when I'm aiming for nonchalant, and Rhodes doesn't miss a thing.

He leans his arms up on either side of the doorway, looking me over, and my breathing halts. Yes, there have been plenty of times I've fought an attraction for my best friend, but I've managed to keep the boundaries resolutely in place.

Every time you've almost wavered, something or someone has prevented anything from happening, I remind myself. Call it divine intervention or poor luck, I have learned from this and now know better than to mess with what we have.

Because Rhodes is truly the best friend I've ever had, and I cannot lose him.

Our kiss was other-worldly good. I doubt I'll ever have another kiss like it in my life. And the other things we did...I relive them in my head multiple times a day.

Still, I cannot be moved on this.

I love him too much to wreck us.

"You can always come to my place, you know," he says. "It's private. No one will see you but the guards, and I trust them."

"I do need to see Levi more..."

"Not me?"

I groan and roll my eyes, but he knows I'm struggling not to laugh at the fool. "I'm thirty-one, Rhodes. I might not even make the team next year, but I want to try. And the season's almost over..."

"With the way we're playing, the season might be over sooner than later for us anyway. I can hang in there for a while."

"You guys will get your mojo back. I heard Henley is working with the wide receiver—what's his name? Cal? And that he'll be around for more practices too. Maybe that will help the morale of the team to have Henley there."

He nods. "Yeah, I think it will. We were all shaken up pretty badly to lose him and now we're just shaken up, period, from all this losing."

"I'm sorry I'm not there for you right now like you need me to be." I point past him and he moves out of the way as Levi and I leave the pantry.

Rhodes wraps his hand around my arm before I'm out of range and I slowly exhale, as his thumb rubs softly over my skin.

"I'm the one who's sorry. I haven't been as supportive of you as I should've been. I love that you made the team." He smiles and his head dips a little closer. "I just don't like not seeing you, but I'll try not to be so selfish."

"Maybe it's for the best that we're not together so much right now." I lift my shoulder and he frowns.

"That's never gonna be for the best," he says.

He lets my arm go and slides his hand over the back of his neck. I loved his curls back in the day, and he still has them, but now his hair is shorter on the sides. This look sharpens his features and somehow makes his eyes and full lips stand out even more.

Levi finishes his snack and takes off down the hall. I panic, hoping he won't go into my office. They haven't been here since I set everything up, and I thought with us trying to maintain distance, they wouldn't be over here until the season was over...and I could hide everything by then.

"I really have to...cut this visit short, I'm afraid," I tell Rhodes.

He looks hurt, but he nods and starts after Levi.

"I can get him!" I rush past him and Levi thinks we're playing a game.

He starts running and I chase him back into the living room. I swing him up in my arms when I catch him and kiss his neck until he's cackling.

"Don't you grow before I see you again, okay?" I say, kissing Levi's face.

"I gwow, I gwow," he cries, cracking up.

"Okay, you grow and grow and then you can carry me around," I tell him.

He frowns and shakes his head. "No, you cawwy *me* awound," he says.

I smile happily and kiss his forehead. "Okay, it's a deal. I'll carry you around as long as possible and I'll love you forever."

"I love you like booty loves cake!" Levi says.

I lose it at that and so does Rhodes.

"Still on the booty, I see." I set Levi down, still laughing.

"The boy knows what he likes and it *is* a stellar word...booty."

Levi laughs now, just hearing the word. He's been on a booty kick for a while now. He just loves the word and works it into random conversations.

"The other day I walked by and he was just singing, "Booty, booty, booty," softly as he played," Rhodes says, chuckling. He swings him up into his arms. "Tell Elle bye-bye."

Levi's face curls up and he starts to cry. My own eyes fill almost every time he cries. I can't stand to see this little guy cry. Ever.

"I'll see you soon, okay?" I lean in and kiss his face and when I back up, I meet Rhodes' eyes. "Yeah, I can't go without seeing him. We just have to be really careful, okay? I'll come to you."

"I'll do whatever you say," he says. "And if we have to wait to see you, we will. Levi will be okay."

"I don't want to miss out on him and whatever new phrases he starts coming up with," I say.

I glance out the window and don't see anyone out there, but I'm regretting cutting our time short. I miss them already.

"You let us know," Rhodes says. "And it's not like we can't FaceTime."

I smile. "Yeah, I'd like that."

He leans against the door. "You're my plus one for Bree and Alex's wedding this weekend. What are we gonna do about that?"

I make a face. "Can you take someone else?"

"*Really?*"

I groan. "How about I call Bree and ask her if she thinks anyone would leak that we're there together...or I could try to get permission to go. I'd feel better about that. I'll talk to Lisa tomorrow and see what she says."

His jaw clenches, but he nods. "Okay. Keep me posted."

When he leaves, I sag against the door and feel the sad quietness in the room without Rhodes and Levi.

I feel like the biggest fraud there is.

I've kept secrets for a long time and it feels like they're starting to catch up with me.

Sometimes I can't believe that I'm cheering again. I've loved being part of the Colorado Mustang Cheerleaders this season, but at thirty-one, all the restrictions can be hard to take.

In a lot of ways, it's like putting on a familiar sweater.

My dad is the pastor of Silver Hills Community Church and the list of rules I grew up with as a PK—pastor's kid—are similar to the rules I have to follow as a cheerleader for a pro team.

No gum in church/no gum in public.
Modest attire/respect the dress code even when off-duty.
Always look your best/Look impeccable at all times.
No tattoos/Conceal any tattoos you may have.
No swearing/No swearing.

I know how to toe the line.

But if everyone knew the latest secret I'm keeping, I'm sure I'd get fired from my job, and my parents would be mortified. My friends would probably get the biggest kick out of it and be so proud of me for doing something like this, because it's so out of character for me.

I feel like the biggest hypocrite.

I've always done things my parents wouldn't approve of and excused not telling them because I'm an adult and I don't want to disappoint them. But for the past ten months, I've been leading a double life, and I'm exhausted from it.

I walk back to the office I was hoping Levi and Rhodes wouldn't see, where books line the walls, mostly of one title: *It Was Always You.*

The book that *I* wrote.

Once I've signed into my computer, I pull up the dashboard to see how much my book has earned today. I can't stop the grin that takes over my face when I see the crazy amount that's in there.

You're doing it, Elle.

I still can't *believe* this is happening to me. I squeal as I check the rankings on Amazon and see that my book is still in the top 100.

I've worked at a chiropractic office for years, and I still do occasionally. Once I knew I'd made the team, I cut down on my hours at Estevez Chiropractic Care. I'll probably need to give this job up soon with the way the book has taken off and how busy I am with the team, but I love the people. In the past, I loved how busy it was, and I needed an excuse for how I was able to afford this condo, because no one would believe that I could afford it on a cheerleader's salary. We make so little compared to the time we put into it.

No one has any idea that I've been writing for a long time, and after I decided on a pen name—Zoey Archer...I know, I know...just another reason for me to be ashamed of myself, using Rhodes' last name—I started to seriously consider putting it out there. I've always thought the name Archer sounded so distinguished, and it was my way of giving my bestie a little secret shout-out. I had no idea anything would ever come of any of this, but wow, has it ever.

I finally had the nerve to put my book up for sale online ten months ago, and it...*exploded*. I did a few anonymous TikToks like I'd seen on Booktok, and while mine didn't go viral, several booktokers who saw it posted about my book when they read it, and *theirs* went viral. Within days, my book sales skyrocketed. Foreign and domestic publishers have messaged me about acquiring rights and I recently sold the audio rights. I should be getting the final files back any day. I can't wait to tap into a new audience who loves audiobooks.

I've also acquired an agent, Rosie, and it's a whole different experience with her on board as my second book gets ready to drop. I have a PR team and the whole works.

It's been the most amazing thing I've ever experienced. I

get emails all the time from readers who love my book, and I'm still pinching myself. I can't believe they're reading my words!

The success of my book is what gave me the courage to go ahead and try out for the team. I'd wanted to for so long, but I didn't want to upset my parents by wearing the skimpy outfits and dancing provocatively in front of millions of people. They don't love it and haven't made any secret of that.

But I would *die* if my parents ever found out about my book.

They would be mortified that their daughter is writing romance...and not clean romance either. My sex scenes have been so spicy, the chili peppers reviewers give to specify steam levels keep growing.

I had to get the steam out somewhere...my ex-boyfriend Bernard sure wasn't enough of an outlet.

Writing about Ryder and Eliza going from friends to lovers helped me school my lusty thoughts into a healthy... and profitable...outlet.

Because that's the secret that I'm most terrified of exposing...

I'm in love with my best friend.

And I have been for a long, long time.

CHAPTER SIX

ROLE REVERSAL

RHODES

Now

> ELLE
> I can go to the wedding, but I'm supposed to stay away from you and the rest of the guys.

I WANT to say *fuck that*, but I don't.

I type:

> You do what you've gotta do.

Delete. Delete. Delete.
Then:

> Okay.

Nope. Delete.
Finally:

> Bree will be glad you're there.

I press send and walk into the locker room after practice and a long workout afterward. I needed to work some of this tension out.

The guys are there waiting for me, looking a bit thunderous.

It's quiet for a second when I walk in.

"Can I just say, if the roles were reversed, you would be giving us so much shit right now." Bowie leans across the table to grab my shoulder and points at me when I meet his eyes.

"What are you talking about?" I mutter.

"Thank you for saying it!" Penn says, throwing his hand in the air. "I've wanted to say it at least a dozen times, but he'll listen to you more than he'll listen to me."

I frown. "Are you guys talking *to* me or about me?"

I turn around to see if anyone is behind me, and nope, it's just the five of us. We at least had the kids with us the other day to help with distraction.

"You seriously left with Levi as soon as you threw out

that revelation the other day about kissing Elle feeling all kinds of right and then ghosted us. We've barely talked outside of the game!" Bowie's normally low, growly voice rises to a level that surprises all of us, and I sit up straighter as he sags back into his bench.

"He's not wrong," Weston says, scowling at me.

"Since when do you ghost us?" Henley adds and I shoot him a guilty look. "I don't think you've *ever* ghosted me."

"You doing okay, man?" I ask him quietly. "I'm sorry I've just been keeping my head down, trying to focus on the game and forgetting about...all that with Elle." I look around the room. "We played well last night." I point at Henley. "You being on the sidelines is not the same as you playing with us, but it's the next best thing."

"Don't try to distract me with your sweet talk," Henley mutters, but his lips quirk up. "You guys did play well last night. I think you're turning the season around, but let's get back to Elle."

"I told her maybe we should rethink the pact," I say, scratching the back of my neck.

"What pact?" Penn asks.

"The one we made in college where we agreed to only ever be friends." I pause for a moment, knowing they'll have something to say about that, and do they ever.

All at once.

What kind of shit is that?

Whose idea was that kind of pact anyway?

That was thirteen years ago!

You've seriously been upholding a pact you made way back then?

What did she say?

And then they all look at me like they're waiting for an

answer. How am I supposed to know where to start after all that?

"She said the pact has never done us wrong and we're not gonna start messing with it now." My jaw clenches as I remember staring at her mouth after she said it, wondering if a kiss from me would change her mind.

"And you agreed with that?" Bowie says, shaking his head like I'm crazy.

The attention turns on him for a second because none of us have seen him this fired up about anything before, not even about a faulty ruling on a play.

"Yes, I agreed to that," I finally say.

And I'm met with four sets of defiant eyeballs.

I pinch the bridge of my nose and take a deep breath.

"Look, I know I talk shit and I push and I'm nosy as all fuck with you guys." I exhale loudly. "I stir it up and am always shoving everyone out of their comfort zones, but this is different." When Weston starts to talk, I lift my hand and shake my head. "*This is different.* I can't dwell on this about Elle. I've gotta let it go for my sanity and you have to let it go too. We are just friends, we will only ever be friends, and that's the end of it."

"But why?" Bowie growls.

I point at Weston. "When I pushed you to entertain the thoughts you were having about Sadie, I knew your friendship was new and you were both being so careful over Caleb. You wouldn't do anything too risky to jeopardize that." I point at Henley. "And pursuing the first woman I'd ever seen you light up over? It was a no-brainer...but the stakes were also not as high. You'd just met her." My eyes drop down at the table before meeting Bowie's eyes. "Elle is my person, my family...my everything. I can't throw away thirteen years to scratch a what-if itch..."

And the way she's treating me now...it hurts. Despite how right it felt to touch her, the way she immediately distanced herself is everything I feared most.

"You're in love with her," Bowie's voice rasps, and it sounds like it's hurting him to say it almost as much as it's hurting me to hear it.

"Yes."

The room is hushed as my answer takes flight and hits each of my friends in the gut. They stare back at me sorrowfully, and I swallow the lump that suddenly feels lodged in my throat.

"Hey, listen, I'll be okay." I reach out and pick up The Single Dad Playbook that we write in almost every meeting. "I've carried these feelings around for a long time. I'll get through this. It's just a little...snag."

"What, the snag is you kissed and realized she feels the same way? How does that not change everything?" Henley asks.

I drop the notebook on the bench and lean back. "It changes *nothing*. She still doesn't want me."

"You need to read something in there," Henley says, sliding the book closer to me. "I saw it earlier and I think it's fitting."

I sigh and open it, going to the last entry.

*When I realized I'd missed out
on Caleb's first couple of months,
I didn't think I could ever get past it.
I can't get that time back.
How do I reclaim what I lost?
But that's one of the most
incredible things about kids...*

they just want you to be present
when you ARE around.
I shifted my thinking,
and instead of dwelling on what I'd missed out on,
I put all my energy into
making that day the best Caleb and I had ever had.
It's actually transformed
the way I think about life now.
All that schooling,
and no one told me I'd learn the most
when I became a father.
~Weston

"DON'T WASTE time thinking about what you've missed or what you think you know about how she feels. Talk to her. Tell her you want a future with her," Henley says.

I nod. I want to do that, but I'm just not sure I can. I tap on the bench and stand up.

"I'm gonna head out, okay? I'll be back to normal the next time we see each other, don't worry." I point at each one of them. "We had a great win again and we've got Bree's wedding coming up. I'm getting my head back in the game... which means I can't turn this Elle shit over in my head anymore." I point at my head like it's a revolving carousel.

"We're here for you, man," Weston says. "Whatever you need."

I open the door and look back at them. "I know you are, and it means so much. Seriously, I don't know what I'd do without you guys."

I walk away before I can look at their desolate faces any longer. You'd think I just delivered them the worst blow, not something that I've been living with since the night I met Elle Benton.

When I'm done working out, there's a message from Carrie saying we need to talk, and I brace myself before calling her back.

"Hey, what's up?" I say when she answers.

"Hello to you too," she snarks.

"Hello, Carrie. How's it going?"

"Well, Levi has had the best day. I think he finally crossed over to liking chicken."

He likes chicken all the time at my house, but I don't bother correcting her.

"The little man likes to eat," I say.

"He's a little pickier than I'd like, but we're getting there. Um, Rhodes, I need a favor..."

"Yeah? What's up?"

"I need you to take Levi a little earlier than we talked about."

"How much earlier?"

"Tomorrow."

"Carrie, you know I've got the wedding this weekend. I can't take Levi until Sunday morning. What happened to wanting him at your family's this weekend?"

"Something has come up."

"What's come up?"

"I need to go out of town," she says.

I stare at the ceiling and count to five. I don't have the energy to deal with Carrie's shit right now. She loves Levi, but what she loves even more than that is trying to keep a constant drama train in motion.

"I'll call my parents and see if they can come. If they can't, you need to figure something out, Carrie."

"I shouldn't be penalized for going out of town one time when you travel *all the time*."

"No one is penalizing you. We share custody over our

son and part of that agreement is that when it's my time to have him, I take care of him and his arrangements. When it's your time to have him, you're supposed to do the same."

"Can you talk for even two seconds without the condescension?" she snaps.

I pick up a stress ball and squeeze it so hard it bursts and little gooey balls spill out onto the floor. The towel I used to wipe my sweat doesn't do a very good job of cleaning it up.

"I said I'd call my parents. I don't know if I can find more help than that this late, so I suggest you look for backup too, if you're determined to go on this little getaway."

"Fuck off, Rhodes. I know your parents have a jillion employees that are thrilled to do whatever they ask."

My parents don't have a jillion employees, but I also don't bother correcting her about this.

"Well, let me *fuck off* this call and find out who can help then." My insides are yelling, but I sound surprisingly calm.

"Was that so hard?" Carrie has the audacity to laugh.

I squeeze my fists and take a deep breath before hanging up on her. I'll blame poor reception if I have to.

After a quick shower, I FaceTime my mom. She picks up, her smile lighting up the screen.

"There's my boy." Her smile falters. "Hey, what's going on, my sunshine?"

"Hi, Mama. It's good to see your face." I try to smile, but my mom just frowns more. "Carrie's just coming in at the last minute, wanting to change the schedule."

"What else is new?" She shakes her head. "I don't know if she will ever grow up."

"I hate to ask this, but...I'm supposed to be going to Bree and Alex's wedding and it was Carrie's weekend, but she has an opportunity to travel...somewhere. Is there any way you could come? You can totally say no, but I told Carrie I would ask."

"We would love to spend a few days with Levi!" she says excitedly.

"Really? You could get here tomorrow and deal with him mostly without me?"

She waves me off. "I know how to handle little boys, you know. Besides, he is an angel."

I laugh. "Yeah, someone is a Gigi through and through."

She tried to get Levi to call her Ouma, like she called her favorite grandma or Gogo after her other grandma, but Levi gave it his own twist, and she's been Gigi ever since. Now even my dad calls her Gigi more than Amara.

"I'm the best Gigi that ever lived and don't you forget it."

"You are. You really are. Are you sure about this? I can pick him up from Carrie's tomorrow and then meet you at the airport."

"No, don't worry about picking us up. We'll try to get in early enough to see you before you have to go and just meet you at the house. It'll be good. I'm excited to see him. *And* you." Her eyebrow lifts. "Why do you look like you're still worrying?"

My mouth parts and I force it closed, shaking my head. "It's...nothing. Thank you for your help, Mama. I appreciate you."

She levels her gaze on me. "Talk to me, my sunshine. You have not been yourself for a while now. Why is that?"

I groan and make a face. "Why you gotta be so perceptive, *Gigi?*"

She giggles and I swear, my mom looks younger than me sometimes.

"You better tell Gigi what's happening before I get there or I'll be all up in your business!"

"Either way I look at it, you're in my business. Do I have that right?"

She giggles again. "Yes, my sunshine. You have that right."

"Things are weird with Elle and it's...messing with me."

"Oh no. What do you mean, weird?"

"Well, for one thing, she was supposed to go with me to the wedding and because of being on the cheer team, she's allowed to go, but she can't be near me or the guys."

"That is the craziest thing I have ever heard," she says emphatically. "You are Rhodes Archer. You do not pay attention to such craziness."

I laugh. "Said as only my mama could."

She shifts her curls back and gives me a regal smile. "Anyone who wants to question this can speak to Amara about it."

I snort. "Okay, got it. I'll send the cheerleader director your way."

She nods slightly, as if to say, *Bring it*.

"And what else is going on with Elle?" she asks.

"What else?"

"You said, for one thing...so what else is there?"

There's no way I can tell my mom that something happened between us. I regret telling the guys and they don't have even a tenth of the grit and determination that my mother has.

So when her eyes light up and she points at me, my hand teeters to hold the phone upright and not hang up right then.

"Rhodes!" she sings. "What happened between you and Elle?"

Aw, hell.

"Nothin', Mama. *Nothing*."

"Oh, this little trip to see you could not be timelier. Daddy and I will be there as soon as we can tomorrow, and you better get ready to spill because I can see that you are *nigh unto bursting*."

"I have no idea what that means," I say.

"Mm-hmm," she chirps. "Love you, my sunshine. I'll see you and that little angel tomorrow!"

Fucking hell.

CHAPTER SEVEN

CHANGE OF PLANS

ELLE

Now

MY PHONE RINGS as I'm finishing up my makeup for the wedding. I glance at it and see that it's Amara. I answer, already smiling.

"Amara, hey! How are you?"

"What is this I hear about you not seeing my boys?" she says.

I laugh and cringe at the same time. "I know it's crazy. I hate it. It's the silly rules of the cheer team. And we haven't done a very good job of following the protocol, to be honest...but I'm trying to do better."

"Well, I don't know if you have heard, but I am in town. And I will not tolerate not seeing you while I'm here." She giggles and I do too.

"Oh, Gigi. You know I cannot resist you."

"I should hope not. So, how about you come over to Rhodes' place and let me see you in your beautiful wedding attire? A hug from me cannot possibly be off-limits."

"Right now?"

"*Right now.*"

"I would love that," I say, not hesitating. "I'll be right over."

I've *never* been able to resist Amara Archer.

When I pull up to the gate, I wave at Rhodes' security guys and they let me through. I gave Rhodes such a hard time when he moved into this place because it looks more like a ski resort than a home. He has good taste though, and between the two of us, we've decorated it so it feels homey. His house is one of my favorite places to be.

Snow coats the tall trees surrounding his house, and I admire the way the sun glints off all of the windows at this time of day. The sun is just starting its descent, and Rhodes has the best view I've ever seen.

Movement to the right of the walkway catches my eye, and I stop and park before going any farther. Rhodes is in his tux, jogging over to Levi, who is...I squint as I step out of the car. Is he—?

"Levi! Get back in the house!"

"I'm watewing the twee, Daddy!"

"The trees need *water*, son, not urine," Rhodes groans.

"What is you-in?" Levi asks.

I can't hold in my laugh any longer and it reverberates around the trees. Rhodes and Levi turn and stare at me in surprise. And then Levi's running toward me as fast as he can, not bothering to cover anything up, and just as he's about to wrap his arms around my legs, Rhodes hauls him up into his arms.

"Look at how beautiful our Elle is," Rhodes says, his husky voice doing dangerous things to me.

My heart does a stutter-step and splats across the driveway, right at his feet.

"So boo-tiful," Levi sings.

"You need to put your Johnson in your pants and go wash your hands before you hug her," Rhodes says in Levi's ear.

Levi wiggles, trying to get out of Rhodes' arms.

"I go wash," he says. He looks at me and says it louder. "I go wash so I can hug."

I laugh. "Okay, little man. I'm all about that hug."

Rhodes sets him down and Levi takes off toward the front door. When he gets there, he looks back. "You coming, Elle?"

"Right behind you," I call.

I move past Rhodes, and I can feel his gaze on me like a match being set off in a forest. I am quickly burning up. I turn and look at him over my shoulder and catch his eyes on my ass. His expression is pained when he finally meets my eyes.

It's like we upset the balance of our world the night we kissed, and now everything we know, everything we are, is crumbling and trying to find a new place to land.

It should not quicken my pulse to see his attraction. It should only terrify me.

"This is a nice surprise," he says. "Did you change your mind about going with me?"

My mouth drops. "Your mom didn't tell you I was stopping by?"

His eyebrows quirk and when he shakes his head, I sigh.

"I just came over to hug your parents really quick."

The door flings open and Amara and Troy stand there, looking like the incredible power couple that they are. Their arms open wide, but Levi doesn't wait around for me to reach them before he rushes over. He wraps his arms around my legs and grins up at me.

"I washed my hands," he says happily.

"God, I love you," I tell him. "You're the best hugger ever."

"Bettah than booty!" he cries.

"Better than booty," I agree, laughing.

"Are you gonna let Gigi hug Elle too?" Amara asks, beaming at me as she puts her hand on my back and air kisses each cheek.

"Gigi and Pop Pop hug Elle too," Levi says. "And Daddy. Evewybody hug Elle!" He runs around all of us, clapping when we hug and zipping around to hug me again when we walk inside.

"He is *pumped* that you're here," Rhodes says, chuckling.

"And so am I," Amara says. She holds my arm out and purses her lips as she looks me over. "My goodness, you are a vision. That dress is perfection on you."

"I've never been to a wedding where they asked the guests to wear certain colors. We had a choice between black and red." My hands slide down the silky material of my dress and when I glance up, Rhodes is tracking the movement.

"You look so striking in red," Amara says.

"Absolutely beautiful," Troy adds, hugging me. "It's wonderful to see you. We've been missing you."

"I've been missing all of you too," I tell him.

Levi runs over and holds up a big red flower. "I picked foh you," he says.

"Such a charmer," Troy says proudly.

"Just like his Pop Pop," Rhodes says, winking at me.

Again with the stomach catapulting to the ground.

"Here, let's make sure we don't get water on Elle's pretty dress." Rhodes carefully dries the stem and I spot the vase where Levi swiped the gorgeous red flower.

Once it's dry, I take the flower and lean down to kiss Levi's cheek. "Thank you, my love."

Levi beams up at me. "You stay and play?"

I shake my head sadly. "I just came by for hugs. I'm on my way to a wedding like your dad."

"Tell me you're not listening to anyone trying to tell you to stay away from my boys," Amara says, looping her arm through mine.

"Mom." Rhodes frowns.

Amara smiles at him and then me, shaking her head. "You are adults, and Elle is family. It's as simple as that."

I pat her hand. "I didn't think they'd be so strict, but they really are." I make a face and she puts her hand on my cheek.

"Well, thank you for breaking the rules to see me," she says. "But I can tell you have not been breaking them very much because there are no Christmas decorations here!"

I laugh and nod, looking around. "I know. It's weird. Rhodes and I usually decorate right after Thanksgiving and that didn't happen this year." My eyes meet Rhodes' and guilt twinges in my chest when I see the hurt there.

"Why don't you come over tomorrow and we can make a party out of it," Amara says.

"Maybe she doesn't want to decorate my place anymore, Mom," Rhodes says. "She's not living at home anymore, you know. She's got her own condo to decorate now."

"You don't have to do a thing," Amara says. "But come on over anyway, it will be fun."

"I *love* decorating with you for Christmas," I tell Rhodes. "Everything has just been—"

"I know," he says softly. "I could leave and hang out with the guys if you'd be more comfortable. Levi would love it if you were here."

I bite the inside of my cheek. "Maybe. I hate to make you leave your house…"

"I don't mind." He clears his throat and glances at his watch. "We should probably head out."

I nod and hug everyone again. "How long are you in town?"

"Just a few days," Amara says.

"Okay, I'll come over tomorrow…"

"Wonderful." She squeezes my hand. "And have such a good time at the wedding. You're going together, aren't you?"

"*Mom.*" Rhodes gives me an apologetic look.

"Well, I'm sorry, but why waste gasoline when you're going to the same place?"

Troy chuckles and pulls Amara's back against his chest. "She has a point there."

"We're out of here," Rhodes says. "Be good for Gigi and Pop Pop," he tells Levi.

"I be good," Levi calls, his little hand in mine.

I give Levi one more huge hug, and Rhodes and I walk to the door. I wave to his parents and Levi.

"You know, Bree assured me that no one would be sharing any photos of the wedding anywhere," Rhodes says quietly. "No one wants to risk you losing your job, but we all want you there with us."

He opens the door and the blast of cold hits me. I'd been so hot getting ready, I didn't bother with my coat on the way over. He puts his arm around me and we walk outside.

"She told me the same thing. I suppose it wouldn't hurt to ride with you," I say.

His face lights up. "Yeah?"

"Yeah. Your mom is right. Why waste gasoline?"

"Gigi's always right."

The mood is lighter than it's been between us in a while as we drive to the venue. Brec is a wedding coordinator, so I have no doubt tonight will be special. Seeing Amara gave me a dose of boldness that feels really good, and I'd be lying if I said I hadn't missed being with Rhodes like this. We don't even have to be doing anything for me to be happy.

"God, I've missed you," I say before I can stop myself.

"I've missed you too."

The sun is dipping lower in the sky, but I can still make out his dimples perfectly. We drive down the long path toward Moonbeam Winery and the lights are shining like a beacon once we reach the main building.

"So pretty," I whisper.

"What do I have to do to get you to save every dance for me?" he asks.

It's quiet when he turns off the ignition, and I turn and stare at him.

"I'm not sure that's—"

"Benton..." he tsks. "You called it yourself back in the

day." He holds up his finger the way he does when he's about to quote me. "'Dancing is our safe zone.'" His grin grows, and I roll my eyes when he continues to quote me. "'When we dance, it's a creative outlet only, so anything goes.'"

I press my lips together and try not to burst out laughing. Yeah, what kind of sadistic eighteen-year-old was I to make up that rule when I just wanted to dance with Rhodes Archer more than I wanted my next breath? It came in handy to have an outlet for all the sexual tension I felt for my best friend, and it also warded off plenty of unwanted attention to dance with Rhodes without worrying about any repercussions.

"I guess I could save you a dance or two," I say.

"Admit it, once we start moving together, you're mine for the night," he says.

My face flames hot enough to match my dress, and I'm glad the sun finally chooses that moment to dip completely.

THE WEDDING CEREMONY IS BEAUTIFUL. I've been to lots of events at Moonbeam Winery over the years, but it has never looked like this. Bree has worked her magic on this place. There are flocked trees with white lights and lit greenery inside and out, a pampas grass-lined arch, and decadent flower arrangements on the chairs at the end of every row.

My heart pounds as Bree and Alex exchange their vows. Sitting next to Rhodes after missing him so much is making me wish for things I shouldn't. His thigh rests slightly against mine, and I breathe a sigh of relief when we make it through the wedding and head to the reception. The arrangements are even more elaborate when we move to the dining hall and find our table.

"I'm really glad you changed your mind and came with me," Rhodes says softly.

He's still being careful with me and I hate it.

"I'm sorry. I realize I'm not making this easy by flip-flopping all over the place. I demand that we be careful and then I show up at your house..."

His chuckle skitters over my bare arm and I lean into his warmth.

"You think I don't know Mama Archer is a force to be reckoned with? I should've gotten her on the job sooner," he teases.

I roll my eyes and laugh.

"Over here, guys," Penn calls. He's at a table with Bowie, Weston, and Sadie.

"No dates tonight?" Rhodes asks Penn and Bowie.

"Nope," Bowie says.

"No date," Penn says, shaking his head. "I thought about letting loose a little bit with it being a bye week. But we're finally on a winning streak again and I don't want to mess it up. I'm not drinking tonight, not staying out too late, resting up..."

"Look at you, being such a grown-up," Weston says. "I'm impressed."

Penn shrugs. "Coach would ream me out tomorrow if I showed up at the meeting looking dusty. He seems to have a radar for when I've had too much fun."

"You better dance with us though," Sadie says. "All of you." She looks at me and grins. "I was so worried you weren't coming."

"Bree reached out specifically to let me know that I didn't have to worry about any guests causing trouble about my job or any photos getting leaked. She's been doing damage control behind the scenes. And after I okayed it with Lisa, I felt even better about things." I glance at Rhodes. "Although she specifically said I needed to keep my distance from all of you." I make a face. "But let's not talk about that tonight."

Sadie reaches out and squeezes my hand, leaning in to whisper, "Let's just forget there's even a Lisa tonight."

"Consider it done," I say, laughing.

Rhodes is quieter than usual. I can tell the guys are even uncertain of how to pull him out of it. After we've eaten and the band starts playing, Rhodes goes to get drinks for us, and Bowie and Penn follow.

"You guys should go dance. You don't have many chances like this without Caleb," I tell Sadie and Weston.

"Are you gonna come too?" Sadie asks.

"Yes...after I have a drink. Go." I grin, nudging her.

I watch as they stand up and then turn to see the guys talking by the bar. Rhodes' eyes meet mine and go from looking at me with appreciation to scowling. I jump when a hand touches my arm and turn to see my ex, Bernard.

Can I not have one night out without drama?

CHAPTER EIGHT

SAFE ZONE

RHODES

Then

I CRAWLED into bed and pulled the covers to my chin. I needed to spend my Sunday catching up on homework, and I would, but first, a nap. I closed my eyes, thinking of the way Elle looked in her tank and shorts when I left her dorm room last night. I couldn't stop sneaking looks at her body and she couldn't stop talking about Alfie, the guy who kept flirting with her in one of her classes. She didn't actually talk about him all that much...it just stood out and made me feel weird. Sometimes I wondered if she talked about guys just to see my reaction. She pointed out cute girls all the time and asked what I thought of them and I tried to change the subject every time because it felt disloyal to her.

I was still trying so hard to keep it straight in my mind that we were just friends. College pact and all that.

Sometimes the lines blurred. There were times when it seemed she was trying to prove to both of us that we were just friends, and times when I saw the way her eyes lingered on me longer than usual too.

My phone woke me up a while later, vibrating under the covers next to me. I picked it up and tried to focus, but the room was dark and quiet and my eyes were still blurry from sleeping for...geez, I'd been out of it for a few hours.

> ELLE
> Meet me at The Big Kahuna in twenty?

I grinned at my phone and hopped out of bed, stumbling to the bathroom. Groaning, I snapped a picture of my bedhead and fingered through my waves, touching up the out-of-control areas with a product from my mom's line. When I was happy with the results, I texted my mom really quick.

> Hey, Mama. I'm gonna need more of this new product you gave me to try. Game-changer. I looked like shit and now I look like your son. :)

> MAMA
> Let me see that sweet face.

I smirked and sent her the bedhead picture and then took one of the new and improved look.

> **MAMA**
> Lord, have mercy. This product works miracles! I'll send you more right away.

I chuckled to myself and then knowing her so well, I waited only a second before the second text came through and laughed harder.

> **MAMA**
> You know I think you're perfect no matter what, baby. But that second shot sure is prettier. ;) You doing anything fun tonight?

> Just hanging with Elle.

> **MAMA**
> Sounds like that's your favorite thing to do these days. You got any updates for me?

> Still just friends, Mama. That's how we like it.

> **MAMA**
> If you say it enough times, you'll start to believe it, right?

I stared at that text a little too long. As usual, I was shaken up that my mom could always see right through me. I hadn't admitted anything to her, but she just knew.

Still, I wasn't ready to admit anything now either.

> JUST FRIENDS.

> **MAMA**
> Whatever you say, my sunshine. Love you.

> Love you too, Mama.

I scrolled to my thread with Elle. What if I pushed a little bit...just to see if maybe I wasn't the only one feeling something?

> I'll see you there, Benton. I wouldn't complain if you're wearing those shorts you wore last night.

She didn't miss a beat.

> **ELLE**
> Have you felt how cold it is out there today? I don't think so!

I smirked. Purposely missing my point or not? It was hard to tell with her.

The noise was jarring when I walked inside The Big Kahuna. I scanned the tables, nodding to a few people who said hi across the bar. This had become one of our favorite places to grab pizza and, depending on the noise level, study or play a game of darts...or just hang in the booth in the back and talk for hours.

When I got to our booth, Elle was there already and her face lit up when she saw me.

The thought hit me hard and certain: *I'm going to tell her how I feel.*

If there was any chance she felt the same way about me, I didn't want to waste another moment. I didn't need to do the whole sow wild oats shit just because I was young. Some people found their person when they were young.

"Hey," she said, leaning forward. "I ordered our favorite, Hawaiian with jalapeños."

I bumped her fist and made a big deal of checking out her legs under the table and acting disappointed when I saw them covered in leggings.

She laughed and lifted her shoulder. "It's chilly out there!"

"You cheer in this weather...what's the difference?"

Her full lips puckered as she frowned. "Yeah, when I'm constantly moving it's not so bad. Are you trying to attack my clothing choices too? I'm showing too much skin for my parents, too covered up for you and Delaney..."

"You look great no matter what you wear," I said, meaning it. "But last night's outfit was my favorite."

She giggled. "Okay, noted."

Our pitcher of root beer came and I filled our mugs to the top.

"I have something to tell you," she said, clanking her glass to mine.

"Oh yeah?" I allowed myself to look at her the way I wanted for once and she faltered for a second, pressing her lips together.

"Do I have something on my face?" She frowned.

"What? No." I laughed. "You look as beautiful as ever."

It wasn't unusual for me to tell her she was beautiful and I knew she thought I was attractive too. Maybe a little too attractive if anything.

She flushed a little and grinned. "You're looking at me funny tonight."

I lifted my eyebrows, smiling at her until she sighed and gave her head a little shake.

"*Anyway*..." She cleared her throat and set her mug

down. "Alfie asked me out!" Her voice rose at the end, giddy.

I sat up and ran my hand over the back of my neck. Did I just hear her right?

"He's cute and safe and...he feels like a good way to put Tristan out of my mind for good."

"Tristan?" I echoed. "You're still...hung up on Tristan?"

"Yeah, I've been out with other guys, but I haven't *been* with anyone since Tristan, and I need to get back on that horse." She laughed and jumped when our waitress set the pizza in front of us.

"And Alfie's the guy you want?" I asked, feeling the steam from the pizza as I leaned in.

"We've talked about this, how we want to have fun in college and not get stuck in anything that would hold us back, right? You've said that as much as I have."

I regretted ever saying those words right now. "But why Alfie?"

She leaned close enough to whisper across the booth. "Honestly? Because I don't see forever with him. *At all.* And that's exactly what I need right now. You know? I had sex with Tristan thinking we were getting *married*..." She shook her head and looked down at the pizza like she'd forgotten it was there. "It feels so twisted now. The whole thing. I'm not saying I want to have sex with *everyone* I go out with," she said under her breath. "But I don't know...I'm trying to figure things out still about what I believe about all of it, and...Alfie seems like a nice, safe bet."

"Elle, I—" I took a deep breath. "I'm not going to try to talk you out of getting over Tristan. You know how I feel about that bastard. But going out with someone because they're not who you want to be with forever doesn't feel like the right move either. Just...don't make any rash decisions without thinking it through, okay? I...I care about you so much and I want you to be okay. You don't have to figure it all out right now. Yes, you should go out, have fun, dance all you want to..."

"I do have fun when we go dancing," she said, raising her eyebrows.

So far the only time I'd gotten my hands on Elle was when we danced. There had been a couple of parties that we'd gone to, and inevitably, we'd end up dancing together for hours. For someone who had been sheltered for most of her life, the girl could dance better than anyone I'd ever danced with, and the best part was that she'd claimed that dancing was our "safe zone."

I was pretty sure she'd felt how hard she made me when she ground against me on our last dance night, but she didn't call me out on it, and I didn't want to say anything that made her stop rubbing that sweet ass against me.

"Except I've already said yes to going out with Alfie," she said, doing a little dance in her seat, "and I think you should say yes to Maren. That girl is *dying* to go out with you, and she's really nice."

I rolled my eyes. "I'm not into Maren, Elle."

"Yeah, but you agreed that she's pretty."

"Lots of girls are pretty. That doesn't mean I'm into them."

"What happened to you being footloose during your freshmen year?"

"Maybe that's not the most important thing to me anymore," I said.

I looked at her and willed myself to go there...to say the next thing that could change everything. It could get me what I wanted and she'd consider being with me. Or it would send her running in the opposite direction. Our eyes didn't break as we stared at each other. I didn't take another breath until she spoke again.

"I just think my heart is still too fragile for anything serious," she said softly. "You know that, right? That's why you're my best friend. You know me better than anyone, Rhodes."

I leaned back in my seat and broke eye contact with her, studying something across the room without really seeing it at all.

Did she know what I'd been about to confess?

It was late that night, long after we'd hugged each other goodbye, that I realized neither one of us ever touched that pizza.

CHAPTER NINE

I SEE YOU

RHODES

Now

IT'S like an endless cycle with me and Elle, one that she has no idea she's on...where I'm about to lay out my feelings for her and I get cockblocked. In college it was Alfie and a few other guys...and for the past few years, it's been Bernard.

When I see him put his hand on Elle's arm at Bree's reception, I don't do the same thing I've always done.

I get my ass over there and put my arm around Elle's shoulder. I can hear her quick intake of breath and the way she stiffens at first, but then she leans into me and it feels so good, so right.

Her red dress hugs her curves like a glove. She looks like a goddess tonight. When her skin and hair brush against my hand, they feel like silk.

Bernard clears his throat and I reluctantly pull my gaze from Elle's. For a second, I'd forgotten Bernard was here. He stares at me with his bulgy eyes, his nose and lip already curling in distaste at the sight of me. He looks between the two of us like he's about to be sick.

I see you, motherfucker. I see right fucking through you.

"You couldn't wait five seconds to get your hands on her, could you?" he says between his teeth.

"Regardless of what you've always believed, Elle is not an object." My voice is level and calm, but inside I'm raging.

He's a fucking narcissist dressed up in a nice suit, who says all the right things to her parents, while treating Elle like shit. The night she broke up with him was one of the happiest nights of my life.

I'm surprised when Elle's hand splays across my chest. My hand skims down her back and lands on her waist and she leans deeper into me. We feel like a force staring down Bernard and this is the only way I ever want to face the man again.

"Bernard! I'm surprised to see you here."

Another surprise is how calm and friendly Elle sounds to Bernard...while her hand moves over mine, her thumb caressing my skin.

"I came as Marissa's plus one." He points toward his

cousin across the winery, his eyes never leaving us. "So, what...the two of you are together now?"

My mouth parts, but before I can say anything, Elle does.

"Yes, we are," she says.

Holy hell.

My insides go on a dancing spree, leaping all over the place, before realizing, *Oh right, this is to throw off Bernard. This is not real. Hard-on, abort. Heart elation, dial down.*

But I can't help but go with it in the moment.

I tilt Elle's chin up and press my lips to hers, and even though it's only a few seconds long and I don't go in deep like I'm dying to, fucking butterflies burst out of my chest, and I swear I can hear violins swelling to a huge crescendo even after our lips part. She stares up at me in shock, and I grin at her and then back at Bernard.

The way Bernard looks like he's been hit in the gut is really fucking satisfying. He smooths back his blond hair and loosens his tie before taking a step closer to Elle.

"You really want to do this, Elle? You know he's going to get tired of you and move on to the next bed like he always does."

I reach out to grip his shoulder and Elle puts her hand over mine, pinning me with her gaze.

"Don't make a scene," she says, her eyes pleading with me.

I shoot her what I hope is a reassuring look, but when I face Bernard again, it's through gritted teeth, my hand still on his shoulder.

"I'm not going to even honor your statement with a response. I don't give a fuck the way you talk about me, but the way you're putting down this woman that I love while doing so? I'm not okay with that at all." I squeeze his shoulder again before letting go. "She doesn't want us to make a scene, so we won't." I look at Elle. "Are you ready for that dance?"

She nods, and when I smile at her, she smiles back, giving my heart another race around the block. We move to the dance floor and her hands loop around my neck, while mine tug her waist close to me. We don't say anything for a minute, our bodies moving in time with the music.

If all Elle and I ever did was dance together, the world would be a perfect place. I don't know how, but being near Elle makes my heart rate skyrocket to the heavens, and yet it also calms my entire nervous system. I don't know how it's possible, but it's always been true.

"I'm sorry about that back there," she finally says, looking up at me.

"You don't ever need to apologize to me for Bernard's behavior."

She bites the inside of her cheek and flushes. "No, I meant what I said about us being together. I don't know why I did that. I wasn't thinking. I'm just so tired of him acting like he stands a chance of getting me back."

I knew what she was doing with Bernard, but it still stings. I want her to say she's mine so bad I can taste it.

"Oh, that didn't bother me at all," I tell her.

She snorts and pulls back, laughing harder when her eyes meet mine. "Yeah, I could tell. Of course you have to go all in and kiss me. Always so dramatic."

I start laughing too and then I smooth her hair back and whisper in her ear. "You didn't think I'd miss an opportunity like that, did you?"

She shivers in my arms and I pull her tighter against me.

"You've just been waiting to give Bernard a piece of

your mind, haven't you?" She smiles up at me and damn, she's so beautiful it hurts.

"You have no idea. But that kiss had very little to do with Bernard."

She tugs her teeth over her bottom lip, trying not to smile when I say that.

"Rhodes," she whispers. "You can't say things like that."

"Right," I say. "Except we're together now, so…"

I would not be Rhodes Archer if I did not tease Elle Benton at every opportunity. I know that little show wasn't for me and am under no delusion that we're suddenly a couple.

No matter how much I wish it was the truth.

She groans. "Forget that even happened. I did the whole foot-in-my-mouth thing with my ex…thank you for filling in as my boyfriend…"

I don't like where her words are going, so when the next song is that sexy throwback, "Let's Get It On" by Marvin Gaye, I let our bodies do the talking. I want so much more than her body, but when her ass sways against my dick, I make the most of the situation. My hand slides down her side and grips her hip as I grind into her before flipping her around to face me. She doesn't look at me, but there's not even a breath of space between us as our bodies move in perfect time.

The next song feels even better, "Leave the Door Open" by Silk Sonic. Elle looks so fucking sexy as she gets lost in the music. She always has. I used to think I had something to do with the look of euphoria in her eyes when we danced together, but it's just her. She comes alive with the music, her body knows exactly what to do, and every ounce of restraint that she typically carries comes undone when she dances.

It's why I'm so glad she's finally doing something for herself. I don't get to watch her out on the field the way I want to, but I know it's her happy place.

It helps get my head back in order. I can chill and wait until she's done with the Mustangs before I try to pursue her. I have no idea if I can change her mind about us being together, but I'm not done trying.

God knows I've waited this long, and she's worth the wait.

My phone has blown up when I crawl into bed after midnight.

> **PENN**
>
> I didn't need a date tonight. I got mine when I watched Rhodes and Elle dance together tonight.
>
> **HENLEY**
>
> No shit. I got mine with my actual girlfriend, but I'm not gonna lie, their little show stoked the flames.
>
> **WESTON**
>
> Sadie was climbing me before we'd even gotten all the way inside the house.
>
> **BOWIE**
>
> I swiped right.
>
> **PENN**
>
> No fucking way, Bowie. Good for you, man!
>
> **BOWIE**
>
> Kidding. But I thought about it, and that's saying something.

HENLEY

I wouldn't blame you, Bowie. The pheromones were hoppin' tonight. Speaking of...Rhodes, you sure are quiet.

WESTON

Maybe he's moved beyond the foreplay and getting his.

I laugh despite my pent-up frustration.

Glad to be of service. 😉

BOWIE

He speaks!

PENN

Tell us you got yours, Rhodes.

I wish.

Fuck, do I ever wish.

CHAPTER TEN

SLIPPERY SLOPE

ELLE

Now

I GROAN when the phone rings and fumble around the covers for it. My eyes squint to read the screen. It's my mother and it's not even eight yet. I stayed up way too late last night, amped up from the wedding and…Rhodes.

I've missed dancing with him and we more than made up for it last night. We danced until the very end. And I was so wired from it that I wrote three thousand words of the hottest sex scene I've ever written before I went to bed.

The phone in my hand buzzes again. I sigh and answer it.

"Hey, Mom."

"Oh, did I wake you up? Sorry."

She doesn't sound one bit sorry.

"It's okay. I didn't sleep much last night. I had that wedding..."

"Yes, I heard. That's why I'm calling. Bernard called us last night so upset. He had a lot to say about seeing you and Rhodes together, looking quite the couple. Sweetheart, how is this gonna work? You're friends, leave it at that. We've all seen how Rhodes goes through one woman after the other, not even bothering to date them. How's that gonna look with your dad being the pastor and you dating this playboy who's all over TV and social media with a different woman hanging on him all the time? Not to mention his ex being in the picture, the mother of his *child*. Levi is precious, you know how much I love that little boy, but he is not yours and neither is Rhodes. He's not the man for you. You're..."

"Mom, I'm gonna stop you right there," I say, sitting up and *waking* up *real* fast.

She goes on like I haven't said anything. "You're thirty-one years old and dancing half-naked every week, and now you're dating Rhodes Archer? What's next? It's a slippery slope and you are not heading down the right path. I'm worried about you. I know you're not praying about this."

If we're talking about prayer, I think there are more important things to pray about than my dancing, or what I wear, or whether I date Rhodes, but that's just me. If she only knew the slippery slope I've already careened down as Zoey Archer. I can't even think about how my parents would react knowing I'm a romance author.

The cheerleading has been devastating enough for them.

"And you think Bernard is the right path?" My words sound brittle, but it's still not as sassy as I want to be saying it.

"He's in love with you and he has been for years. He's at church every Sunday and has served on the church board for a long time now. We *trust* Bernard. Can you say the same about Rhodes?"

"I trust Rhodes with my life. And Mom...Bernard is not exactly Mr. Innocent."

My mom scoffs into the phone. "Between the two men, I'd say their reputations speak for themselves."

She has no idea. I've never badmouthed Bernard to my parents. They love him and he's needed them in his life too, not having the best relationship with his parents. I haven't wanted to deprive them from that relationship just because I don't want to be with Bernard. But this just isn't right.

I blink back tears, frustrated that Rhodes has never gotten a fair chance with them, while Bernard still manages to be a saint in their eyes.

"Anyway," my mom sounds brisk again, "are you still coming over for dinner tonight?"

This is one of the few free nights I've had in a while, but I wish I hadn't agreed to dinner now. I love them so much, but I don't want a rerun of this conversation. And then I remember Amara and Troy.

"Oh, Mom, I'm so sorry. I totally spaced and told Amara

I'd go over there and decorate with them. They're not in town long. Can I have a rain check? I could do Thursday night, but then my schedule is gonna be crazy for a while. I miss you guys and need a quiet dinner at home soon."

"Are you sure you're not trying to get out of tonight because you don't want to talk about Bernard anymore?"

"Well, yes, I would also like to table the Bernard discussion, but that's not why I'm bailing tonight."

"For now," she says, laughing. "I've said my piece."

If only she'd leave it at that, but we'll be revisiting it later, no question. Louisa Benton doesn't just drop a topic.

I can't believe I've created this mess about Rhodes. I'll tell my parents on Thursday that it's fizzled out, and we'll leave it at that.

I get up and clean my condo and then run to the grocery store. The day after tomorrow, I'll be back to my crazy schedule with work and practice and writing, so the day off has been nice. When I get home from the store, I write for as long as I can until it's time to go to Rhodes' house.

My phone buzzes on my way to the car. I check it, expecting it to be Rhodes, but he's been quiet all day. I did sort of fly out of his SUV when we pulled into his driveway last night. I didn't trust myself not to do something insane like climb his body and never let go.

I really shouldn't be going to his house. For all the reasons. And the cheer team is honestly at the bottom of that list at the moment.

> TRU
>
> Oh my God, why have I not read this book sooner?

SADIE

> I know. I'm OBSESSED. I stayed up until three this morning finishing it and the ending is so satisfying.

CALISTA

> Sigh. I read it in one sitting. I wish I could be experiencing Ryder and Eliza for the first time. The joy it brings me to know you are is just as good though! 🎉

Since I can't stay quiet forever, I finally chime in.

> Guess I better get on the bandwagon and read this book!

CALISTA

> Girl, get after it! We need to discuss!

TRU

> I'm dying for you to read it, Elle. You know who it reminds me of? You and Rhodes! Especially after seeing you guys on the dance floor last night, which was OH SO HOT. I don't want to give any spoilers, but dancing is kind of their thing too, and it is steamy AF. Henley is loving that I'm reading all this steam and needing an outlet. 😉

SADIE

> It's so crazy you said that because I've gotten Rhodes and Elle vibes reading this too! The way they're each other's ride or die like you guys are. Please tell me after last night, the two of you have fully made up again because it's too traumatic when you're upset with each other.

My face flames, and I pause outside my car door,

fanning my face. Never in a million years did I think my friends would be reading my book. I thought I'd be lucky if ten strangers found it and enjoyed it, and now I'm having group chats with my best friends who see the similarities between me and Rhodes.

I am so screwed.

> I think we're getting there.

I decide to leave it at that.

CALISTA

> Damn. I was hoping you'd tell us you spent the night together. The way the two of you dance is clearly a sign that you would be FIRE in the sheets.

TRU

> Calista's not wrong.

SADIE

> I'm just glad she said it because we are ALL thinking it. 😂

> Not happening, you guys! We're FRIENDS. And we've always danced together like that. It doesn't mean we need to sleep together.

CALISTA

> But what if you did? Sleep together, I mean. Don't you think you'll always wonder what it would be like with him?

There's never been a time I haven't wondered. Yes, I

will always wonder! But the heartache I would feel if it didn't work out...I can't fathom it. We just can't go there.

I keep all of that to myself, even though I'm dying to say all of it.

> We decided in college that we would never cross that line. And when we crossed it even a little bit, it turned everything upside down.

SADIE

> Did it REALLY turn everything upside down though?

These girls with their questions.

> We fought for the first time! It's been weird between us ever since.

CALISTA

> But hasn't that mostly been you trying to shut things down?

Damn Calista for knowing me so well.

> Hopping in the car. Catch up later. XO

And then my dad calls. When I don't answer, he leaves a message, and I listen to it on the way to Rhodes' house.

"Hi, sweetheart." Heavy sigh. "I've been with Bernard this afternoon and he's crushed. And I have to say...I'm... confused about your decision to date Rhodes. You've been so adamant all these years that you'd never date Rhodes. Why now? I'm really concerned. And Bernard is too. Call me. I love you, sweetheart. I want to make sure you've given this a lot of thought."

My hands are shaking as I pause and chat with Rhodes' guard, one that I don't recognize. He waves me through after calling Rhodes, and I sit in my car for a second, trying to calm down.

I know my parents are controlling, but why did I imagine that one day I'd be considered old enough to know my own damn mind?

CHAPTER ELEVEN

IT'S A PARTY

RHODES

Now

"WHAT TIME IS ELLE COMING?" my mom asks as she walks into the room. "Soon, I hope," she adds. "You've got one more tub to bring in before she gets here."

Large, red containers have taken over my house. Levi is sitting in the only one I've emptied and I feel a twang of guilt that I haven't decorated before now. I've been so upset about where things stood with Elle and me, I almost didn't decorate for Christmas.

"Did the two of you talk about a time?" I ask.

She gives me an exasperated look. "No, I hoped the two of you would take care of those details. What do I have to do? Force you guys to communicate? What's going on, honey? Why were things so weird with the two of you last night? And don't tell me it's the cheerleading business. That isn't adding up, because I barely had to do anything to convince her to go with you last night."

"It is adding up. Thank you, by the way, for talking her into going with me last night." I grin at her and she rolls her eyes but smirks, looking pleased with herself.

"Text her and see what time she's coming over," she says.

"I'm trying to respect her wishes. She doesn't want to get in trouble and I don't want to make her lose her job."

"Don't you think if you talked to the head of that cheerleading team and told her Elle is your child's godmother, and she's been your best friend for years, that she'd get over herself and not make a big deal about this?"

"We've already tried that. Well, Elle has tried that, and it hasn't worked. I'm lucky Elle went with me to the wedding…I'll be surprised if she comes back."

The way she bolted when I pulled into the driveway last night. I'd barely parked and she was already to her car. It made me question every bit of progress I'd thought we'd been making all night.

"I'm not going to push it. I, uh…I pushed things with her before Thanksgiving and things still aren't quite back to normal."

"What happened before Thanksgiving?"

"Nothing." I look up at the ceiling. "Let it rest, Mama. We'll be lucky if we see her tonight."

My phone rings and it's my guard, Mitch.

"Hey, man," I say.

"Elle Benton is here."

Mitch is a recent hire and further proof that things haven't been normal around here. The other guards know to let her through.

"You can always let Elle through the gate," I tell him. "She's on the list."

"Got it," he says.

The doorbell rings a couple minutes later and Levi runs next to me to help open the door. When we open it, Elle looks tense. I open it wider.

"Come in. What's going on? Why do you look so stressed?" I ask.

She hugs Levi and he runs off to grab one of the Christmas decorations to show her.

"Bernard told my parents that you and I are dating and now they're—" She flings her arm out and shakes her head. "I can't believe I did that last night. Rhodes, what was I thinking?"

I want to say, *You were realizing I'm the only man for you*, but of course, I don't.

Instead I say, "You were thinking you wanted that jerk off your back."

She sighs, "Yes, I was."

"You're just too nice. Why did he blab that we're dating to your parents? It's something that should have come from you."

"It's not even true," she says, her hand going on her hip.

She looks hot as hell in her soft cream sweater and

skintight black jeans. I want to bury my face in the whisper of cleavage I see and stay there all night.

"Did I hear right?" My mom squeals. "You told your parents you guys are dating?" She claps her hands together in excitement. "Where has this news been all my life?"

"Settle down, Mama."

"No, no," Elle says. "It's not true. We're not. And I should've just said that to my parents." She plops down on my couch and puts her head in her hands. "I have totally screwed everything up, and next, Lisa will be calling to tell me I'm fired just because I don't want to deal with Bernard."

My mom's nose scrunches up when she looks at me. She has never liked Bernard.

"Well, good riddance to Bernard," Mama says. "I have been dying for the two of you to get together...for at least a lifetime. Why didn't you tell me last night?"

I guess she's just choosing to ignore what Elle just said?

"We're not dating, Mom," I say.

"Well, why not? Anyone can see that you should."

Elle starts laughing through her hands. "Because we would be a disaster if we dated," she says.

Levi runs over and puts an elf up to Elle's face. She drops her hands and makes the elf do a little dance, while I stare at her, probably looking a little green. Levi laughs and runs to look for the other elf.

I need to know where she's going with this because I don't think we'd be a disaster at all. I think we've been fine-tuning this relationship for years and she's just taking forever to catch up to it.

"Define disaster," I say.

"Well, you've never been in a relationship." She looks at me like that's my answer.

"So I'm the disaster, is that what you're saying?" I say it

in a teasing tone, but part of me wonders if she really believes that's true.

"No, I know you're not a disaster," she says softly. "You're the best guy I know, but if we didn't work, it would be so messy."

"The best relationships are," my mom says.

My dad comes up behind her and pulls her back against his chest while he nuzzles her neck. "The best relationships are what?"

"Messy," she reiterates, smiling up at him.

"Mm-hmm." He kisses her while I pretend to gag.

I think Elle swoons a little bit as she stares at them. She clears her throat and when I take another look, I realize there are tears on her cheeks.

"Hey," I say, walking over and sitting next to her on the couch. "What can I do? What would help you right now?"

"Can we just forget about everyone else and decorate for Christmas? I've missed you guys so much and I need us to just be *us*, Rhodes and Elle, best friends until the end of time, the way we've always been. I don't want to think about the Mustangs or my parents or Bernard right now."

I put my arm around her and tug her into my side. Her hand lands on my chest and slides up my neck as she leans into me and takes a shuddering breath.

"I've got you, Elle baby," I tell her.

When she sniffles, I pull back enough to look at her and wipe her tears away. "You're nicer than most jocks I've met," she says, rolling her eyes when another tear drips down.

I repeat what I said to her the night we met, when she said the same thing. "I'm not that nice. It's you bringing it out in me."

She smiles and takes a deep breath, sitting up straight.

Levi runs up with the next best thing to an elf, the Christmas giraffe that Elle gave him last year. When he sees her face, he freezes and leans into her.

"Elle cwy?" he asks.

She puts her hand on his cheek. "Not anymore. I'm so excited to be here. Are we ready to put your tree up?"

He nods tentatively, like he still isn't sure if she's okay, and she hugs him.

"I'm okay. I just had to get a little cry out, like that time you were sad when we couldn't go to Pet Galaxy."

"You want to go to Pet Galaxy?" he asks.

We all laugh.

"Not tonight, but that does sound fun," she says.

"I made a batch of my South African eggnog just for you, Elle," my mom says.

That perks her up.

"That's exactly what I need," she cries. "I've been craving that since last Christmas." She looks at me and points. "Just don't let me have a second cup, no matter what."

I chuckle and nod when her gaze intensifies. "Okay, I won't. But you can be hard to reason with when you've had Mama's eggnog."

"It's the amarula," Mama says proudly. "I like it heavy on the amarula."

"We know." I laugh. "Your eggnog is dangerous."

SEVERAL HOURS LATER, my house has transformed, and so has Elle. Any sign of sadness is gone and she's animated as she slides around the hardwood floor in her socks with Levi. We've all worked hard and the house is so much cozier with all the holiday spirit. The clock in the living room chimes and Elle turns to face me a little too fast. I reach out to ensure she doesn't run into the tree. She's only had one glass of my mom's eggnog, but it was a large glass and this batch was extra strong.

"I had no idea it was so late. Oh my goodness. I need to get home." She slaps her hand over her mouth. "I cannot drive. What—" She laughs when Levi runs into her and puts his arms around her legs. "You're up so late!"

"It's a party," I say. "And I can't deprive him of seeing you."

Her lower lip pokes out and wobbles. "I love him so much."

"I know you do, love. He loves you too. Don't you, Levi?" I bend down and pick Levi up as he's nodding. "Give Elle kisses and then Gigi said she'd read you a bedtime story," I tell him.

He leans over and kisses Elle, a loud smack on the lips, and then she kisses all over his face, making him crack up.

"Night-night, little man. Sweet dreams. Love you."

"Luh you," he says back.

I hand him to my mom and give Levi a kiss too. "Love you, son."

"Luh you, Daddy."

Never fails to make my heart melt when he says those words.

When my mom takes Levi up to his room, I look at Elle. "I texted my guards earlier. I'll drive you home and Bobby will follow in my SUV."

"Thank you. I should've thought of that before I had Gigi's eggnog. I'm gonna be feeling it at practice tomorrow."

I make a face. "Yeah, I bet you will."

"IGNORE the mess in my car. I've been going like crazy. My car is overdue for a cleaning, as you can tell," she says, putting a pile of papers in the backseat.

"I haven't been around enough to do my job." I give her a cocky grin.

I've been taking care of her car for a long time now.

"No one takes care of me like you. I've missed that," she admits, laughing.

"I see now what you miss me for—" I start the car.

All of a sudden, a low, sexy voice comes over the airwaves.

"Yes. Fu-u-uuuck. Fuck me harder, Eliza. That's right, baby. You feel so good, so right. I love the way you're clenching my cock right now. Take. Every. Inch. Of. Me."

"Good *God*, what is this?" I stare at Elle and then crack up as she fumbles with her phone and drops it, yelping as she tries to find it.

"That's it. You're so fucking tight. I feel your pus—"

While she clambers around with her phone, trying to turn it down, I nudge her hand away.

"Don't turn it down. I want to hear what happens!"

"No, Rhodes. Stop." She laughs. She's fanning her face and I have no doubt that if it weren't dark out, her face would be flaming bright red. She clutches her chest like she can't breathe.

"What do you *listen* to when you're driving? *Elle Benton*." I'm still laughing and batting her hand off of mine as I turn up the volume in the car.

"Ryder, I'm so close. You feel so good, too good," plays extra loud.

"Can you take the shortcut?" Elle tries to shout over the erotic words and sounds of heavy breathing.

"Harder, harder..."

"Only if we can listen to this all the way...my little dirty bird."

"Well, I've got to get some satisfaction somewhere," she says lightly, her voice shaking slightly.

I shoot her a look, unable to stop laughing.

"How did I not know this is your kink? I knew you liked to read, but...do you like to *hear* sex scenes in that sexy man voice? *'Fuck me harder, Eliza,'*" I mimic the narrator, and when she presses her legs together, I nearly lose my shit. "Fuck *me*. Don't you dare try to turn that off again. She's so close. I need to know if she gets there. I need to see if *you* get there."

She rolls her eyes. "You're ridiculous," she says, fanning her face.

"Am I though?" When I laugh, it's low and I don't miss the way she shivers.

Ryder and Eliza take it on home as I pull into her driveway. Holy fuck, the way he rides her is hot as hell and Eliza is one happy woman when the job is done. I'm so into the story that I miss it when Elle reaches over and turns off the ignition. The silence is shocking and Elle jumps out of the car, waving over her shoulder.

"Thanks for the ride. Night!"

Holy. Hell.

My dick was all about that little sexy time story. I get in the SUV and Bobby has the decency not to give me a hard time about my situation. It's a long ride home before I can take care of it in my shower, thinking about Elle the whole time I do.

CHAPTER TWELVE

SUCH A GUY

ELLE

Then

I GOT to the party late and looked all over for Alfie. He'd been planning this party with his friends and when I told him I wasn't able to come because of a dinner with Rhodes and his parents, he got so mad at me. Alfie and Rhodes tolerated each other, but lately, Alfie had been more annoyed than usual about any time I spent with Rhodes. I tried to reassure him that he didn't need to worry about anything, but he thought Rhodes was into me no matter how hard I tried to tell him otherwise.

My dinner with the Archers ended up getting moved back to tomorrow night. Troy's flight back from London was delayed, so he'd just flown into LA tonight and wouldn't be in Palo Alto until even later.

The house was packed. As I wandered through the crowd, I said hi to a few people from my lit class. When I saw some of Alfie's friends, I asked if they'd seen him.

"I didn't think you were coming," Jesse said.

"Yeah, I wasn't, but it worked out at the last minute."

He smirked and nodded and I kept walking.

Eventually, I wandered down the back hall to find the bathroom. There was a short line outside the bathroom door and I waited, smoothing down my outfit.

Rhodes had stopped by my dorm to let me know his parents weren't going to make it and whistled when he saw me.

"Damn, girl. What have you got on?" he'd asked, swiping his hand down his jaw.

I must have flushed a million colors because then he'd laughed at how pink my cheeks were.

"You look *good*," he said. "I love this dress."

"Thanks. I've been trying to branch out," I told him.

I glanced down at the little black dress that made me feel both classy and sexy before shyly meeting his eyes.

"Well, it is *working*," he said, grinning as he looked me over again. "Let me take you out to dinner anyway. You can't let this dress go to waste."

I was about to say yes and then paused. "You know what? I should probably go to that party Alfie was throwing with his friends. He was pretty upset that I was missing it."

"Oh." He nodded. "Okay. You sure?" He lifted his hand. "Steak dinner?" And then the other hand. "Or college party?"

I laughed. "Yeah, there's no comparison, but I don't like how Alfie and I left things last night. I've been a pretty sucky girlfriend lately."

"You could never be a sucky girlfriend," Rhodes argued. "He needs to lighten up."

I knew it wouldn't lead to anything good if we started talking about Alfie, so I shrugged my shoulder and Rhodes nodded.

"Okay, got it. Have fun," he said.

When he walked away, I felt like I'd upset him too.

A girl in front of me moved up and it drew me out of my thoughts. When it was my turn, I took care of business fast, washed my hands, and hurried out. I veered to the left instead of the right to avoid the growing line and the door across the hall opened. Alfie and a blonde girl stumbled out of the room, his hands on her waist. She leaned up and kissed him while I stood there in shock, watching. When they stopped, Alfie turned and saw me standing there and I finally snapped out of it and started moving. I heard him calling after me but didn't stop, and even after I went outside, he called after me, telling me to stop.

Instead of driving to my dorm, I drove to Rhodes' house, and the whole time I thought, *I just caught my boyfriend kissing someone else and I'm not even very upset. What is wrong with me?*

I just needed to see Rhodes. He would make everything better. He always did.

Because you belong with him. That little voice inside

my head had gotten pretty persistent with those thoughts lately, despite having a boyfriend for the past couple of months.

What if I told Rhodes that I'd thought about us being more than friends? A *lot*.

I parked on the street and knocked on the front door, opening it when I realized there was a party going on here too. When I didn't see Rhodes on the first floor, I went up to his room and knocked. He didn't open right away, so I knocked again.

"Rhodes, are you home?" I called.

I heard something on the other side of the door and then Rhodes opened the door. His shirt was unbuttoned and there was red lipstick on his neck. I looked past him to see Lila French on his bed. I'd known she was interested in him by the way she was always hanging around him after games, but I didn't know he was into her too.

"Oh, God. I'm sorry. I didn't—" I backed up and he stepped out of the room.

"What's wrong, Elle?" He moved toward me and I kept backing up, my throat closing up as tears started to come.

No, do not *cry now*, I told myself.

I held up my hand. "I'm fine. Go back to Lila. It's all good."

"Elle, wait," he called as I turned and bolted down the stairs.

I cried all the way to my dorm and when I got to my door and saw Alfie standing there, I knew he thought the tears were for him.

"I'm so sorry, Elle. What you saw...she kissed *me*," Alfie started.

I shook my head. "This isn't going to work," I said.

He tried to talk me out of breaking up with him, but I

didn't change my mind. He left, swearing he'd make it right, but I told him not to bother.

Once again, I'd given too much of myself to someone who didn't value me at all.

When I got to my room, I saw a few missed texts from Rhodes.

> **RHODES**
> Are you okay? I wish you'd stayed.

> **RHODES**
> Did something happen at the party?

> **RHODES**
> Just let me know you're okay.

I didn't answer and half an hour later, he knocked on my door.

"Are you in there?" he called.

My phone buzzed and I looked down, sighing when I saw it was him.

> **RHODES**
> Are you ignoring me?

He knocked harder. "Stop ignoring me, Elle. What's going on?"

I opened the door and his eyes narrowed when he saw I was wearing my fleecy elephant pants. He held up a bag and stalked inside, pulling out Ben & Jerry's Phish Food for me and Half Baked for him.

"I thought we could watch whatever you want on Netflix," he said.

I take the Phish Food out of his hand and grab spoons. "You don't have to stay. I'm good with the ice cream."

He leveled me with a look. "Not a chance. If you don't

wanna talk about what's going on, fine, but I know you're upset and the elephant pants prove it. You only wear those when you're mad, hurt, or on your period." He frowned. "Are you cramping?"

I groaned and shoved him away when he got in my face. "No, I'm not cramping. God, you're so nosy. I'm sorry I interrupted your date with Lila."

"It's okay. She's really only after one thing and I'd already given it to her before you got there."

He laughed when I flicked him.

"You're such a guy," I groaned.

"Guilty," he said, opening his tub of Half Baked.

"I caught Alfie kissing someone."

Rhodes froze mid-bite and stared at me, his jaw clenching. "You can't be serious."

"Oh, I'm serious. And he showed up here, apologizing and acting like she kissed *him*, so that meant it didn't *count*, but I saw him kiss her back without hesitation...after he came out of a bedroom with her. Looks like you both got lucky tonight," I said, attempting to sound light-hearted, but it came out sounding foul.

"Elle. I'm so sorry. That guy is an idiot if he doesn't see what he has in you."

"*Had* in me. He has me no longer. I broke up with him." I waved my hand over my elephant pajamas. "All of *this* is no longer available to him."

And honestly, it didn't feel like a huge loss at the moment.

I climbed on my bed and Rhodes moved next to me. He put his arm around me and I inhaled his cedar and citrus smell. The feel of his arms around me was so perfect. I allowed myself twenty seconds near him and then I forced myself to move into my own space and ate my ice cream.

We started watching "Bob's Burgers" and I fell asleep to Rhodes playing with my hair.

When I woke up, he was gone and there was a note next to the bed.

> Elle,
>
> Any fool who would cheat on you is not worthy of you.
>
> Remember that.
>
> And remember that I love you, I've got your back, and I will kick that fool into next week if you say the word.
>
> Yours,
> Rhodes

CHAPTER THIRTEEN

FLAILING

ELLE

Now

I'VE AVOIDED Rhodes all week. His texts, his calls. I know I'm being weird and it's like I can't even stop myself. Every time I think back on the other night, I die all over again.

I wasn't expecting to have Rhodes in my car anytime

soon, and I've been listening through the audiobook of *It Was Always You* before it goes live next month. I've been so excited about getting an audio deal, I've tried to listen during every break from work, and I have to say, these narrators have brought the book to life in ways I wasn't expecting.

Like the sex scenes, for example.

But *damn*...of all the idiotic things for me to forget to check before letting Rhodes in my car.

He's been funny, saying things like, *Have I lost you to that sexy man voice?*

And, *Where are you? Wait, you're driving again, aren't you? Damn, my dirty bird.*

I've cracked up and simultaneously endured another mortification with each message. Neither one of us likes when the other doesn't respond right away. We're very co-dependent that way. So I know it's probably bugging him that I've gone radio silent.

I drive home from the chiropractor's office, exhausted. I stayed up late writing, then worked a few hours at the office after practice this morning. I barely have time to change out of my work clothes for dinner at my parents' and still make it on time.

I love Dr. Alan and Dr. Sarah so much. They're a dream to work for, but it's getting harder to keep up with it all. The chiropractor's office has been the perfect job and they've been willing to have me fill in when I can, but I don't know how much longer I can keep pulling it off. I'm drained when I get home from practices and it's been harder to write because of that. Being a Mustangs cheerleader is really more than a full-time job when it's all said and done, and as much as I love it, I don't want anything to get in the way of my writing.

I got a call from my agent last night, excited about

potential movie interest in *It Was Always You*. I can't even let myself get too excited yet. She insisted that these things take time, but the fact that I'm even on a movie exec's radar just blows my mind. She also brought up, as she always does, all the requests she gets for me to make appearances at different bookstores and libraries and book events all over the country, and I let her down gently again, saying I'm still not willing to go public with my identity.

I pull into my parents' driveway and walk up to their door, giving it a slight knock before carefully opening it. It always feels weird to come home and not just walk right in the door, but walking in on your parents naked on the couch is not something you can unsee.

"Hey," I call. "Anybody home?"

"In the kitchen," my mom calls.

I walk through the living room and inhale when I step into the kitchen. It smells like pasta and garlic bread. My stomach growls. I haven't eaten like that since I started cheering. But what's one night going to do? I did pay for the eggnog the other night, but it was worth it. If I had been sober for that car ride home with Rhodes, the whole experience would have been a thousand times worse.

My mom stops in her tracks when she sees me and looks me over.

"What are you wearing?" she asks, expressionless due to the Botox, but it's all there in her tone.

She's wearing a silk blouse and black dress pants despite making an Italian dinner. I know better than to show up looking sloppy, but I tried to make an effort with my sweater dress. Yes, it's a shorter length and has a lower neckline than what I would've been allowed to wear growing up, but I'm fully covered.

"A sweater dress," I say, laughing awkwardly.

She tsks. "That's an awful lot of cleavage you're showing," she says.

I try to pull up the neck to hide the millimeter of cleavage I see, but it's no use. This material is not going anywhere.

"Can I help?" I change the subject.

"No, it's all ready. Everything's on the table, but this dish and the bread. Doug, it's ready," she calls. "Why don't you head to the dining room?"

"Okay, babe," he calls back from his office.

I pick up the bread basket and follow my mom into the dining room and am about to sit down, when my dad walks in.

With Bernard right behind him.

"Hi, sweetheart," Dad says.

Bernard lifts a hand at me in a stiff wave, a sheepish expression on his face.

"What are you doing here?" I mutter.

"Bernard just stopped by and I invited him to stay," Dad says, grinning his wide *isn't this amazing* smile.

"That's...something." My voice is deadpan, as is the look I shoot Bernard, and he has the decency to look embarrassed.

My dad comes over to hug me and then lifts his eyebrows in exaggeration. "Goodness...who do we have here? Britney Spears?"

He thinks he's saying something inflammatory, but he has no idea what a fan I am of that woman. I was a preteen when Britney Spears' song "Toxic" came out and I watched the music video in secret so many times, eventually making up my own choreography that I taught Rhodes six years later in college. We also have a routine for "I'm a Slave 4 U" that we still pull out when we want a good laugh. It's sexy as all hell to see Rhodes shaking his fine body to that song. I like to think I'm somewhat responsible for the Britney dance numbers I've seen Rhodes and his Mustangs besties do over the years. *It is gold.*

"Elle?"

I blink and turn to my mom, who's waiting for a response.

"I'm sorry. What?" I clear my throat.

"I was just asking if you'd seen Bernard's new house yet," she says.

"No." I shake my head. Why would I have seen my ex's house?

"It's beautiful," my mom gushes. "Four bedrooms, a nice big yard..."

"That's great," I tell Bernard.

"It'll be the perfect place to raise a family," she says, smiling at Bernard before directing her gaze on me. "It's a much more practical space than that huge place Rhodes has. I worry about Levi near the lake..."

"Mom—"

"Well, you have to know we're all worried about you... with this news about Rhodes," she says.

I'd intended to set the record straight about Rhodes over dinner tonight...when it was supposed to be just the three of us. Now I feel cornered and it puts me on the defense.

"Yes, you mentioned that on the phone. I really wish you'd give Rhodes a chance. You said yourself that you love him...I know you do. So I don't understand why this news isn't being better received?"

"We love everybody. And I don't judge Rhodes for the lifestyle he leads, that's between him and God. But that doesn't mean he's the right man for you!" My mom's voice raises and I glance at Bernard, who is sitting smugly in his seat.

I expect him to toss popcorn in his mouth at any moment.

I shake my head. "You may think you're not judging him, but you are. You always have. I can't believe you're doing this right now. But since you are, I'm just going to say it so you *all* hear me...I'm with Rhodes. He is the best man I know. He always has been, and I wish you'd be happy that we have...what we have."

Okay, that wasn't the best declaration I could make, but I'm flailing here.

"He doesn't deserve you," Bernard says.

"And you do?" It's out of my mouth before I can stop it.

He flinches and looks afraid, like he's just waiting for me to drop the secrets he'd never want my parents to know, but I don't.

"*No one* deserves you," he hurries to add.

"Sweetheart, we just don't want to see you get hurt," my dad says. "Rhodes' track record isn't a good one. And the choices you've made lately..." He lifts his hand up in what I'm assuming is to call attention to my clothing choice this evening on top of all the other revelry I'm partaking in. "Well...it's just not you. And I know the pull of the world is strong, but you've gotta resist..."

I pull the napkin off my lap and set it on the table. "I have an early morning tomorrow. I love you. Thank you for dinner tonight. It clarified some things for me," I say, including Bernard, as I look around the room. "I'm not coming back to you, Bernard. I'm happy and I wish all of you could be happy for me."

I stand up and walk out of the room. My mom follows me out.

"Are you really leaving?" she asks.

"Yes." I turn and hug her.

Her face is getting blotchy, and I want to leave before she gets more upset.

"What if you and Bernard went to couples counseling?" she asks.

"If I go to couples counseling, it will be with Rhodes," I tell her.

Her face looks stricken. "Are you moving in with him?"

Where did that come from?

"No, Mom. I just—"

Her shoulders relax. "Then there's still hope. Please keep an open mind, Elle. Remember that preacher that came through and predicted you'd be with Bernard…"

I remember it well because it messed with me so much to be told by a visiting preacher in front of our whole church congregation that it was God's will for me to marry Bernard.

"I remember," I say softly. "Do *you* remember that it's recently come out that that man has had affairs with women all over this country? You think his wife thinks it's God's will that they're still together?"

"We can't judge them for trying to make their marriage work," she says, folding her arms.

I swallow and nod, knowing that this conversation is going nowhere.

"I love you," I say softly. "I'm gonna head out."

I turn and leave before she can stop me. Once I'm in the car, I select Rhodes' number and his voice fills the car when he answers.

"There you are. I thought I'd scared you off for good with all my sexy man jokes."

"No, sorry, I—"

"What's wrong?"

He's always known with one word, one look, if I'm upset.

"I went to my parents' tonight for dinner and Bernard was there."

"Fuck. They're not letting up on that, huh?"

"No. And I messed up, Rhodes. I was going to let them know we aren't really dating and it just...I got us in a way deeper mess."

He's quiet for a second. "What do you mean?"

"Well, one of the last questions my mom asked is if we're moving in together. I told her no," I hurry to add. "But the point is, I let her think we're serious."

"Why don't we just go with it? Let 'em think we're dating, so they stop pushing Bernard on you. No one else has to know."

"It's a disaster waiting to happen. We can't."

I pull into my driveway and groan when I see Brock outside.

"What is it?"

"Brock is just always outside lately. It's freaking winter. Why is he always around? Oh, and Tuesday night, he left a mug by my door that says *My Favorite Mustang* with a very voluptuous caricature of me on the front. How do I respond to that?"

"Fucking creeper," Rhodes says. "I'm coming over."

"What? No. Don't—"

"I dropped Levi at Carrie's and I'm not even two minutes from your house right now. I can stop by and make my presence known so he backs the fuck off."

"Okay, alpha."

"Is that what your favorite book guys would do?" His voice is low and gravelly, mimicking the narrator he heard the other night. *"I'm coming, deeper...harder."*

I snort and as I pull into the garage, I see Rhodes' headlights behind me. Instead of closing the garage, I walk out to meet him, ignoring Brock next door.

He surprises me when he puts his hands on my waist and leans in, whispering in my ear, "Should we let Brock think we're dating too?"

I stand on my tiptoes and put my hands on his neck, leaning up to his ear. My breasts brush against his chest and he grips my hip tighter.

"If you think it'll make him stop leaving weird things by my door," I whisper.

The next thing I know, he picks me up and buries his face in my hair as he stalks into the garage. I peek through his arm to see Brock staring at us from his driveway.

CHAPTER FOURTEEN

LET'S DISCUSS

RHODES

Now

AS MUCH AS I want to carry Elle all the way to her bedroom and toss her on the bed before leaning over her and kissing my way down her soft skin, I don't. I set her on her feet carefully as soon as we're inside the door, and even move across the room, so I'm not tempted to change my mind.

"Thanks for coming. You didn't have to. I'm not very worried about Brock. He's just a little weird sometimes."

"The fact that you're worried at all is enough for me to check on you."

She tilts her head and lifts her shoulder slightly. "Yeah, I guess I'm a little creeped out by him, so thank you."

She walks over to the couch and I work to school my expression before she turns around. It's always been a battle. She has long legs and the most perfect ass I've ever seen, and in this little sweater outfit she's got on, both are displayed to perfection. It's no better when she turns around. Her tits are calling my name and I want to get my hands on her hips and sink into her more than I want my next breath.

Since hearing what she sounds like when she comes, it's all I can take to be in the same room with her. We haven't talked about the way she cried out my name when I dipped my fingers inside of her. We've talked about the kiss and skirted around everything else, but God knows I haven't stopped thinking about the way she felt, the way she sounded, the way she tasted when I licked my fingers clean. I wanted to lick her everywhere.

I must not clear my expression entirely because she stares at me like she's trying to figure something out.

"What?" I ask. I have to clear my throat because it barely comes out.

"Just wondering what you're thinking."

"Let's figure out what we're gonna do. This dating thing. I wanted you to move in with me when I bought that house, so why *not* move in?"

She looks at me like *come on now*. "I just got my condo. Why would I move in with you?"

"To save money? To avoid your creeper neighbor. To get your parents off your back about Bernard. To get *Bernard* off your back. It's not a ridiculous idea."

"I know we've been hanging out more lately and it's been...nice. Really nice. I've missed you so much. My job situation hasn't changed though. I know I went to the wedding with you...and hung out at your house. But if too many people see us together, it's going to backfire." She pauses. "And, I don't think we've fully recovered from what happened. Pretending to be dating—hell, moving in together—it could get confusing."

I stare at her, waiting for her to keep going. "You're worried about my feelings."

"Well, yeah. Aren't you?"

When she fell apart in my arms, I thought it was because she felt everything I did, that she wanted me with the same unrelenting desire that never seems to let up. Now, I think she'd just been bottled up too long, too stifled under her parents' thumb and Bernard's inability to see past his own dick. If the guy ever made her orgasm, I'd be shocked. She's never talked about it much, but she mentioned one time that he preferred the missionary position. When I asked her what she preferred, she got a wistful expression and said sometimes she wished she was more adventurous.

I took that to mean their sex life wasn't very satisfying, and it's eaten me up, knowing all the ways I could show her a *world* of fun.

"I'm not worried, no," I say quietly.

She seems surprised by that. "Oh. I—I guess I..." She shakes her head and leans forward, her elbows on her knees.

I keep my eyes steady on hers, so I'm not tempted to stare at the creamy expanse of skin, that dip between her breasts that I traced with my tongue that night.

"Then if you're really okay with it, I'll keep acting like we're together with my parents and Bernard."

I nod. "Yeah, that's fine by me."

Her brows furrow and I'm not sure if it's a scoff or a laugh that comes next. "You're so nonchalant about it."

I put my hands in my pockets and laugh quietly. "I'm not sure what you want me to say. I'll fake date you for the rest of our lives if that makes you happy."

There's definitely a laugh from her now. "I'd never ask that of you, don't worry."

"I'm not worried, remember?" I smile at her.

"Right. You're not worried. Don't you think your *real* dating life would suffer if you were stuck fake dating me forever?" Her lips pucker as she stares me down.

"I would not be suffering."

"What does that mean?" She stalks toward me, her finger jabbing into my chest. "You think you could go a week without getting laid to keep pretenses up? Because if we lived together or if word ever got out about us dating, it would really cramp your style."

I grab her finger and hold it, watching as her mouth parts and her eyes flicker up at mine, uncertain.

"I guess you haven't noticed that nothing has been going on in that area for a while now."

"You're finally getting tired of playing the field?" she rasps.

"Something like that."

"Well, don't you think lines might get confusing if we're together all the time after—"

"I'm. Not. Worried."

"*Why not?*" Her teeth clamp over her bottom lip, sliding over it as her eyes bounce between mine.

"Because I've been living with how I feel about you since the night we met."

Her eyes widen and I let her finger go, stepping back from the heat between us. I walk to the door and look back. She hasn't moved an inch.

"Think about what I said about staying with me. Keep your place, sell it—you don't have to decide now. It can be for however long you want. If you need the option or just like the idea, it's there. Bonus would be that it's one way you could see Levi without getting caught. Since he's with his mom half of the time, he'd just think he was getting to see you more often."

And since I plan to convince you to stay with me forever and fall madly in love with me, Levi will never have to get used to being without you.

"We'd set boundaries, of course. He could schedule time to see you just like we have to do now, so you still have your privacy when you want it," is what I say instead of sounding like a creeper myself.

I'm thinking about Levi though. I don't want to confuse him, so if she moves in, I want her to stay.

My lips lift when hers do and deepen as I allow my gaze to trail down her body for just a second.

She's fucking beautiful.

I smirk and she shifts, rubbing her hand over her arm like she's suddenly chilly.

I point at her now, playful but just telling the damn truth. "And I've proven I can control myself around you, so you don't have to worry about that."

She blinks and I turn to face the door.

"Make sure you keep your doors locked. And promise

you'll call me if Brock so much as breathes wrong in your direction."

When she still doesn't say anything, I look over my shoulder.

She swallows hard and eventually nods.

"Yeah, I promise," she whispers.

I smile. "Night, dirty bird."

She groans and rolls her eyes as I walk out. The neighbor isn't outside anymore, but I sit in my SUV for a few minutes just to be sure he's not lurking around out here. When it doesn't seem like he is, I pull out my phone and text the guys. If it were offseason, I'd call an emergency meeting in person, but we're all exhausted right now.

> Anyone around? I know it's been a long day with practice...but I need someone to tell me if I'm doing something crazy.

PENN

> You're never too crazy for me, dude.

WESTON

> Lay it on us.

BOWIE

> I'm tired, but wired. What's up?

HENLEY

> What have you done now?

> Turns out, Elle let Bernard and her parents think we're dating. As you know, I would not be opposed to this idea whatsoever, but she's apologetic and worried about it. And I think, why doesn't she just move in? So I suggested it, you know, to keep the theory alive and all.

WESTON

Sacrifices. Lol.

BOWIE

Isn't this what you're wanting?

HENLEY

Sounds like the perfect opportunity, man.

> You guys think so? I just feel like she's my best friend. She's always going to be my best friend. So we play house for a little while, fake date. What's the harm in that? Why the hell not? It's not like she's saying she's really going to be with me. But at least I'd get to be around her, right?

PENN

Shit, Rhodes. You've got it so fucking bad. I can't believe I just thought you've been having a slow roll for the last…what the hell has it been now? You haven't been my wingman for months. Fuck, you've been off for longer than that. A year or more.

> I miss sex, but hooking up with random women just hasn't felt right to me for a long time.

They'd be so shocked if they knew how long.

PENN

I feel like everything I've thought about you is a lie.

I chuckle, but it's hollow in my vehicle. That pretty much describes how it had started to feel with sex—empty. Not that there's anything wrong with it, but I never planned on being thirty-one and single. My parents' marriage is something special and I've always wanted that. I started the casual hookups trying to get over Elle when she started dating that jerkoff Alfie in college and it just sort of ballooned from there.

I'm not old, but I'm too old to be *stupid*...and knowing I'm in love with Elle and continuing to stand by and not do more about it is stupid.

> She was with Bernard so long, I'd numbed myself.

PENN
> But she ain't with Bernard no more! 🌍 🕺

> Damn straight, she ain't.

BOWIE
> I don't want to, but I'm just gonna say it. It will cause you a world of hurt if she doesn't want to be with you.

> I know. But I already don't have her the way I want. So it's not like it's going to hurt any worse than it already does.

WESTON
> Man, this is heartbreaking. I can't believe you've loved her like this all this time.

I stare at her condo and sigh, finally cranking up the SUV. I can't believe I've loved her like this all this time either, but I do.

And I always will.

HENLEY

I think this is your chance. Remember when you guys told me I needed to pursue Tru? What better way to pursue her than while you're doing this fake dating thing?

WESTON

THIS. You need her to move in, Rhodes. You can see her without getting her into trouble with the team, and I'm telling you, once she's under your roof and with you all the time, she won't be able to resist.

PENN

Like Sadie couldn't?

WESTON

Exactly. 😏

HENLEY

Whether she moves in with you or not, it's time to woo.

PENN

Yes. WOO THE FUCK OUT OF THIS GIRL. Fuck me, I'm all torn up about losing my favorite wingman, but I can't stand to see you suffering. You and Elle belong together.

> Thanks, guys. I'm fucking terrified, and I don't know exactly what to do, but I'm going to try to put all my cards on the table. If she just wants to be my friend after it's all said and done, I'll know I've tried.

I'm tempted to go knock on her door and start trying tonight, but decide I need a better approach than startling her when she's getting ready for bed.

When I get home and am in bed myself, I send her a text.

> You looked absolutely beautiful tonight.

It's quiet for a few minutes and I worry that I've already blown it.

ELLE
> Are you already practicing fake dating me?

> It's never been fake when I tell you how beautiful you are.

ELLE
> Well, thank you. You can stay. 🩶

I smile at my phone.
Let Project Woo begin.

CHAPTER FIFTEEN

NO ONE COMPARES

ELLE

Now

"BECAUSE I'VE BEEN LIVING *with how I feel about you since the night we met.*"

I've thought about Rhodes saying this nonstop. Throughout practices. Throughout the charity events all weekend. While I watch the recording of the Mustangs' game in Indianapolis on Sunday in the comfort of my bed and rewind every time there's a close-up of Rhodes.

The way his eyes heated as he said it, the way his eyes roamed over me before he left—all of it has been excellent inspiration for writing. Lisa has worked us so hard this week at practice and I'm dragging by the time I get home, but when I open my laptop, the words pour out of me. I've sent a few chapters to my agent Rosie and she said, "I wish you would quit everything else you're doing and finish this book!"

I know I can't do that, not without everyone in my life wondering how in the world I'm surviving financially... unless I did move in with Rhodes.

I feel guilty even contemplating it.

Hiding my identity while I'm living under Rhodes' roof and using him for inspiration for every book boyfriend I write?

My parents are right—I have slipped down that slippery slope.

But the more I think about it, the more it feels right. I don't want to quit cheering, I love it too much. The season is almost over, but if I'm lucky enough to get in next season, I have to do it. The thought of seeing Rhodes and Levi at home while I'm keeping my distance in public the rest of the time...it feels like the only way I can survive another year of this.

My phone buzzes and it's Calista in the group thread.

CALISTA

Hey! I'm just reminding you that this Thursday night is Shop by Candlelight on Jupiter Lane and I'll be having some worthy treats and drinks at Twinkle Tales! Like don't even bother eating dinner, just come eat with me if you want.

I'd almost forgotten that I'd agreed to stop by Twinkle Tales later this week with Sadie and Tru. We might hit a few other shops too, but if it goes the way it has the past few years, I've mostly hung out at Twinkle Tales.

The team is away again for this Sunday's game, and I only have one Mustangs event scheduled on Friday night in Denver. When the team is away, the cheerleaders' schedule is packed with events. Sometimes it's just one or two of us going to a store opening or a luncheon, and other times it's a charity performance or a fundraiser. This weekend, we're all required to be at the Winter Ball.

I'll be there!

SADIE

I can't wait. Hey—do we know when Zoey Archer is putting out her next book? I'm having major book withdrawal.

CALISTA

Not until March. But guess what, you guys? I've emailed her! I found an email through her newsletter and I've invited her to the shop. It's a long shot and I probably should've gone through her PR team, but I thought, what the hell, I'll try it!

My heart starts pounding. I open my email from my

phone and scroll through the zillion emails. When I finally find it and read her sweet note, I blink back tears.

DEAR MS. ARCHER,

I hope it's okay that I'm emailing. I don't fangirl very often, but I'm such a huge fan of It Was Always You. I own a bookstore in this really charming little town in Colorado, Silver Hills, and I tell everyone who comes through the door about your book. It's such a beautiful story of friendship and perseverance and love. I laughed and cried reading about Ryder and Eliza's ups and downs as they found their way to each other. The way they pined for one another just gave me all the feels, and when they finally surrendered to their love and put down every wall between them, knowing their love would survive taking it to that next level, it was EPIC.

I've scoured the internet for any news about your signings and haven't found anything. I hope you'll consider coming to Silver Hills. Our town is small, but the love growing for you here every single day is huge. We're not far from Denver or Boulder and people come from all over to our Pixie Pop-Up Market (see link). If we coordinated your visit during one of those weekends, the books would fly off the shelves. Please think about it!

Sincerely,
Calista Hart

THERE'S no way I can do it, but this makes me wish so bad that I could. Another wave of guilt washes over me. I mark it as unread so I can go back and respond later.

TRU

I can't tell you how much I'm looking forward to a night out. My students this year are so much rowdier than last year's! Warning, Henley will probably be with me since he doesn't have a game that night.

SADIE

Weston's already asked when the Twinkle Tales party is. Caleb loved your storytime last year.

CALISTA

The more, the merrier!

I look at the time and try to calculate where Rhodes would be by now. I doubt he's on the plane yet. I haven't seen him since the other night, but he's texted every day. Not to tell me I'm beautiful again, but...definitely a little...I don't know...sweeter. The last one was right before the game.

RHODES

I don't like away games anymore because you're not here.

I snuggle under the covers and text him back.

You guys are BACK! That was such a good game tonight.

RHODES

It felt good. I'm tired though. We had to work for it.

You worked that tight end off.

RHODES

I see what you did there.

> You like that?

RHODES

I like everything about you, Elle.

Gah. See what I mean? He's always been so sweet to me, but I don't know. This just feels...a little more.

> You're pretty okay too.

RHODES

Mm-hmm. Remember when you wrote that short story in your creative writing class senior year and it was published in the school paper?

> You'll never let me forget.

RHODES

It was an excellent story about a brilliant guy who never gave up.

> Hmm. Did I use the word brilliant? I don't think so.

RHODES

I'll check when I get home because I'm almost positive the story said he was brilliant and super sexy.

I snort.

> I know I didn't say he was super sexy. And what do you mean you'll check it—you still have the story?

> **RHODES**
>
> Hell yeah! It's in a special box I keep with everything you ever wrote. I miss reading your stories. Do you ever miss writing?

I swallow hard, fingers pausing over the keyboard. It's been painfully difficult not sharing everything that's happened with my book with him. He would be so, so proud.

> I still write sometimes.

It feels good to say even this much of the truth.

> **RHODES**
>
> Really? That makes me happy, Elle. You never talk about it anymore. I thought you'd given it up. You've always had such a way with words.

> Thank you. You always made me feel like my writing was important.

> **RHODES**
>
> It was. It is. You are.

My eyes fill with tears and drip down my cheeks. How did I get so lucky to have him in my life all these years?

No one compares to him.

CHAPTER SIXTEEN

SOULLESS

RHODES

Then

"LET ME SEE." I tried to peer over her shoulder and she flipped her laptop shut.

"Go away." She laughed, shooing me away with her hand.

"But you always show me what you're writing."

"Not always, and not yet."

I wasn't pretending when I pouted, but she laughed again, not taking me seriously.

"Come on, Elle. I need something good. It's been a hard week. We lost and—"

"Well, there *was* something I wanted to ask you..." She stood up and leaned against the chair.

I nodded. "Okay. Shoot. You can ask me anything."

I straightened the stack of books on the end of the table. We were at the lounge in her building where we often worked on homework together. If we weren't here, we were at my house.

She bit the inside of her lower lip, her tell that she was nervous.

"What's going on? You're scaring me."

She laughed, but it sounded nervous too.

"Elle, what is it?"

"Would you go to the Senior Formal with me?" She said it so fast I wasn't sure I'd heard her correctly.

"You're asking me to the Senior Formal?"

She nodded tentatively.

"Elle..." I blew out a long breath. "Dammit. I would've killed to go with you. You said you were going with Isaac."

"We broke up a few days ago."

"What? Why didn't you say something? Are you okay? I thought you liked him."

"He said pursuing writing as a career was like working for a pyramid scheme. You've gotta be able to sell yourself and whatever product you've got, nonstop, and the guys at the bottom make nothing."

"That's bullshit." I scowled. I moved toward her and put my hands on her arms. "I never liked that guy. What an asshat. Your writing deserves to be read. Don't listen to that joker. He might do well on Wall Street one day, but he has no soul."

She cracked a small smile and I leaned down so my eyes were level with hers.

"Okay?"

"Okay." She bit her lower lip again. "I'm not heartbroken. I wasn't feeling it anyway. It just...stung, and it felt like he was trying to put me down on purpose."

"It might take time and be tons of work, but I have faith in your talent," I said, holding my fist up.

"Thank you, Rhodes." She bumped my fist. "So, you have a date to the Senior Formal?"

"Yeah, I told Farrah I'd go with her earlier this week."

She looked winded and I frowned, about to ask her if she was sure she was okay when she said, "You've seen her more than once. You must like this girl."

I shrugged. "She's nice, yeah."

She nodded and ducked away from me, picking up her laptop.

"I'm gonna go take a shower and get to bed early," she said.

"Are we good? Elle, I totally would've preferred going with you. I can back out of it with Farrah and—"

"No, don't you dare. That would be so rude."

"But I—"

"*No.*" She gave me a tight smile and lifted her bag over her shoulder. I'd thought we'd probably end up in her room watching a movie after this and I'm sad to see her go.

"Night," she said.

"Night."

I watched her walk away and wondered if there was a way to *politely* tell Farrah that I couldn't take her to the formal.

But Elle had another date by the next night.

Grant Elliot.

It felt like I'd blown my chance with her. It was senior year and we didn't have much time together. I'd wanted to take her to the dance in the first place, but she'd been with that jerkwad Isaac. She'd shown vulnerability in asking me and I didn't know if I'd imagined it, but I almost felt like I'd let her down somehow.

I made ruthless fun of Grant's slicked-back hair and uptight attitude from the get-go and told her she could never seriously consider being with him because Elle Elliot was a sucky author name.

SHE WAS STILL DATING HIM—WHICH I fucking *hated*—by the time her short story was published, but after I read her story, I felt like I'd won.

It was about a girl and her best guy friend, Lane Bow... get it? Rhodes Archer in *code*. I'd shared my obstacles in becoming a football player with her. I'd grown too fast and had a lot of pain in my knees for years as I was developing, but football was my passion. It meant I had to work extra hard, often feeling like I'd never get there, and at the expense of a social life a lot of the time. In the story it wasn't football, the guy was heading to the Olympics as a runner, but everything else was the same. His parents were famous and he often felt like people didn't care about getting to know the real him. They wanted to meet his parents, have an in with someone in Hollywood, or just be close to the money.

And the friendship between Lane Bow and Elsa Wilson...Elle Benton in *code*...everything about it made my heart hum. It was sweet, poignant, and in places, damn funny. She brought the story to life on the page and also made me feel like I was ten feet tall.

The last lines said, "I only hope when he's won a gold medal and wined and dined with the world's most famous people, he'll remember that he loved me once. Because no matter where life takes us, I'll love him most of all."

I'd read those lines out loud to her, shaking her while she laughed.

"As if I could ever forget that I love you. And I love you most. You and I both know it," I yelled, making her cackle harder.

I pulled her to me and hugged her tight.

"I love this story, Elle. I love it so much. I'm so damn proud of you."

I leaned back and smoothed her hair away as she looked at me with wide eyes.

"And I sent six copies to my parents. I told Mama it's coming and she said she's gonna put it in a shadow box so it'll stay safe, but I'll be able to get to it to read it whenever I want."

She burst into tears and I tugged her back to my chest.

"Fuck. What did I say?" I pulled back again, trying to wipe the tears falling so fast.

"I'm just going to miss you so much. You promise you won't forget about me when you're in Florida and I'm in Colorado?"

"We're still going to see each other. You'll visit me in Miami and I'll see you every time the Dolphins come through Denver..." I wiped more tears from her face, feeling close to tears myself. "It won't be enough. We'll have to FaceTime all the time."

"We'll be in different time zones," she sobbed.

"I know. It's the worst thing. I hate it. Are you sure you can't ditch that job in Denver? Try for a job in Miami instead?"

"I'm hoping I like the job more than I'm imagining. It's writing...even if it is about pets for a blog. My parents would kill me if I ditched it and you wouldn't be in Miami all the time anyway. But I wish I could." She sniffled and leaned back, her arms around my neck. "I'll be cheering you on during every game still, I promise."

Her face crumbled again and this time when I hugged her, a few tears ran down my face too.

CHAPTER SEVENTEEN

NIP SLIPS

RHODES

Now

"ARE YOU KIDDING ME? Who moved my towel and clothes? I am the one who should be pranking all you rookies. I've done my fucking time," I yell.

I hear the guys trying to control their laughter, but one of them is laughing so hard it makes me snort. Shaking my head, I walk out of the showers and into the locker room, holding my arms out wide, naked as the day I was born.

There are only a few guys here, and they're all trying not to laugh. Weston doesn't bother to hide his laugh, the fucking traitor.

"Who'd you piss off, Archer?" he asks.

"No one. I played my ass off this weekend and again at practice today." I slap my ass to prove my point. "All right, 'fess up, assholes, where are my clothes?"

They're all in on it because not one of them gives me a towel or my clothes. In fact, the cabinet where we usually have extra towels is completely empty. Fucking mutiny.

"Come *on!*" I whirl around, my dick whipping heavily against my leg. "I didn't know you wanted to see all this so bad." I hold my hands out and have to press my mouth firm to keep from laughing.

Jon Carlos, the shyest rookie I've met yet, points out the door. His hand shakes. "I-I think I saw your pants out there."

I give him an assessing look and the poor guy looks like he's going to hurl. "Thank you, Jon Carlos. I'll remember that you helped me out."

I turn and glare at everyone else, and the snickers quieten. Roscoe shifts on his feet and looks away first. Yep, I thought this was his doing. He is cocky as shit and pure trouble, but I like the kid. He reminds me of how I was my first year with the Dolphins. Hell...I can still be that way when I want to be.

I walk out the door, going into the main hallway of our athletic center. I glance around and don't see anyone, but my clothes and towel are in the doorway across from me.

I mutter a string of curses and walk over, bending down to pick them up.

And then turn around to see Elle walking out of the bathroom one door down. We freeze. Her eyes widen and journey downstairs, while I remember to cover my dick with my folded pants just a little too late. Fuck me.

"Roscoe," I yell, still staring at Elle. "Your ass is mine."

I hear Elle cracking up as I run into the locker room, and Roscoe hides behind Weston when I come after him.

"He won't save you," I tell him, pulling out my scary voice as I grab him and force him toward the showers, turning the water on as cold as it'll go.

He shudders at the frigid temperature, but he takes it.

When I turn the water off, I bop him on the shoulder. "That was a good one, kid. But do it again and I'll shave off every strand of hair on your body."

"Respect, man," he says through his teeth chattering. "I've got nothin' but respect for you."

I grin at him and go dry off. When I'm dressed and heading out, I look for Elle, but don't find her. I call her on my way home and her voice is quiet through my speakers until I turn her up.

"Taking a break from streaking through the halls?" she asks, hardly able to get the words out from laughing so hard.

"Are you wheezing, love? Is that why I can't turn you up loud enough?" I crack up myself.

When we finally stop laughing, I clear my throat and she coughs before doing the same.

"I noticed you didn't look away," I say smugly.

"Um, yes, I did...after you ran away." She starts laughing again. "Do you blame me? I haven't seen your ass since 2014, when you and the team streaked through the campus on our last night. And I...I've never quite managed to *see* what else you're packing, which is ironic since it's not like you're modest or anything."

The unspoken is ringing out between us. She hasn't seen me, but she sure as hell has felt me. I get hard just thinking about it.

"I didn't know you were so curious, Elle baby. I would've shown you a long time ago if I'd known you wanted to see so bad." My voice has gotten all hoarse and I'd give anything to see what color her cheeks might be turning right now.

"You're ridiculous," she says, but she sounds breathy too.

I can't help but grin. "I'm curious too, believe me," I tell her. "*But—*" I drag the word out. "How do I tell you this? There's something I've never told you."

"What?"

When I'm quiet, she groans.

"Rhodes, what? You're making me nervous."

"I saw your nipple once," rushes out of me. "On your right side. Senior year. Must've been the year we lost all inhibitions." When she doesn't laugh, I hurry to say, "I'm kidding. It was...we fell asleep in your dorm while watching a movie and you had on a baggy shirt that slid to the side and...I covered you up as soon as I woke up and saw."

"That is *so* embarrassing."

"Trust me, Elle, you have nothing to be embarrassed about when it comes to your body. That nipple was..." I let out a rough exhale. "Stunning."

That nipple sighting played a role in my fantasies that whole next year when I moved to Miami. Hell, who am I kidding, I still picture it when I'm jerking off...although I do also manage to envision the other side that I never actually saw. I feel like I know Elle's body as well as I possibly can, having seen her in bikinis and skimpy cheer outfits, but seeing her rosy pink nipple was the highlight of my life.

The level of regret I have that I did not strip her bare the night I touched her...well, I have a lot of regrets about that night, but that one's up there.

I can't help it if I'm pathetic. Everything about this girl has always done it for me.

"I've made it awkward, haven't I?" I finally say.

She giggles. "No. *Yes*. I just can't believe you've never told me this until now."

"Yeah, I wasn't exactly sure how to bring that up. Nip slips happen. It's actually surprising it hasn't happened more often. We really need to work on that."

She laughs again and I'm relieved.

"It seemed only right to tell you after you admitted to being curious," I say softly.

"What other secrets are you keeping from me?" she asks.

Girl, if you only knew.

"I'm *pretty much* an open book when it comes to you," I say.

"Pretty much," she echoes. "Yeah, same."

We talk about our practices that day and about the week ahead before hanging up. When I pull into my garage, I wish she was pulling in next to me. The house is always especially lonely on the weekends I've had an away game because I have less time with Levi. When I have a Sunday game out of town, Carrie has Levi from Saturday until Monday or Tuesday, depending on my unpredictable travel schedule. This week, she's got him until Wednesday while she has family in town and it's another away week coming up, so I'll only see him in the evenings after practice, Wednesday through Saturday.

The house looks beautiful after my parents, Elle, and I decorated, and when I walk past the tree, I realize Elle still hasn't said when we'll get together to exchange our gifts. In the past, we spent every Christmas Eve together, and the first year I moved to Silver Hills, we hung out on Christmas night too, after celebrating with our families. It got complicated when she was dating Bernard, but we still stole away on Christmas Eve to spend an hour together, just the three of us...Elle, Levi, and me.

Bernard hated that, and I don't blame him.

I've dropped my keys in the dish I keep in the kitchen when my phone buzzes. I grin when I see that it's Elle.

Before I can say anything, I hear, "Rhodes," and the crack in her voice makes me break out into a cold sweat.

"What's wrong?" I demand.

"Can you come? I'm—scared."

I already have the keys and am sprinting to the garage.

"What's going on, Elle? Talk to me, love."

"I'm okay. I'm just trying not to freak out. I was...pulling into the driveway and something caught my eye. There was a...one of those..." She pauses and the suspense is killing me, but I try not to rush her. "A blow-up doll, like one of those," her voice lowers into the phone, "sex dolls? It was leaning against Brock's truck. Rhodes, it looks like me!" She talks faster. "And that was just starting to register when Brock walked over to it and just stood there next to it, *staring* at me!"

"Fucking creeper," I mutter. "I'm on my way. Are you inside, doors locked?"

"Yes." She took a deep, shaky breath. "I didn't react until I got inside and now I can't stop shaking."

"I'm two minutes away, baby. I'll knock, but make sure it's me before you open the door. Are you able to get some things together? If not, just wait until I'm there and I'll help you. I'm bringing you back home with me, okay?"

"I can get some things really quick. I'm going to my bathroom right now to get my overnight bag."

"Stay on the phone with me, okay? And as soon as we get back to my place, we can make a few calls about how to handle this."

"Okay."

"Breathe," I tell her, and it calms me when I hear her taking deep breaths, each one sounding less shaky than the last. "That's it."

"Thank you," she says and I can tell she's put me on speakerphone. "It's helping."

"I guess I'm getting my wish today after all," I say.

"What wish?"

"You're moving in with me tonight."

She laughs. It's light, but the sound calms me even more.

"This will probably be the craziest thing we've ever done," she says.

"I think it will be the best thing we've ever done," I say. "And it's been a long time coming."

CHAPTER EIGHTEEN

REBELS AND DECEPTION

ELLE

Now

I'VE NEVER BEEN SO relieved to see Rhodes in all my life. It's not that I necessarily think Brock is going to storm over here and act on the scary sexual vibes he's putting out there, but I'm also not sure he won't. The whole thing creeps me out way too much.

As soon as I let Rhodes in the door, he hugs me tight and then pulls back to look at me.

"Are you okay?"

I nod and he frowns, still not sure.

"What do we need to take? I can grab as much as you need now or come back later." He points at the bag sitting by the door. "Or we can just take that and get out of here."

"I like that option. Let's get out of here," I say.

"Okay."

He picks up the small bag and puts his arm around my shoulder protectively, glancing at me.

"I should take my car."

"Okay."

He walks out with me and I nod before he opens the garage door. I don't even look to see if Brock is around.

"He's not out here," Rhodes says softly. "I checked before I came in and I don't see him now either."

I feel his eyes on me, but he doesn't say anything as he helps me into my car. Then he gets in his and I follow him to his house. When he pulls up to the gate, he motions for both guards to come to his window.

It's too hard to hear him clearly, but I make out his last sentences.

"It's important that you don't let anyone know she's here. No one. Do you understand?"

They both nod.

"Yes, sir," they echo each other.

As I drive down his driveway, the stress levels out. I've always loved Rhodes' house. I helped him pick it out. His realtor showed us four houses that day, and this is the one I immediately loved. It's way too big for Rhodes and Levi, but he's made good use of this space. We've spent a lot of time here, thrown some great parties with his family and the guys from the team, and before I joined the Mustangs cheerleaders, it wasn't uncommon for me to spend the night occasionally.

It feels different tonight.

The place is massive, but it's cozy, with oversized furniture and plush faux-fur blankets thrown on every sitting area. In the summer, he swaps out the faux furs for soft linen throws. We've watched a lot of home decorating shows together over the years and I've happily taken credit for some of the choices he's made—the furniture in the bedroom he's always called *my* room, for one. While Rhodes' bed is a massive black wooden frame with beautiful detailing and a cream comforter, the furniture in my room is cream and has cream and black linens. The color comes from a huge floral painting that I absolutely love, and the view outside the windows is spectacular. His home is striking, yet everything is comfortable.

I feel better just being here.

"Thank you," I say, as he sets my bag down in the room.

"If you think of anything you're missing, I can go back to get it or...we can buy it online and have it delivered."

I smile. "I'll be fine. I know for a fact I have a toothbrush and deodorant in this bathroom. And I *will* be soaking in that tub later."

He looks so pleased, so like the Rhodes I first met, that I laugh.

"Not that I'm complaining, but what are you laughing about?"

"You. You just look so excited."

He moves until he's standing in front of me and puts his hands on my waist. "I hate that you were scared tonight, but having you here...I'm not gonna lie...it's exactly what I've wanted." He makes a face. "That's not coming out right. I mean, I *do* want you here, that's clearly true. But when I heard your voice on the phone tonight, it scared me so bad, Elle..."

I put my hands on his chest and then wind them around his neck. He's so tall that when we're this close, I have to look up, despite being tall myself.

"Thank you for coming to my rescue. I've always known that anytime I need you, you're there. I was..." I pause and press my lips together, my nerves ticking up. "I'd already been thinking that staying here maybe...sounded like...a good option. I don't know that I would've done it tonight or right at Christmastime, but—"

I lean in and hug him and his arms wrap around me tight. I close my eyes, inhaling him. Rhodes smells like cedar and citrus and cinnamon. I want to dip myself in his bodywash and bury my nose in his neck, but I settle on just inhaling deeply.

"I'm glad I'm here," I finish.

His voice is husky when he says, "Right where you belong."

We stand there for a few beats longer than is probably healthy for either one of us, and I pull away first.

"I called my lawyer on the way back, and he said we could try filing a temporary restraining order, but they'll want proof of what he's done."

I nod. "I thought it might be difficult to prove how creepy he's been. I'd rather just stay out of his way."

"I think you should at least tell the sheriff what's happened. He can go have a word with Brock if you don't want me to."

"Okay, I'll make a call."

"Great. I'll work on dinner. You hungry?"

"I didn't think I was, but the thought of your cooking could change my mind."

Again with that boyish smirk, but on this sexy man, it's almost sinful.

"If I'd thought about it, I would have lured you here with my cooking a lot sooner. Does anything in particular sound good?" He moves toward the door and turns back.

"Anything you make is always good. I *have* been missing your whatever's-in-the-fridge soup. And your throw-everything-in pasta. Even though I'm *trying* not to eat like that anymore."

"Elle, your body is slamming. You don't need to do anything different than whatever you're already doing." His voice darkens. "Is Lisa giving you a hard time?"

"Uhh," I hedge. "Not me specifically, no...but we do have to weigh in, and that is driving me crazy a little bit."

He scowls. "I hate that. You dance better than anyone I've ever seen. You learn your routines perfectly. I've seen you out there. That should be the only thing that matters."

"You're right. I know. I don't know why it's like that in this industry, but...it is. I have to admit, I do feel better when I eat lighter and not so carb-heavy, but still. Dodging them completely will never work for me, and when I do have them, I shouldn't feel like I'm doing something wrong."

"Agreed," he says. "You just tell me when you want all the carbs, and I'll bring it. We can go lighter if you prefer, but you've been traumatized tonight, so you get whatever you want."

"There's something else I should probably tell you...in case it comes up with Carrie. We had a little run-in a few days ago when you were out of town. Not a big deal, but... you know how things can sometimes go sideways with her." I make a face. "I stopped by Serendipity and she was there with Levi. He ran over when he saw me and she chewed me out, saying I didn't need to encourage that."

"What? Why? She knows how much he loves you."

"She was all over the place. First, it was that it sends him confusing messages to see me all the time and then not...and that it's weird for him to see us together," I point between the two of us, "but not her with you. I said that's what co-parenting a child with someone you don't have a romantic relationship looks like...which she hated." I laugh. "She told me to watch my place and said I needed to back the hell off of her child."

My eyes well with tears and I bite down on my lip, frustrated to be weepy over this.

"Elle baby, I'll talk to her," he says softly, rubbing my shoulder. "That's not gonna fly. I'll set her straight. She has no right to talk to you that way. She knows how important you are to me and to Levi."

"Yeah, that's why she said it when you weren't around." I exhale and blink up at the ceiling. "Anyway, then it turned into...I should know better than to let him run across the restaurant away from his mom when he's out in public. Someone could grab him because you're famous. And I'm like, Carrie, you're the one who didn't stop him from running to me. I know how to watch out for your boy. Trust me. I've been looking out for him since the day he was born and you know it. You weren't complaining when I took care of him when he was sick because you guys were both sick too. You weren't complaining when you wanted to go see your sister and Rhodes had an away game, so I watched Levi." I shake my head. "That slowed her down for a second, but when she tried to start in on me again about it confusing Levi, I got out of there."

"I'm sorry. Sometimes I can't believe this is my life. She

makes it so fucking hard. I'm just sorry *you* ever have to deal with her."

"I love Levi. He's worth it. All of it. I love you, Rhodes. Thank you. I feel better already, just being here."

"I love to hear you say that." He leans in and tips my chin up, his lips curling in a grin. "I plan on things only getting better."

He walks out and I stare after him for a few seconds before catching my breath. Whew. *You can't be losing your willpower here, Elle.*

I call Sheriff Davis and it's a relatively painless process. He says he'll pay Brock a visit. I feel much better already that I let someone know what's happened.

Next, I unpack my bag. I brought enough clothes for the next few days and hang them up in the walk-in closet. When I walk into the bathroom and open the cabinet next to the sink, I realize more of my things are here than I thought. One of my favorite perfumes, my deodorant, lipstick and a brush I've been missing for months, and all the bobby pins and elastic bands I could ever want.

Since it's getting late and I am hungry, I decide to just take a quick shower instead of getting sleepier in the tub. I hop in and out and get into something comfortable. I walk into the kitchen and sigh.

"It smells so good in here. How did you do that so fast?"

He's changed into his sweats and the vision of him standing by the stove, stirring soup, is almost as good as when I've watched him reading a book. It might only be beaten out by watching him work out. I've had to go take many cold showers after watching him lift weights like it's nothing.

I take him in for a second and he holds up a spoon.

"Wanna taste it?" he asks.

I walk to the stove and blow before taking a taste of the soup.

"Oh," I moan, "so good."

He's staring at my mouth when I look up at him and we stay suspended there for a few seconds.

He swallows and slowly lowers the spoon.

"I'll grab the bowls," he says.

"I can do that. And I'll get the ice. Do you want anything besides water?"

"Water's good."

I set napkins, spoons, and glasses of iced water on the large bar where we eat more often than the table, and take the bowls to the stove. He fills our bowls and I thank him and take both to the bar.

"I made the call. Brock will be paid a visit soon." I frown. "I guess I could've called Lisa about it..." I frown. "Actually, I probably will need to tell her about it, won't I?"

"I think you should. Just leave out that you're staying here now...obviously."

"I'm feeling like such a liar these days. I don't like it."

"You haven't ever lied about being close to me."

"Yeah, but disobeying the rules so blatantly...it just doesn't sit right with me. And yet, I'm not going to stop seeing you and Levi." I look at him. "Tried that and hated it more."

His dimples sink in and I have to look away again.

"Sometimes I feel like growing up with such strict rules that I didn't always agree with created a liar." I take another taste of the soup and nearly moan again.

"What do you mean?"

"I acted like I was working on the newspaper at school when I was really dancing..."

"Didn't you also work on the newspaper?"

"Yes, but...way less than my parents thought."

"But you tried to get their permission to dance and be on the cheerleading team, right?"

"A little bit. I didn't push it though, because I knew they wouldn't change their minds. So I found ways to still do what I wanted to do."

"Part of that is just being a teenager. My little rebel." He nudges me, laughing.

"Except here I am, still sneaking around." I laugh, but it's bittersweet.

I'd love it if I could be exactly who I am and know there would not be huge repercussions.

My fist hits the granite. "Dammit. You know what I forgot? My dress for the Winter Ball."

"When is that again, Friday?"

"Yeah."

"I'll get it. I can ask the guys to go with me and we can clear your place out if you want."

I think of my office and my cheeks heat. Yeah, I'm a liar all right.

"Oh, that's okay. I can go. I can even ask the girls to go with me."

"I don't want you going over there without me. Please, Elle. I know you're capable of taking care of yourself, but I don't trust that guy."

"Okay, we can go together...and the guys too if they're available."

I'll just have to work on the office while they're working on everything else. Oh, God. This is going to be a disaster. And how do I expect to keep this secret from Rhodes when I'm living in his house?

By the time we've finished eating and put the dishes in the dishwasher, the exhaustion from the day has caught up with me. When Rhodes puts his hand on my shoulder, I sag into him, my forehead on his chest. I smile when I hear his low, raspy laugh.

"Should I carry you to bed?" he asks.

"I'm almost tired enough to agree," I tell him, propping my chin on his chest and looking up at him.

He's wearing my favorite expression, the adoring one.

"Have I said I'm really glad you're here?" he asks.

"You have. And I'm really glad I'm here too."

He leans in for a second, and my airwaves halt. I just know he's about to kiss me. He seems to come to his senses and pauses long enough for me to step back.

"Night. I'll see ya when I see ya," I finish lamely. "I've got to work a couple hours at the chiropractor's office early in the morning and then I'll be going to practice."

"All right." He nods. "You know I want to kiss you, right?"

My insides get shaky, stunned that he's just coming out with it. I try to nod nonchalantly.

"Yeah, I kind of thought so."

He stares at me, his hazel eyes glued on me. "We already know how fucking amazing it would be."

"It would also be confusing though. Right?"

"Right," he says finally. "*Right.*" Firmer this time.

When I get into bed, I'm wide awake and unable to stop thinking about that near kiss. I hear him walk past my room and pause, and my heartbeat nearly pounds out of my chest.

I wonder if he'll knock lightly or maybe crack open the door to see if I'm sleeping...

When he keeps walking down the hall, I'm disappointed.

CHAPTER NINETEEN

PLAY IT COOL

RHODES

Now

I GET UP EARLY the next morning, having barely slept.

I'm going to love having Elle live here...and it's going to be fucking torture.

I still hop out of bed feeling pretty damn great.

Things are good. We're winning again with the

Mustangs. I don't think it's enough to turn our season around entirely, but we're playing much better than we were.

It's been a huge loss not having Henley playing, but Cal's coming around. We're getting there and this weekend, we're going to win again.

I chuckle under my breath when I hear Elle singing in the shower. She's a horrible singer and it's the cutest thing ever. When she walks into the kitchen half an hour later, looking all cute and perky, I lift my protein shake to my lips to keep from smiling too big. I need to maintain my cool a little bit.

We're going to make this work. I don't want to send her running right back to that condo next door to the creeper just because I can't get ahold of myself.

"Good morning! I hope I didn't wake you up."

"Not at all. Would you like a shake?" I ask.

"Sure," she says.

I empty the blender into a glass and hand it over.

"You really don't have to wait on me," she says. "I'm going to get my bearings. I'll be helpful. I won't be in your way." She pauses like she doesn't know what else to list and I laugh.

"You don't need to do anything to make me happy. Rachel cleans this place. I get meals brought in half the time. I like to cook the rest of the time. All you have to do is get comfortable, make yourself at home, and treat this place like it's yours, because as far as I'm concerned, it is."

She beams up at me and it's damn addicting.

"I promise I'm going to find something to do around here to make a difference. And I want to help financially too." She lifts an eyebrow, daring me to argue, and I'm already shaking my head.

"Quit it. You are not helping financially. No. We're not even going to entertain that thought. And seriously, just seeing your face around here this morning is enough for me. You don't owe me anything."

"I owe you everything," she says.

"Quit with that talk."

She walks over and kisses me on the cheek. When she leans back, her eyes are bright. Her lips are...full and kissable. I want to kiss her so bad I can taste it.

"I haven't forgotten a single second of that night," she says softly. "Just in case I didn't make it clear. It meant something to me. It meant *so* much," she adds. "Which is exactly why I don't want to play with fire. And I think that's what we would be doing. I should have just said it like that all along instead of getting upset with you and icing you out. I regret that, but I was scared."

"Elle baby. You don't need to regret a single thing. But I seriously want you to reconsider your decision about breaking the pact."

I put my hand on the back of my neck and exhale. Subtlety be damned.

She takes a step back and stares at me.

"I don't know what to say," she finally admits.

"You don't have to say anything. I plan on working my charm and convincing you otherwise...just so you know where *I'm* going with this."

She laughs, her cheeks flushing. "Okay. We're going with full disclosure."

"Yep, I guess so." I smirk. Hell, I'm just winging it as I go. "Have a good day."

"You have a good day too," she whispers before bolting.

WHEN I GET TO PRACTICE, Roscoe is waiting for me and hands me a towel to use for my workout. Then he offers to carry my bag in.

"Well, that's more like it," I say, laughing.

He tries to take my bag and I shake my head.

"Kidding. We're even. Do it again and I'll stick your head in that fountain over there," I growl.

He laughs. "You know I have such mad respect for you, man. I just thought maybe it'd be fun to...I don't know what I was thinking." He rubs the back of his neck. "I just hope there are no hard feelings."

"Of course not. I've been the new brat plenty. You're a good player. You'll do well. Don't make the wrong people mad though." I stare at him pointedly and then grin.

He laughs, relieved. "Yeah. My mom always tells me I'm more trouble than I'm worth. I know I'm not for everyone."

"You're all right," I tell him, pounding his back.

After practice, I motion for Weston, Penn, and Bowie to walk out with me. As soon as I'm sure we're out of hearing range, I tell them what happened with Brock and ask if they'll help me go pick up Elle's things.

"Son of a bitch," Henley says. "Yeah, I can go today, the sooner the better," he adds.

"Me too, this is important. We'll make time," Bowie says.

"I'm in too," Penn adds. "Although I can't promise I won't beat that guy's head in if I see him."

"No." I shake my head. "Trust me, I want to, but we're not getting in trouble over this asshole, and we're not going to draw attention to Elle. That's the last thing she needs. She called Sheriff Davis. I'm hoping she'll talk to Lisa about it today, and the less my name is ever brought into it, the better." I lean in. "You get this means she's moving in with me, right? You think I want to mess that up?"

"You're right," Weston says.

"I'll be on my best behavior," Penn adds. "We'll let Davis do the work, but can't we just scare Brock a little bit?"

I laugh. "Yeah, let me think about it."

I message Elle when I'm walking out and look for her car in the parking lot, but don't see it.

> The guys are in. Just let us know how you want us to do this.

She texts back right away.

ELLE
> Oh, that's wonderful. How soon are they free?

> We're ready now. I can pick you up if you want to go over there too, or just send us there and we'll get the job done.

ELLE
> I'd like to go. I can meet you there. I just got to your house.

> You just got home, you mean? 😉 All right, I'll let them know, and I'm leaving practice now. I'll meet you at your condo in thirty.

ELLE
> Thank you. 🩶

WHEN WE GET to Elle's condo, there's no sign of Brock. It's just as well. Sheriff Davis let her know he'd given Brock a warning and hopefully he'll stay away. Whatever the case, I'm going to be on alert.

The guys are already parked near her place and heading in with boxes when I pull up. Elle pulls up behind me and I hurry over to open her car door. We walk inside and Elle exhales.

"Are you okay?" I ask.

"Yeah, I just really don't want to see him. But I'm glad we're doing this."

The guys and I are all wearing sunglasses and caps, but it hits me that this might not have been the best way to go about this.

"What's wrong?" Elle asks.

"I should have hired movers to get this done. If anyone's looking too closely, they could recognize us. I didn't think this through."

"No, I didn't either," she says.

"If you get in trouble over this, just tell them the truth. We had to get you out quick. There wasn't time to hire anyone."

She nods. "Yeah. We're not going to worry about it. Let's just take the basics. And I'll hire someone to get the rest later, okay?"

"Whatever you say."

"Thanks for bringing boxes. I picked up some too and the tape's on the table," she says.

She starts walking down the hall and rushes to close her office door.

"Just not in here, okay? There's...private stuff. I'll pack up in here while you guys are working on the other stuff."

"Kinky stuff?" Penn asks. He frowns and shakes his head. "I don't want to imagine you that way."

"*Don't* imagine her that way," I growl.

He wrinkles his nose. "I might have to scrub my eyes with bleach or something because now it's there…"

"Shut it." I point at him. "Shut your mouth."

He holds up his hands.

Elle laughs, covering her face.

"I'll start on your closet. Does that work?" I ask.

"That's great," she says.

"I'll take the kitchen," Henley says.

"I'll do—is the bathroom safe?" Penn asks.

I growl again and Elle laughs.

"*Yes,*" she says.

The guys and I scatter toward our respective places, and I hear Elle go into the office and shut the door.

Now I'm curious about what she's got in there too.

CHAPTER TWENTY

OCEANSIDE DANCE

ELLE

Then

THE RIDE TO RHODES' house in Miami was gorgeous.

"I can't believe all these palm trees are really here. I thought that was kind of...I don't know. Not a myth exactly...there are just way more than I expected!" I laughed and so did he.

He was driving a fancy new sports car and looking over at him, with the sandy beaches and turquoise water in the background, was almost more than I could take.

"It's really beautiful. Are you still liking it?"

"I do," he says. "I miss California, but I do like it here. And the team is great. I just miss seeing you."

"I miss you too."

And it was true. Missing Rhodes was an everyday occurrence. I woke up thinking about him and fell asleep thinking about him. We had done a good job staying in touch, but it wasn't the same, not seeing him every day like I had for four years. He had become a hot shot, just like I knew he would, but thankfully he hadn't forgotten me.

It was weird though, staying updated about his life through his social media and looking up articles about him. He always had a sexy girl by his side when he was at a party, never the same one twice. It was hard to get used to that, but he'd always had plenty of willing girls in college too. But in the nine months since we'd graduated and his world expanding in professional football, the opportunities were vast. The women he came across now were hotter and more accessible.

It was too hard to think about all the beautiful women, so I tried not to.

For the most part, we both steered *somewhat* clear of discussing our love lives with each other. I told him when I had a boyfriend and tried to ask about who he was dating now and then, but he'd always say, "I'm focusing on my career right now and these girls that I meet...it's just fun, you know? I don't trust them beyond a fun night."

"What are you thinking?" he asked as we pulled into a driveway. "Your cheeks are pink."

He grinned over at me.

"Oh my God, is this your house?"

I couldn't tell him I was wondering about all the women he'd met. As long as it didn't get in the way of our friendship, it wasn't my business. That didn't explain why it *hurt* to think about, even when I was in a relationship.

"Yes, it is," he said proudly. "What do you think?"

"Wow. It's *beautiful*."

It was in a nice neighborhood and looked bigger than I expected it to be, but not too big. He grabbed my luggage and opened the front door, the anticipation on his face tugging at my heartstrings.

"Welcome," he said.

His hand landed on my lower back and I warmed all over just from that brief touch.

Yeah, some things never changed. I would always have a thing for Rhodes Archer.

He showed me around and I oohed and ahhed. The place really was nice, although a little bare in some rooms.

"You've got more room than you know what to do with," I said, laughing when we came to the last bedroom and it was completely empty.

"Yep, you need to come move in with me. Fill up my house," he said.

"Yeah, right. I'm not sure I'll ever leave Colorado now that I'm back."

"Are you sure? Maybe I can convince you otherwise while you're here." He lifted his shoulders when I laughed. "Hey, you can't blame me for trying."

"What if you switched teams?"

He put his hand on his heart. "I'll never switch teams, Elle love. You have my word on that. I love women too much for that."

I laughed and shoved him, making him laugh. "You

know what I mean. Anyway, Denver's not bad. I miss California too...a lot," I admitted. "And I miss seeing your parents regularly. Their visits were always a highlight."

"Well, you know how we can fix that—we've got to go see them."

"I'm game. As long as I give enough advance notice at work, I can pull that off."

"Should we go out to eat or stay in?" he asked. "Are you tired?"

"I'm a little tired. It's been a long day and the time change is kind of doing a number on me."

"How about we stay in?" he said. "We can watch a movie, pretend like we're at school."

"I'd love that. I'm good with ordering a pizza or something too, so you don't have to make anything."

"How hungry are you?" he asked.

"I'm starving."

"All right, pizza it is. I'll make a big breakfast for us in the morning and take you out tomorrow night. There's a party too, if you wanted to check that out."

"Sure, anything."

We ordered pizza and ate in front of the movie playing in the background. When we were done eating, I leaned back on the couch and he put his arm around me.

"It's nice having you here," he said. "It's been a big adjustment. The guys on the team are great...it just doesn't feel like home yet."

"It's been hard to imagine you here. Seeing your place helps. When I'm talking to you on the phone or even FaceTime, I still picture you in California...at school or even your parents' house."

"It helped once I saw your condo in Denver too."

He'd played in Denver a few months before and we'd

only seen each other for one night, but I went to the game and then brought him back to my condo. We'd stayed up all night talking until I took him back to the hotel to meet the team before flying out.

"I know you think I was kidding about you moving, but seriously, Elle...everything would feel right if you were here."

I turned to face him, crinkling my nose. "You really think you'd want me here *all the time*? I'm sure the women in your life wouldn't appreciate that much."

"I don't bring women here." He shook his head. "They're too much already. I keep that separate because I can't trust that they wouldn't share everything about my house on social media. And anyway...you're the one who always has a boyfriend."

"I don't always have a boyfriend. I do date guys for longer than one night, so sue me."

He poked me in the side and we laughed when I jerked, too ticklish for his grabby hands.

"I don't know. There are things I really miss about Silver Hills. It's not that far, so I'm close enough to go visit my parents and get my Silver Hills fix. I do like having my independence. My job is still just okay though. It's not really improving." I made a face and he put his hand on my neck and started playing with my hair.

I sighed and we were quiet for a few minutes.

"That's nice," I whispered, yawning.

I'd missed him playing with my hair.

"I'll do my best to show you the best Miami has to offer," he said.

My eyes drifted shut. "You are the best Miami has to offer." I wasn't sure if I said it out loud or just thought it.

The next thing I knew, I was being carried to my room. He set me carefully on the guest bed and I smiled up at him.

"Thank you," I whispered.

"Can I get you anything?" he asked. "I didn't want to wake you up by taking your shoes off, but you'd probably be more comfortable if we got rid of those." He laughed when I just let out a big yawn. "Or I could get your shorts. I know you're usually in the 'soft things' for sleep." He did quotes because I had strong opinions about wearing soft things to sleep in.

I grinned. "You know me well. That would be great. Sorry, I'm *so* tired. It hit me hard all at once."

"You've had a long day," he said. "Okay, what side would they be on?"

"The left side," I said. "My shorts and a tank top."

"All right." He opened my suitcase while I pulled my shoes off.

All of a sudden, a buzzing came from my suitcase. He paused and I froze, horrified about what I knew was about to be one of my most embarrassing moments.

"I'll get that," I said, jumping off the bed, rushing toward him.

He held up my large, hot pink vibrator and waved it. "What have we here? Elle love. *Girl.*" He laughed his head off and studied the vibrator then turned it up to the next level.

I snapped out of my coma and swooped in to grab it away from him.

"I'll have you know this has been the greatest thing ever...since being single."

"I can see why. No need for those puny guys you go for anymore." He tilted his head. "Does this seem big to you? It's not all that long...and not much girth."

"Rhodes!" I yelped. "Don't you know size doesn't matter?"

He snorted.

"And just because they're not six-foot-four doesn't mean the guys I go out with are puny."

"Well, I don't imagine they've got much going on, if you know what I mean."

"Okay, Sexiest Man Alive."

He rolled his eyes. I had teased him for months about being on *People's* list. He acted embarrassed when I called him that but loved every second of it.

"And yeah, I know what you mean. So rude." I tried to sound annoyed, but I couldn't stop laughing.

"If they're so good, you wouldn't need this thing." He shrugged.

I buried my face in my hands. "You're not wrong," I said, laughing.

He smirked while I tried to hide it back in my suitcase.

"My little Elle and her hot pink vibrator." He shook his head. "That is a sight I will never forget. I'll let you...get to sleep. Don't worry. These walls are probably soundproof."

"Get out," I said, throwing a pillow at him and cracking up.

Of course I was too afraid he'd hear me if I used the vibrator, so I woke up the next morning still keyed up from being near Rhodes again. I was shy when I walked into the kitchen, but Rhodes just gave me the dimpled smile that made me melt and said, "Pancakes?"

"You know it."

All the shyness faded away as we talked and ate and then went to the beach. He smoothed sunscreen over me and I tried not to think of his length and girth as he did so. It was a losing battle. I hoped I'd meet a man that I didn't constantly compare to Rhodes, but he was the gold standard for me. Once every few years—less now than in the beginning of our relationship—I was tempted to tell him how I felt about him.

But how embarrassing would that be? He didn't feel the same about me. There had been pockets of time when I'd wondered if he did, but he never said anything, never made a move. We'd always been touchy-feely, so I didn't count the times he played with my hair or even held my hand when we'd go into a restaurant or put his arm around me on the couch...that was just us. I'd wanted to forget the pact and yet, I knew it was what was best for us. He didn't want to settle down and both of us wanted to keep what we had forever.

That night he took me to a gorgeous restaurant overlooking the water. We were dressed up and it was hard to tear my eyes away from him. Throughout the meal, every time I looked at him, he was staring back.

"You look so beautiful, Elle," he said softly. "I love your dress."

I wore a simple white sundress, but it made me feel pretty.

"Thank you." I looked at his broad shoulders and the way the candlelight made his eyes glow. "You do too."

His full lips lifted. "Thank you. Want to walk down the beach before we head to the party? We can actually get to the house from out there."

I nodded and after he paid for the check, we walked onto the deck and down the stairs. I took off my heels and let them dangle from my hand, as he took my other hand. We took our time walking in the sand. He unbuttoned his dress shirt and took it off, revealing a white T-shirt underneath.

A combination of music came from either side of the beach, the nightlife of Miami just getting started, but the water was completely calm.

"This looks like a good place to dance," he said.

"Yeah?" I giggled, but then I dropped my shoes onto the sand and he dropped his shirt, and we started moving to the song that was playing the loudest.

I felt dizzy and alive and happier than I'd been in so long. He twirled me around and dipped me back and I laughed, but it quieted when I saw the expression on his face. His gaze lowered to my mouth and when he lifted me back up, one of my hands was on his waist and the other on his head. His hand lifted to my neck, his thumb tracing near my mouth—

"Rhodes Archer, I didn't know you had moves like that!" A guy yelled, and we turned in slow motion, the moment dissolving.

Two of Rhodes' teammates and three girls materialized. We must have been in our own world to miss them walking up. One girl came straight to Rhodes and put her hand on his chest. His hand dropped from me as she pushed into him.

"There you are. I thought you'd be at the party a long time ago," she said.

"Uh, Elle, this is Crystal." He held his hand toward the girl and then introduced the rest. "Jordan, Al, Mina, and Leanne."

They all said hello and Crystal turned to look me over.

"Oh my God, you're Elle?" She looked up at Rhodes. "I thought Elle was a dude...like short for Louie or Elliot or something. You didn't say your bestie was a girl!"

"Pretty sure I did," he said, looking at me.

I couldn't tell if his expression was an apology or embarrassment, but I tried to laugh it off.

"Not a dude," I said.

I grabbed my shoes and we walked the rest of the way to the house together. Once we were inside, he tried to stay close and tell me who everyone was, but people kept coming up and interrupting us. Eventually I gave up trying to have a conversation with him and just people watched.

This was a whole different world that I wasn't a part of...his friends here hadn't even known I wasn't some bro from college. He'd made a life for himself and I was happy for him, but I felt on the outside for the first time. The longer the night went on, the more painful it got to realize things would change between us, whether we wanted them to or not. Life would take us in different directions.

We didn't talk about the moment on the beach. I didn't even know if it really was a moment or if I'd just wanted it to be one so badly. When we got home from the party, he suggested turning on a movie, but I told him I was exhausted, and I went to bed.

He brought up me moving to Miami a few more times that visit, but I knew following him wherever he was drafted wasn't a path I could take.

It would only lead to heartbreak.

CHAPTER TWENTY-ONE

EUPHORIA

ELLE

Now

"WHOA, THESE BOXES ARE HEAVY," Rhodes says as he brings the last few boxes from my office into his house.

All that's left at my condo are the larger pieces of furniture—my couch, the dining table and chairs, my bedroom set, and my desk. Bowie said he knows someone who can move the rest of it, so I jumped on that. He said he'd take care of it, so it could stay quiet that I'm moving in here, which sounds ideal.

We offered to get the guys dinner to thank them for their help, but they all had other plans.

"You know me and my love for books," I say, grinning.

"Would you like them in your room or what if we set up the room next to yours as a library or, I don't know...an office? What do you think?"

"I feel bad taking up two rooms, but—"

He shakes his head, lifting his hand. "Nope. Not hearing that anymore, roomie."

I laugh. "Then yes, I'd love to set that room up as a library slash office."

I have no idea how I'm going to keep him from seeing my books, but for now, I'm thrilled they're hidden away in boxes. He moves them into that room while I go to the kitchen to find something for us to eat. He has the ingredients for a chicken cobb salad, so I work on that. When he walks into the kitchen, he's carrying a bottle of wine, and I'm putting the huge wooden bowl of salad on the island in front of our plates.

"Should I open this? Feels like we need to celebrate."

"Sure." I grin.

He opens the bottle and fills two glasses, handing me one. I clink my glass to his and we both take a sip. He leans against the island and stares at me, lips quirked.

"What?" I ask.

He tries not to grin, but those dimples give him away. "So, what was in your office that was so secretive?"

I lift my eyebrows. "Wouldn't you like to know!"

"I would." He laughs and puts his hand on his hips, his muscles bulging.

It's like a feast for the eyes at all times around him.

"I thought when I found your vibrator in Miami, I was inducted to the *know all your secrets* club."

I put my hands on my flaming cheeks. "There's no way I can let you in on *all* my secrets."

"Why not? You don't think I'm trustworthy as your secret keeper?" he teases, his dimples popping out.

"I trust you with my life," I tell him, my voice getting husky.

He steps closer and pulls me closer to him by the belt loop on my jeans. My stomach flip-flops and my heartbeat skips ahead.

"I trust you with my life too," he says. "What's one secret about you that I don't know?"

With him standing so close, it's like I'm on a pheromone high.

"I've never admitted...to you...that you were right about the vibrator and the puny men in my life."

He lets out a surprised sound—half-cough, half-laugh. "How so?"

"You said...if they were so good, I wouldn't need one, and...you were right. Not necessarily that they've been puny, but maybe just didn't know..."

"How to work with what they had," he finishes, a husky laugh sending skitters down my arms.

He notices and runs his hands over my arms like he's trying to warm me up.

"Do you need someone to love that body right, Elle?" His expression has turned serious now and I could swear we're standing closer to each other than we were a second ago.

"What do you mean?" I laugh awkwardly and try to play dumb.

"You know what I mean. I think we should go there, Elle. Don't you know we're gonna wonder if we don't? You know what? No, I'm not gonna wonder. I already know we are going to be so fucking good. I'm just ready for you to realize it."

"What are you saying, Rhodes? This is...this is crazy. I can't...we can't...I can't stay here if that's what you think this is going to be."

I don't think I can survive it if I experience sex with Rhodes and he realizes he doesn't really want more than a one-night stand. But at the same time, do I want to go my whole life and not know what it's like to be with him like that?

No, I don't.

He puts his hand on my face and leans in until his forehead touches mine.

"Baby, when are you gonna see it? I'm tired of waiting for you to see me standing here, only wanting you. I've been patient for so long. I don't think I can wait another day to—fuck, yes, I can. I've waited for thirteen years." His lips lift and I want to lean in and kiss them. "I'll wait however long it takes for you to know how I feel about you. I just don't *want* to wait anymore." His eyes don't leave mine.

"What do you *mean*?" I whisper. "How do you feel?"

I back away slightly so I can read his expression better. A flash of fear crosses his face, but it's gone so fast and replaced with something more like determination.

"I don't care how we phrase it, whether you want to pretend this is a fake relationship for your parents and Bernard, or...if it's more than that and you're ready to give us a real chance. That's what I really want, a life with you, a *relationship* with you. I'm afraid I'd scare you off if you knew how much I want that. But I'll take whatever you want to give me. We can test the waters slowly. For now, just let me show you how good it can be between us."

"Things never line up for us, Rhodes," I say. "There's a reason we've gone this long without going there. We're friends and we don't want to wreck that."

"They're lining up now."

"But—"

"No buts," he says. "I know you want more. You're scared, and I am too, but you will never lose me. We will always be friends. I hope to change your mind, and convince you that we can be more than that, but we can focus on the physical for now." He reaches out and slides his thumb over my lips, staring at my mouth. "You came so fast before—I'd barely even touched you. Your body is begging for me. We've always been able to talk about everything else. Why can't we talk about this? You don't have to decide what you want with me long-term. It's okay. But I'm in this. I love you, Elle. I'll take whatever I can get. We're perfect in every way."

Somehow while he's been talking, our bodies have moved together as if they've got a mind of their own. A mind that's giving the middle finger to any resistance I might have left. He's saying all I've ever wanted him to say. Is this really happening? Our lips are barely a breath apart. My hands are around his neck and his body is flush against mine. I can feel how much he wants me, and I let out a whimper.

His lips are on mine in the next second and it's like the most perfect choreography, the way everything falls into place while simultaneously exploding. We fit. The way our lips and tongues and teeth and hands and bodies come alive when we touch is the most beautiful dance. I kiss him with every ounce of longing I've been holding back. The years of wishing I could do this and it coming true are almost too much. He picks me up and my legs wrap around his waist, my head falling back for a second when I feel him against my core.

"Rhodes," I whimper before my mouth finds his again.

We kiss and kiss and kiss and my hips buck against him. His hands grip my ass and he rubs me against him until we're moving with a steady rhythm.

"Take what you want, Elle. I've got more. I'm gonna do this all night—"

He slides his fingers under my yoga pants and dips into me once before sliding back to my clit and staying there with the perfect amount of pressure. Oh, he's so good at this.

I cry out, coming embarrassingly fast like I did the first time he touched me.

"You're perfect. So ready for me," he says. "I can't wait to—"

Despite the euphoric state I'm in, I think I hear the doorbell, but he doesn't seem to. When it rings again, I pull back and he looks at me, eyes dazed. Then his focus clears and he curses and sets me down.

"I'm so sorry. That's Levi. I—I'm off because we changed days. I—"

"It's okay. Go. I'm good."

He smirks when I let out a shaky breath. "You're so good."

I shoot him a look, and he just laughs.

"Not funny. Carrie is right outside with your son and we were just—"

"Hold that thought," he says, holding up his finger when the doorbell rings a third time. He turns around, eyes on me as he walks backwards. "We are not finished."

"Yes, we are," I hiss.

He just grins and shakes his head. "You look so fucking beautiful when you come."

My cheeks flame and I'm glad when he finally turns and jogs toward the door.

I try to sneak into the mudroom off of the garage, so I won't have to see Carrie, but just as I'm rounding the corner, Levi comes running into the kitchen and spots me.

"Elle!" he yells.

He comes barreling into me. I bend down and hug him.

"Hi, little man."

"What the hell?" Carrie says from the other room.

Rhodes doesn't say anything. I know I'm putting him in a bad position. It would be normal for him to let the mother of his child know when a woman is moving into his house, especially the woman she's always hated.

Rhodes calls Levi into the other room.

"Go say bye to your mama," I whisper.

"I want to stay heah," he says.

"I'll be here when you come back. Just go say bye to your mom."

He shakes his head and buries his face in my stomach when I stand up.

"I stay wif you," he says.

Carrie comes into the kitchen and Rhodes is right behind her, shooting me an apologetic look.

"I thought it must be you," she says, coldly.

"Yep. How are you doing, Carrie?"

"Fabulous, Elle," she says.

The snark in her voice is impossible to ignore.

"Come say bye to Mommy," she says to Levi when he holds on to me.

I pat his back and kind of push him gently forward,

encouraging him to go to her. When he doesn't, she huffs and walks over, bending down to kiss him.

"Love you," she says.

"Love you too," he says. "Bye, Mommy."

She shoots me a hateful look and stands straight, walking stiffly toward the door.

"It's looking real cozy in here," she says over her shoulder.

"I'll call before I bring him in a couple of days," Rhodes tells Carrie.

When she leaves, I let out the breath I didn't know I was holding. This is not going to go well. None of it is.

Rhodes looks at me and says under his breath, "Please don't freak out."

I don't say anything and when Levi comes over with a book, I take it and sit with him on the couch and read. Rhodes sits by us and Levi happily brings over more books and toys. I read him a few more stories before it's time for bed. When Rhodes picks him up and leans Levi over me to get kisses, I kiss all over his face and we laugh at the way Levi cackles.

When they walk out, I go to my room and shut the door.

CHAPTER TWENTY-TWO

DREAMING

RHODES

Now

AFTER I PUT Levi to bed, I'm on a mission to get to Elle. Disappointment slaps me in the face when I realize she went to her room. I stare at her closed door and walk toward my room, then stop and turn back toward hers...more times than I want to admit.

I respect a closed door...but I *know* her. I know she's in there worrying about what happened between us. I know she's never quite right after seeing Carrie, no matter how many times it's been now.

I know that she kissed me back and that her body is *begging* to be worshipped, begging for *me*.

I know that she wanted me as much as I wanted her.

Without overthinking it another second, I knock lightly on her door.

"Yes?" she calls.

"Can I come in?"

There's only the briefest pause before she says, "Come in."

I open the door and chuckle when I find her room dark. "You didn't waste any time getting into bed."

"I didn't know how long it would take Levi to settle down..."

"Mm-hmm." I walk toward her bed so I can see her a little better. "Once I told him you'd be here tomorrow too, he took Pretzel and laid right down."

"That teddy bear is the best investment I ever made."

I hear the smile in her voice and it warms me from the inside out.

"I wanted to make sure you're okay after...earlier," I say.

She looks up at me, her hair splayed out on the pillow, the moonlight and nightlight shining from the open door of her bathroom casting an ethereal glow over her.

"I'm okay...besides the lingering embarrassment that I'm a complete hussy."

I choke back a laugh. "Tell me how you can possibly define yourself as a complete hussy."

"You saw the way I—" She waves her hand toward my

body, and I lift the covers, motioning for her to scoot over. "What are you doing?"

"I'm not letting you get out of talking about this, my filthy hussy."

She snorts. "I can call myself that, but you're not allowed...and I never said filthy..."

I laugh and turn to face her, tugging on her to face me too. We stare at each other for a few moments, and I'm nervous, but this also feels more right than anything ever has.

"I have so many favorite memories with you, but the two times I've seen you fall apart...next level."

"Yeah?" she whispers.

"Yeah."

She waits a beat and then, "I'm scared, Rhodes."

"Of what, baby?"

"You and me. We're so good, Rhodes. I can't live without you. You're my best friend, and doing anything physical...it will change things."

"Why does it have to? Or...what if the change is better?"

"You're gonna be thirty-two next month and you've never had a girlfriend."

"*You're* my girl. For thirteen years, you've been my girl."

She makes a face and I tug her lower lip out from under her teeth and then smooth it with my thumb.

"You know what I mean," she says. "We shouldn't mess with us, Rhodes. What we have is too important."

"You're right. I could tell you why *I* think I've never had a relationship work out, but I'm not sure you're ready to hear it."

Her expression is conflicted. My fingers trace down her neck and I feel her pulse quicken.

"What if I show you what it can be like between us? It

will be explosive, Elle. You know it will. We can do this tonight and go from there. We will still be best friends, *us*, but here in this bed, I'll be your lover."

"What happens when you get tired of me or you want someone else?"

"I will never get tired of you. I've never wanted anyone else."

She reaches out and puts her hand on my cheek. "That sounds like a relationship."

"Well, we are fake dating, so..."

She laughs and I pull her to me, hugging her.

"Where is this coming from?" she whispers.

"Woman, you and I have been participating in the longest foreplay known to man."

She giggles again and my hand slides down her back until it reaches her ass. I squeeze it and she arches into me.

"So, you're hot for me, is that it?" Her voice is husky and through my thin T-shirt, I feel her nipples pressing into me.

"It's more than that and you know it, but if you're more comfortable calling it that, we can," I say, kissing down her jawline and neck.

"One time and we get it out of our systems?"

I pause and look at her. "If you seriously think that's true, I have my work cut out for me."

"I'm just giving you an out, *us* an out...in case we do this and it's...bad?" Her hands clutch my head to her chest when I lick my way down to her tits and tongue her peak through the soft satin tank.

I lift her shirt and she whimpers when my tongue connects with her skin.

"Tell me you think anything we do together will be bad, Elle love," I say against her other breast.

"Do you call everyone love and baby?" she asks between gasps.

I squeeze her ass again. "No one else. Ever. And I've called you these things from the beginning."

She smiles. "You have."

She leans up and pulls her tank over her head and I fully see her for the first time. My Elle.

"Fuck. You take my fucking breath away. Can I see all of you?" I ask.

She nods and slowly pulls her shorts down, tossing them aside.

I curse under my breath. "So beautiful, I can't think straight."

I lean down and kiss her stomach and then keep going until I'm between her legs. When I inhale and take in her sweetness, I can hardly believe I'm here.

Right where I want to be.

I press a chaste kiss on her pussy and she squeaks. Amused, I glance up and she's leaning up on her elbows.

"I think this didn't feel real until—" she says.

"I kissed your pussy?"

She covers her face with her hand and peeks between her fingers. "God, Rhodes. Yes. Are we really doing this?"

"Oh, I think so. I've been waiting way too long to taste you—"

"You don't have to do that. I—I have a hard time relaxing and usually can't—"

I prop her legs on my shoulders. "You can watch or you can lie back, but I'm doing this."

She whimpers again and the sounds change drastically when I start licking her. I take my time, kissing and sucking and devouring. She is everything I've craved. Her legs tighten around my head and she starts moaning louder. I hear her shift the pillow over her face and I smile against her skin.

"That's it. Let it out."

When my fingers dip into her wetness, she bucks against me and I suck harder.

"Rhodes," she cries. "So good."

And then her cries are indistinguishable as she covers her mouth with the pillow. She's so close. I can feel the flutters beginning and when she clamps down hard against my fingers, her moan goes straight to my cock. I only slow down when she pulls my hair.

I look up, mouth still clamped on her and she says, "I want you. Now."

I still and then press one more kiss on her before I move up, my hands near her head as I hover.

"You sure?" I ask.

"Positive."

"I'll be right back." I'm jogging to my room and back with a condom before she can miss me.

She's exactly where I left her, and I pull my shirt off in one swipe. She leans up on her elbows and then sits up and advances toward me like a lioness on the hunt.

"Fuck, you are something else," I say, gripping my dick so I don't blow my load right here. "There's so much I want to do with you."

"Let's start by taking these off," she says, slipping her fingers under the band of my sweatpants.

I can't take my eyes off of her, can't stop smiling. "Seeing you look at me this way..." I shake my head. "It's intoxicating."

I step out of my sweats and her eyes drop to take me in. I'm hard as stone.

"God, Rhodes," she says reverently.

Her eyes meet mine in what I can only describe as awe before they drop back down.

"You are...unbelievable," she says. "Now I know what you meant about puny."

A laugh bursts out of me and I try to scowl. "You're calling me puny?"

She gasps and starts laughing, reaching out and wrapping her fist around me. "No. Everyone else before you."

I rip open the condom and slide it on. "I don't care about everyone before me, only that I'm the only one from here on."

Her gaze meets mine, surprise flickering through them. She doesn't fully get that there's never going to be anyone for me but her, but she will. It might take time to deprogram the friend zone out of her, but I will.

I put my hand on the curve of her hip. When I lean my knees on the bed, I surprise her again by picking her up. Her legs wrap around me and both of us take a deep breath when my dick hits her soft, warm center. My forehead touches hers.

"It's still us," I whisper.

She nods.

"But I'm going to fuck you every way I've imagined for the past thirteen years, so it's going to take more than one night."

"Okay," she says shakily.

I can't help but smile at her, and then I kiss her as I gently lay her on the pillow and lean over her.

"Are you okay?" I ask.

"I feel like I'm dreaming."

"I assure you, this is real."

CHAPTER TWENTY-THREE

FOREPLAY DANCE

ELLE

Now

HE SLIDES his tip over my wetness.

"More," I gasp.

When he gives me more, little by little, pausing with something between ecstasy and pain in his expression, I feel every sensation. I was in this before, having the best orgasm of my life when he worked wonders with his mouth and tongue and fingers, but this.

It's a holy experience.

And it's Rhodes.

I lose my breath, lose my mind, lose all earlier restraint and pull my legs up, wanting him deeper, all of him.

He's right. We've been dancing this foreplay dance for so long, he's got me perfectly primed for him, and when he bottoms out, we both let out a ragged exhale.

"Feel how right we are?" he whispers.

"Nothing has ever felt so good," I tell him.

I flutter around him.

"Don't you make me come yet," he groans.

I smile and he kisses it off of me, playful nips until he starts to move and then his kisses feel more like what he's doing inside me.

I can't take it. It's too good. The solid drag of him builds an unbearable ache inside of me.

"Rhodes," I cry out.

He looks at me and my eyes blur, as he pulls slowly out and pushes so slowly back in.

"Like we were made for each other," he says, the veins in his arm twitching with his restraint.

"So right," I whimper.

I reach up and bite his lower lip and his breath hitches. His thrusts go faster, his skin hitting my clit with each slide. My body heats, the pleasure snaking through every part of me. He grips my hips and my breasts bounce, as I arch into every thrust. Until we're going so hard and fast, I don't know where I end and he begins. He tells me I'm doing so good. That I'm perfect. How he's never wanted anything but this and it's even better than he imagined.

I gasp *yes* and *please* between this pure bliss he's giving me, and his eyes take me in, relief and hunger and restraint crossing his face all at once. Watching his reaction does as much for me as what he's doing to me with his body, and I start to fall.

He looks so happy as I crest over the edge and I cling to him, pulling him deeper. When I bite his shoulder as I desperately try to take him as deep as I can, it unleashes something in him and he groans, his rhythm becoming crazed. It makes my orgasm ride on forever.

"*Oh*," he moans.

His head falls into my neck and he stiffens inside of me before the pulses rock through him. I arch into him, wishing it would never end.

When we've both caught our breath, he lifts his head and kisses me, slow and sweet. Our tongues tangle together and I gasp when he twitches inside of me. Just like that, desire kicks in and I'm ready for more.

His hand slides up my neck to my cheek and when we break the kiss, we stare at each other in wonder.

"Hello," he says.

"Hello," I whisper.

He kisses me again and I nearly cry with how complete I feel. My body has never been so completely sated and alive.

I just had sex with Rhodes and it was transcendental.

"I'll be right back," he says, kissing my lips, my nose, my forehead before getting up and going into the bathroom.

I run to the bathroom across the hall, do my business, and the world's fastest sponge bath, and still make it back before he does. When he comes back, he smells like soap too and he pulls the covers back and picks me up.

"Where are you taking me?" I laugh.

"I want the next time to be in the king-size bed. More room to spread you out."

I bury my face in his neck. "Awfully presumptuous, picking me up out of bed like you own me."

"Baby, if I could own you, I'd be the happiest motherfucker there ever was."

"What are these things you're saying?" I whisper against his skin, kissing my way up his neck.

"Mmm," he hums. "I'm not missing my chance. While I've got you where I want you, I'm saying it."

I look at him, full of so many questions, but too afraid to ask them. Now that we're here, I don't want to do anything to burst our bubble.

When we reach his bed, he tosses me on the bed and we both grin at each other. It's still unreal to me that we're doing this, the barriers we've carefully constructed demolished after tonight...or at least for right now. I'm terrified to think of what happens beyond tonight.

He prowls over me and tilts his head up. "On your stomach. I want to see you from every angle."

When I turn over, his hands guide my hips up, until my backside is in the air. Heat flushes my neck and face. I'm comfortable with my body, but I'm not used to this level of exposure.

My sex life has been vanilla ice cream, not even the melty kind, but the freezer-burn vanilla where you kind of wince with every bite like, *is this still good?*

But I trust him.

His hands run over my cheeks reverently as he curses under his breath.

"Elle love, I'm obsessed with your tits, but this perfect peach," he squeezes me, exhaling a rough breath, "goddamn, baby."

His hardness slides up and down between my cheeks and I drip in anticipation. His breath hitches and his fingers reach up between my legs to rub the wetness all over me. His lips brush against my ear.

"You ready for me?" he asks.

"Yes," comes out shakily.

I hear the rip of the condom wrapper and one of his hands leaves me briefly to slide it on. I turn to watch him over my shoulder, and his eyes are trained on where he guides himself inside. I gasp when he enters me and his eyes squeeze shut for a second when he goes in a little further. At my moan, he stares into my eyes before looking down at where we're joined again.

"Take it, Elle baby. That's it. I always knew you were mine."

His words. God.

My head drops forward and I push back into him, making him go deeper. The sensation is already too strong. I already feel close.

"You're swallowing me up, fucking greedy for me," he rasps, dragging in and out of me.

"I am," I moan. "Don't go slow, I need more."

"I will, Elle. I will. But first, you've gotta be desperate for it."

I cry out when he goes deeper and then drags out again. His hands tighten around my hips when I try to go faster.

"I'm not going anywhere," he says. "Do you think anyone else can love your body like I can?"

I bury my face into the bed and he leans down, his chest against my back, his lips against my ear as he continues his painfully slow glide in and out.

"Answer me, love. I need to know that you feel what this is between us."

"I feel it," I say into the bed.

He wraps his fist around my hair and tugs it back so my face is off of the bed and turns me, kissing me the way he's fucking me. It gets so intense that his movements become more haphazard, picking up tempo, but it's still not as fast and hard as I want him. He goes in deep and it's heaven and then pulls back until I'm feral for him.

I break away from his kiss and moan, my body trembling with this insatiable need, and I hear the smile in his voice when he asks again, "Do you think anyone else can love your body like I can?"

"No," my voice breaks.

His chest lifts from my back, and I miss his warmth, but he makes up for it right away. One hand stays on my hip, while the other moves between my legs, rubbing circles over me, until I'm panting his name. He moves in earnest now, the sounds of our skin slapping together erotic.

"I've. Wanted. You. For. So. Long." His words hiss through gritted teeth as he pounds into me.

My thoughts somersault over themselves, but only in my head.

You have? I've wanted you for so long. Every time I looked at you, every time I was near you, every time we've laughed together, cried together, were quiet together...every time you called me Elle love and Elle baby.

"Elle. Talk to me, love. Tell me you're here with me."

"I'm here," I cry. "With you."

White dances over my vision and my eyes scrunch closed, tears rolling down my face as my body experiences pleasure like it never has before.

"Rhodes," I moan. "I—can't wait."

"You're doing so good...taking me perfectly." He hisses

when I clench around him, groaning. "Elle, it's never felt like this."

His words stoke the fire in me and I crash and detonate. He lifts my back against his chest, holding me tight against him as we both fall apart. Tiny explosions erupt through me and he holds me through it all, his own raspy groan the most satisfying sound.

Finally, my body is limp and he lays us down, spooning me for a minute while we catch our breath. Then he leans over to see my face and I turn until I'm on my back. My hand winds around his neck and we stare at each other...

Entire books are spoken without us saying a word.

CHAPTER TWENTY-FOUR

CROSSED WIRES

RHODES

Then

I DIALED Elle's number and waited. Still no answer. Dammit. We were supposed to FaceTime tonight and I'd been running late. There was a long press conference after the game and I couldn't text her to let her know.

Lately, that had been happening more often than I liked. More often than not, it was my fault. Not intentionally. But my schedule had become a beast. Our team was doing well, which meant more exposure all the way around. I'd played for the Dolphins for a few years but I still hadn't acclimated to Miami.

If I wasn't playing or training, I was at charity events or speaking at schools. And when my coach and team didn't have me working overtime, my agent, Bob, did.

It had been weeks since I'd talked to Elle. The void felt like a massive crater had been hollowed out in my chest.

I was tired, and I needed to see her. It had been too long. We tried to not let three or four months pass without seeing each other. Even if it was just for a night when I played in Denver, her coming to see me for a weekend, or us meeting in California at my parents'. Her schedule had been busy too. We hadn't seen each other in over six months and our calls and texts had become less frequent too.

I tried her again and got hopeful when my phone buzzed. Diego. I groaned.

> **DIEGO**
> Are you coming to the bar or what?

> Not tonight, man. I'm exhausted.

> **DIEGO**
> There are some fine ass girls here, dude. They're asking for you. 😀

I ran my hand over my face. Going out had helped to take my mind off of missing Elle at first, but it had lost its appeal for a while. It was getting old, working my ass off and then going out drinking with my teammates and meeting women who only cared about me because I was famous. It was easy. There was always someone everywhere I went, ready to party, flirt, and spend a few hours in a hotel room as an escape.

I never saw myself becoming this person, but sometimes the loneliness was consuming. Other times I thought, why the hell did I care if the tabloids portrayed me as the biggest player out there? I was single and it wasn't hurting anyone.

In college, I'd hoped Elle would see the girls flirting with me and realize she wanted me after all, but she never did. She had months-long relationships and I had to endure watching her hold hands with the guys, lean into their shoulders, stand up on her tiptoes and kiss them...and it killed me every time.

Lately, it felt like the only one my lifestyle was hurting was me.

"Fuck, answer your phone, Elle."

When she didn't, I went on Instagram to see if her stories told me anything. As always, I got a little rush of adrenaline when I saw that she'd shared something and clicked her picture. She was at a club in Denver with Calista, her best friend from Silver Hills. They were dancing with a few other girls, and Elle looked like a smokeshow in a tight, hot pink dress. Damn, how did she just get better and better?

My eyes narrowed on the guy leaning close to her in the next frame. I'd seen him in her stories before. Who was this joker?

I went into my room and paused before leaning against the headboard. Diego texted again, but I ignored it. It wouldn't make me feel any better to go out tonight.

I closed my eyes and woke up later to my phone

buzzing. My light was still on and I'd slept an hour. The phone screen blurred, so I rubbed my eyes and answered it.

The screen blinked and there she was.

"Hey, Rhodes!" she sang.

"Where are you?" I said, sitting up straighter.

"The back of an Uber." She grinned at me and my eyes narrowed. She sang all her words when she'd had a little too much to drink.

"Are you alone?"

"Yep." The *p* popped.

"Fuck, Elle. Where is Calista? You shouldn't be alone in an Uber when you've been drinking."

"Who says I've been drinking?" She turned the camera toward the driver. "And say hello to Shelby. She's a very lovely human."

"Hello, Shelby," I grumbled. "Please get my girl home safely."

"Will do," Shelby said.

"See?" Elle sang, turning the phone back to herself. "I'm being totally responsible." She pointed at me. "You, however, are not."

"I'm really sorry I was late calling you. It was out of my control tonight, Elle. But it's no excuse, I've been shit at staying in touch and I'm sorry."

Her voice flattened, as if she was suddenly sober. "Yes, you have." She sighed. "And so have I."

"Come see me."

"I can't, Rhodes. I just changed jobs and...I don't love how I feel after a visit to Miami."

I brought the phone closer. "Really? Why? What do you mean?"

She angled the screen away from her face, but not before I'd seen her glassy eyes.

"Elle love. Talk to me. What's going on?"

I heard a sniffle and wished I could reach through the phone and hug her.

"Elle," I said louder.

She cleared her throat and the screen showed shadowy lips that only brightened with an occasional streetlight. "I just miss you. I miss the way we used to be. Everything feels so...you've got such a different life now and I don't fit. I come to see you and I feel like a stranger."

"With me? I'm not a stranger. I'm still the same."

She laughed, but another sniffle quickly followed. "The first time I visited, your friends didn't even know your best friend was a girl. The second time, you were called away to an unexpected event...which wasn't your fault. The third time, I liked the new crowd fine, but it didn't seem like any of them were interested in getting to know me beyond your guy friends flirting with me."

"I fucking hated that they were such assholes," I said.

I'd taken Elle to lunch and we ran into some of the guys from the team, who wouldn't stop flirting with Elle.

"How do you even remember that? You were preoccupied with those girls..."

"What girls?"

She snorted. "What girls? One sat in your lap and the other one put a chair between me and you—when there wasn't *room* for a chair—just so she could sit by you."

"I don't remember them. I just remember hating that we got interrupted."

"I love that you're successful doing what you love. It's just hard when our time together is short, and every time, there are girls hanging off of you nonstop."

"There are not girls hanging on me nonstop." My feet

swung to the floor and I leaned my elbows on my knees, trying to calm down.

"Feels like it," she snapped.

"How would you know? You've had a guy hanging on you from the time we met." I ran my hand down my face.

Fuck. Why was I picking a fight?

She gasped. "I'm trying to do better at not jumping into a relationship just because I've had a few dates with someone." She started crying harder. "But you really can't talk, Rhodes. At least I try to let people in...*really* in."

"I let people in. You're about as far *in* as anyone can go. Who's the new guy? Does he have a problem with me too? Because all your boyfriends do. Is he why you don't call me as much anymore?"

The phone jostled and I saw her face. She looked livid and her face was streaked with tears. I felt awful knowing I was causing this.

"I don't call you as much anymore because you don't answer half the time. Do I have to remind you that you flaked out on *me* tonight? Not the other way around."

For a second we just stared at each other, both breathing hard and hurt.

"I'm sorry, Elle. I miss you. I never want to flake on you. I'll do better."

She wiped her face and nodded. "We're pulling up to my place. I'm gonna go."

"Talk to me until you get in the door, so I can know you got in safe?"

"I'm a big girl and doing this most of the time without your supervision." Her mouth quirked up slightly to soften her words.

I nodded. "I know. I'm—"

"Bye, Rhodes. I'll talk to you soon."

She hung up and I fell back, pounding my fist on the bed. She texted a few minutes later.

ELLE
Inside, safe and sound.

Thanks for letting me know.

ELLE

I sent her one back and then grabbed my laptop and checked flights. I wouldn't have much time, but if I could spend a day with her...I *needed* a day with her.

I forgot to ask what you were up to this weekend.

It took a second and I wondered if she'd already fallen asleep, but then my phone buzzed and I grabbed it like a man getting his next fix.

ELLE
It's a low-key weekend. The most exciting plan I have is to go to the bookstore across the street and get some new books. What about you?

The most exciting plan I had was surprising her.

Surprisingly chill for me too. Maybe I'll crack open a book too. 😊

ELLE
OMG. Don't go out of the house with one unless you want to get mobbed!

I chuckled, feeling lighter already and bought my ticket.

MY FLIGHT LEFT at 6:50 AM and I landed in Denver at 9:22 AM with nothing but my backpack. I convinced the Uber driver to stop by a florist so I could get a bouquet of flowers and since he liked the Dolphins, he agreed to take me to Elle's place too. I tipped him well, signed his shirt, and he vowed to be a fan for life.

I hoped Elle would be happy to see me. I'd have to leave the next afternoon to make it home in time to sleep a little and play the next night, but it'd be worth it to see Elle's face.

When I knocked on her door, there was no answer. I glanced at my watch; it was already after 10:30. Highly possible that she'd already gone to the bookstore, her favorite place in the world. It wasn't far from here.

It didn't even take ten minutes to walk there.

But I saw her before I made it that far. I always seemed to sense when she was near. As I approached a restaurant, the patio overflowing with people talking and laughing outside, I scanned the tables.

There she was. Beautiful. Her hair was pulled back with a red scarf and it blew in the breeze. She looked serious and then nodded and smiled when the guy from the pictures the night before reached out and took her hand.

Maybe it was nothing. Maybe he was just a friend and this wasn't the beginning of a new relationship at all, but I didn't think I was up for sticking around to find out. Not today anyway.

I tossed the flowers in the trash, went back to the airport, and got an earlier flight home.

Once I got over myself, I felt like an idiot for leaving.

She'd said what she wanted from me from day one. I was the one who kept wanting to rewrite things.

I texted her a few days later and made a point to call at least once a week. Things felt better between us and I could tell we were both trying harder to make each other a priority.

I needed to just be happy to be her friend.

CHAPTER TWENTY-FIVE

MORNING HOURS

RHODES

Now

"I CAME to see you in Denver once…that time after we fought, when you called me from the Uber." I stroked her arm and she leaned her chin on my chest.

"You did? When? Why didn't I see you?"

We were naked in my bed. It was about four in the morning and we'd had sex four times. Each time was the best thing I've ever experienced in my life.

"I felt so bad about the things I'd said...for the distance between us. So I booked a flight, arrived around 9 or so the next morning. Got to your place and realized you weren't there. I walked over to the bookstore because that's what you'd said you'd be doing that day, and on my way there, I saw you with that guy."

"What guy?"

I look at her to see if she's serious and she is.

"The guy that we argued about that night. He had been in your stories and hanging around in pictures before then. You were at a restaurant with him, sitting outside."

"*Oh*, Jeffrey," she said. "That's right. Well, what did you do? Why didn't you say something?"

"I saw him take your hand, and I just thought I better leave before I said or did something else I'd regret."

"So you left without seeing me?" she says in shock. "I can't believe that."

"I know. As soon as I did, I felt so stupid that I'd missed a chance to see you. I knew that even if you were with the guy, you'd still ditch everything and hang out with me."

She swats my chest but laughs. "You're right. I would have. You must have not stuck around long enough to see him try to kiss me...and for me to pull away and tell him, no, I wasn't into him that way."

I laughed. "Uh, yeah, I did miss that. Fuck."

She grins up at me. "That was a hard weekend. I remember being so shaken by our...well, it wasn't really a fight, but it was kind of the closest we'd ever come to fighting at that point. I hated feeling so far from you."

"I hated it too. Those years living away from you were not my best."

We're quiet, and I wonder if her thoughts are going to those years like mine are.

"Elle," I whisper.

"Yeah?"

"I'm so glad you're in my bed."

She laughs against my chest. "I think I'm in shock."

I turn to face her, my hand moving to her cheek. "A good kind of shock?"

Her fingers trace circles over my chest. "Can't you tell by the way I've moaned your name at least ten different ways?"

We both crack up.

"I did think that was a really good sign," I say through my laughter.

"I've always wondered what your come face was," she says. "You did not disappoint."

"Ugh. I don't even want to know what it looks like."

"It's the best. You're beautiful. You're so in control all the time. You rule out there on the field and you...know what you're doing in bed..."

My heart swells at her praise.

"But watching you lose control...and knowing that I played a part in it...it's—" She shakes her head.

"It's what?"

"It's addicting. I'm already addicted to it," she says, her laugh somewhat shy now.

"*Please* be addicted to it," I say, leaning in and kissing her neck. "Because you don't just play a part in it, you *are* it."

She pulls my head back and stares at me. "You keep saying things that are—"

"Say it," I urge.

"I'm scared to."

"Don't be scared. It's us, remember?"

She sits up and faces me, and I prop the pillows against the headboard and sit up too.

Her lips pucker as she studies me and then her shoulders relax and she shakes her head. "You know what? Let's not talk about it tonight...or this morning." She laughs. "It's been the best night I've ever had, and we're tired and on an orgasm high."

She laughs again, and I reach out and weave my fingers through hers.

"I don't want to do anything to mess this up," she says.

"I know that feeling. I've been teetering back and forth on this high wire of not wanting to do anything to make you run."

She scoots closer, and it's impossible to not touch her soft skin now that I've experienced it.

"I'm never running from you, Rhodes. When I've withdrawn, ever, it's only for self-preservation, not because..." Her voice trails off.

I wait, but she doesn't finish. I trace barely-there patterns on her skin, wondering if she needs me to pour my heart out at her feet or to respect what she's saying and not talk about it tonight.

I decide to respect what she's saying.

"I will never hurt you, Elle."

"That's not something we can really promise each other."

Our eyes are locked.

"Then I promise to never intentionally hurt you, and if I do, I will do whatever it takes to make it right."

"I can get behind that. I promise the same."

I lift her and place her in front of me, straddling my legs. My dick has been hard just staring at her this whole time.

"Should we bring in the sunrise the right way and seal that promise?" I ask, planting soft kisses along her neck as I palm her perfect tits.

"Yes, please," she breathes.

Never breaking eye contact, we fuck each other nice and slow, and once again, my mind is blown. I've imagined this happening a thousand different ways, but nothing could prepare me for how good we feel together.

As we drift off to sleep later, her head against my chest and leg over my hip, I feel like I finally have everything I've ever wanted.

"DADDY! ELLE!" Levi's voice is pure elation as he runs and dives between the two of us.

"What—" Elle mumbles, pushing her hair out of her face and blinking. "Oh!" She pulls the covers over her chest as Levi leans his forehead onto hers.

"Elle," he says happily. "You sleep in Daddy's bed?"

Elle's eyes shoot to mine, mortified.

"He's excited," I tell her, groggy but laughing. "No one's ever slept in Daddy's bed but Daddy," I say pointedly.

Her eyes widen and I nod.

"Besides Gigi and Pop Pop, you're the only one who's ever slept in this house."

"Is this gonna be traumatizing?" she whispers before smiling at Levi.

He's nestled next to her on top of the blankets and looks like he could snooze a few minutes longer. As I'm thinking that, he pops up and grins down at her again. Tricked me there for a second, no chance is he gonna fall back to sleep with Elle here.

"Not even a little traumatizing. You're his favorite person and getting to see you first thing in the morning is the happiest thing he can imagine." I reach over and grab the sweats that are draped on the chair nearby and slide them on. "My boy and I have that in common, don't we, son?"

"Yep," Levi says.

Once I'm up, I grab Elle a shirt and shorts and hand them to her. She smiles at me gratefully and puts them on under the covers.

I lean over and kiss her forehead. "We can let you get more sleep now."

"No way." She sits up and tries to calm her bedhead. I grin and mess it back up as she bats my hands away. "I'm up, and I want to see him as much as I can before we have to leave."

God, I love her.

"Do we have time for pancakes?" I ask, knowing we do or there's no way I would've said that word out loud in front of my pancake-loving son.

"Pancakes!" Levi cries.

"All right, let's have some pancakes!" I high-five him and he and Elle bounce on the bed before getting up.

It's like any other breakfast we've ever had together and yet completely different. Elle and Levi crack up about the shape of their pancakes. Elle thinks hers looks like a clown once she's added the strawberries and whipped cream. Levi thinks his looks like a booty. It doesn't, but it makes us all laugh anyway. But between laughing and eating and playing with Levi, Elle shoots me these looks that are shy and sexy, looks that remind me of everything we did last night.

It's everything.

CHAPTER TWENTY-SIX

OVERTHINKING AND CLOUDS

ELLE

Now

THROUGHOUT THE DAY, I bounce around from a short practice to the chiropractor's office and back home to get ready for Calista's event at Twinkle Tales as if I've had twelve hours of sleep instead of two. All day long, people have been complimenting me or asking me why

I'm so happy, and I can't even turn the joy down a little bit.

I am on cloud nine.

My night with Rhodes was unlike anything I've ever experienced. I know I should be panicking because it's him and it's what I've wanted for so long, but also what has terrified me more than anything...but it's hard to deny a night like we had.

I stopped Rhodes from saying anything more, because all the things he's said so far have made me hope for too much, things I'm terrified to hope for, but that I want so badly. I just want to live in this moment and not let any fears get in the way.

Part of me feels guilty for so blatantly ignoring the Mustangs cheerleaders' rules, but I can't even stop myself.

I put on a cute outfit and head over to Twinkle Tales. Jupiter Lane is in the dreamiest part of their holiday spirit, with so many lights everywhere that it's dazzling. It takes a while to find a parking spot, but I manage. When I walk in, Sadie and Tru are already there. Stephanie, Tru's mom, walks in as I do, and she puts her arm around my shoulders.

"Elle, you are glowing. You've got to tell me about your skincare regimen. I need to know your secrets."

I laugh and it causes Calista and the others to turn and look at us. When they see me, they do a double take.

"Damn, you're looking fine tonight," Calista says. She studies me more intently. "Girl, what have you done?"

I just laugh.

I texted them about the Brock stuff and the move into Rhodes' place, which elicited a gif rainstorm. But I did not say a word about our night.

"Okay, talk," she says.

She pours me a glass of wine and motions for me to

come over to the table covered with food. Customers are milling around the store, and it's fuller than it's been in a while. It's always like this at Christmastime, and this Shop by Candlelight event is always one of her best of the year.

"Calista's right," Tru says. "Did something happen?"

Sadie leans in with her glass of wine, eyes wide.

"Tell us everything," she says.

"Well..." I lean in and they all do too. "I slept with Rhodes last night," I whisper.

There's an audible gasp from all of them. I look around to see if anyone else heard, but everyone is busy looking at books and taking bites of their hors d'oeuvres.

Tru and Calista high-five and Tru whispers, "I owe you five dollars," to Calista.

My eyes narrow on them and they look slightly guilty.

"From the look on your face, it went *so* well," Sadie giggles. "I had no doubt it would," she adds.

Tru squeals. "I am *beside* myself."

Calista comes over and throws her arms around me. "I want to weep, I'm so excited. Tell us everything. I mean, I know you're not going to tell us *everything* because you're not like that..." Her voice lowers, "But tell us everything."

I crack up. My phone buzzes and I shoot an apologetic look as I grab it out of my purse.

> RHODES
>
> Where are you? I'm home and I've looked forward to kissing you all day long. Not that you're supposed to be waiting for me when I get home every day, but...

RHODES

> I can't believe I sent that needy ass message. Don't mind me. But I do miss you. And your lips. And every other part of you.

I smile and the girls laugh at me.

"Look at her face. She's lovesick," Calista says.

I hold up a hand. "Let's not get ahead of ourselves. We slept together. We're fake dating," I whisper. "And trying not to let anyone but my parents and Bernard know it."

"Well, good luck with that," Calista says. "Anyone who sees your face will know what's going on in like, ten seconds."

I put my head in my hands, laughing. "People have been asking what's up with me all day. They're complimenting my glowing skin..."

Stephanie nods. "It's true. I did. As soon as I saw her, I had to know. Guess I just need to have earth-shattering sex to have good skin," she says, as we all burst out laughing.

"Also, it sounds like you skipped right over the faking and went straight to the dating." Calista looks very pleased with her deduction.

I groan. "I know. I don't even want to think about it too hard. Just let me have this one night to bask in the incredible way I feel."

"Baby girl, you don't even have to say it." Calista puts her hands on my shoulders and squeezes. "I can see it all over your face that you have never felt like this a day in your life. I know I sure as hell didn't see you even close to this with Bernard."

I shoot her a look. I don't even want to think about him right now. All the years I wasted, trying to make something work that I knew wasn't *my* idea of happiness, but my *parents'* vision for my life.

"Yeah, this feels completely different," I say. "I'm terrified." I lift my hand again. "Not going there."

I shoot Rhodes a text.

> I like your needy ass messages. I miss you too. I'm at Twinkle Tales. It's Shop by Candlelight on Jupiter Lane.

A LITTLE BIT LATER, Rhodes walks into Twinkle Tales with Levi on his shoulders.

"Elle!" Levi yells.

My eyes widen and Rhodes shoots me a guilty look. He sets Levi down and Levi runs over to hug me.

"Hi, little man."

I lean down so we're at eye level, and Levi puts both hands on my face. "We look for you and find you," he says happily.

"What a great surprise," I say.

"Sorry, I thought we could pretend like this was a chance meeting, but my son kind of blew our cover," Rhodes says under his breath.

"Couldn't wait even a second to see our girl, could you, lover boy?" Calista says, smirking.

He grins, the dimples out in perfect display, and I don't miss the elation that crosses his face when he realizes that I've talked to the girls.

"Guilty." He looks at me. "But we will be going...just in case anyone from the team happens to see us together." He looks around and holds up a finger. "After I've done a little shopping." He winks and makes a show of going over to the table that has an assortment of books and blindly grabbing a stack.

He sets them on the counter and then sees a few kids' books and grabs them too. Calista goes over to help him and smiles when she starts ringing up his books. She waves a book and my heart races when I see it.

"Excellent choice. This one was a crowd-pleaser, right, ladies?" She sets *It Was Always You* in his bag and keeps ringing up the rest.

"Oh my God, I have never loved a book more," Sadie says. She smirks at Rhodes. "I can't wait to hear what you think about it."

Rhodes grins good-naturedly. I don't think he has any idea that he just picked up smut.

My smut.

Our smut.

Book Rhodes is pretty damn great, but real-life Rhodes puts him to shame.

But oh, the sex scenes I could write now that I've experienced the real thing. I laugh and fan my face when everyone looks at me.

"It's toasty in here," I say.

"Mm-hmm," Calista says, seeing right through me.

"You look exceptionally beautiful tonight," Rhodes says, staring at me.

We're probably four feet away from each other, but he says it like we're in a room alone.

"We've been telling her that all night," Sadie says.

Tru runs her hand down my arm, smiling. "My mom even said it looks like she's got a whole new skincare regimen."

"And that I might have to take up sex," Stephanie says under her breath.

The girls and I laugh way harder than we should, while Rhodes' brow crinkles up.

"What did I miss?" he asks.

I try to wipe the goofy grin off my face, but it's impossible. Calista hands Rhodes the bag and he thanks her.

"Ready to go?" he asks Levi.

Levi looks up at me and I lean down and whisper, "I'll come read one of your new books to you, okay? Help your dad get home and I'll be there soon."

He nods excitedly and runs over to Rhodes, taking his hand.

"Well, that was easy. Whatever you said worked miracles," Rhodes says to me.

Several customers walk to the counter and recognize Rhodes. He signs a few autographs and sends me a look that sends a fire blazing through me before he walks out the door.

"Elle, if you don't get home to that man immediately, you have way more willpower than me," Sadie says. "Just seeing the way he looked at you makes me want to go jump Weston." She looks at Calista. "After hanging out here, of course."

Calista waves her off.

Tru fans her face. "Same. Henley is so getting some tonight." She covers her face. "Sorry, Mom. I forgot myself for a minute there."

"Honey, no one could be happier than I am that you've got a man like Henley," Stephanie tells her daughter. "And this feels like a good time to add that I wouldn't mind having a grandbaby around."

Tru chokes on her wine.

Calista motions for the next customer to come forward. "Hey there! Welcome to Twinkle Tales."

"Thank you! I love it here!" She's a cute blonde, and when she sees us all standing there, she does a double take. "Oh wow, hi." She lifts her hand in a wave. "Sorry, I'm totally fangirling. Big Mustangs fan." She points at me. "So envious of your dance moves." And then she smiles at Sadie. "Team Baggy Clothes, all the way. The press was so wrong and so rude to you." She lifts her eyebrows. "You've shown them. And I love the way you dress, whether it's for comfort or this cute outfit you've got going on."

"Well, you have made my night," Sadie says. "What's your name? I'm Sadie."

"I'm Poppy," she says, grinning. "Fairly new to Silver Hills, and I've been dying to come into this shop."

We all introduce ourselves and chat for a few minutes. Poppy is adorable.

"You should come to one of our girl nights," Sadie says.

"Totally!" Tru adds. "They're a little crazy right now because of the holidays and football season, but yes, please come out with us!"

"I would love to," she says.

We exchange numbers before she leaves.

When Calista is done with the next customer, she points at me. "I can't believe you're still here. Go." She holds out her arms and I go hug her. "Don't be afraid of this. I have never seen any two people more perfect for each other than you and Rhodes."

"Same," Sadie says.

"We're all in agreement here, and I know the guys feel the same way too. We've all discussed it," Tru says.

"Really?" I look at each one of them.

"Even when I've been around," Stephanie says.

"Wow. Well, I don't want to get anyone's hopes up because I have no idea what's going to happen next—"

"What's happening next is that you're gonna get home and do sexy, sexy things with that man," Tru whispers. "Don't overthink this, okay?"

"What she said," Sadie points at Tru.

"Okay." I nod. "*Okay*," I repeat more emphatically.

I drive to Rhodes' and crank "Now I'm In It" by HAIM the whole way. When I pull into his driveway and get out of the car, Rhodes opens the door before I even reach his steps and walks toward me. His hands twist through my hair and he pulls me in for a toe-curling kiss.

"Welcome home," he says when we break apart.

Oh, I could *so* get used to this.

CHAPTER TWENTY-SEVEN

LET ME COUNT THE WAYS

RHODES

Now

I WAS afraid that a day away from me would give Elle time to think about what we did last night and send her running for the hills. When I got home and she wasn't here, it sent me spiraling a bit. But the way her eyes shone at the bookstore every time she looked at me...the way she kisses me back when she gets home, leaning up on her tiptoes to get closer...all feels right with the world.

We go inside, Levi running to grab her hand, and we spend the next hour and a half playing with him. She reads book after book to him and he falls asleep with his head on her lap. He's overjoyed having her here. And I know the feeling.

After I've carried him to bed, I find her in the kitchen, cleaning up the Honey Nut Cheerios Levi was snacking on earlier.

I come up behind her and nuzzle her neck.

"I can get this," I say. "You don't have to clean up after us."

"I've gotta pull my weight around here," she says, her head falling back on my chest. "And you know I can't leave a mess for two seconds."

I laugh against her skin. "I do love how tidy you are."

"I love how tidy you are too."

I hum. My nose trails up her skin until my mouth reaches her ears. "Lotta love going on around here."

"Hmm." I feel her cheeks lift with her smile.

"I'm already hating that I have an away game this weekend. I don't want to leave you."

"There's still tomorrow." She gasps when my hands slide under her shirt and palm her tits. "I've got the day off because the Winter Ball is tomorrow night."

I tweak her nipples and she presses her ass into me, sighing when she feels how hard I am. I lift her blouse over her head and toss it over the stool.

"It's gonna be hard as fuck to stay away from that...you all dressed up in God knows what."

"Oh, you'll like my dress." She puts her arms back, pulling my head closer, and turns to say, "I'll give you your own private show, if you'd like."

"I would *love* to have my own private show."

She laughs softly. "Lotta love going on around here…"

"Mm-hmm."

Her pretty lacy bra comes off next. It drops to the floor. I turn her around to face me and kiss her deep, until we're both breathless, and then I kiss her some more. When we pull away, her lips are swollen and red and her eyes are heavy with lust.

"I can't believe how beautiful you are," I say, my thumb caressing her lower lip and then dropping to her rosy nipple. "I *love* how beautiful you are."

Her lips lift with the sweetest smile. She gasps when I pick her up and set her on the island and undo her jeans, tugging them and her panties down until she's bare. Her pussy glistens and I run my fingers over her slit before bending down and tasting her for myself. She arches into me, crying out my name, and then grabs my head and holds on for dear life.

We desecrate that island.

I lap her up like I'm starved because when it comes to her, I am.

I spread her wide and when I suction onto her clit, her cries become urgent. My hips jerk into the air, I'm so hard it's painful, and when she comes violently around my tongue and fingers, it's a spiritual experience. I stare at her, my fingers slowing when she arches into me, and I think, *I am exactly where I'm supposed to be.*

"Please get inside me," she pants.

She leans up on her elbows and watches as I slowly drag

my fingers out of her. A whimper escapes her when I lick them clean.

"You need my cock, Elle?" I rasp.

"Please."

"I love how desperate you are for my cock."

She bites her lower lip as she grins.

I take a condom out of my pocket and hold it up.

"Prepared," she says.

"Hopeful."

"Why are you so slow?"

I smirk at her and get my dick out and wrapped so fast it's not even funny. A laugh bursts out of her and I pause to lean in and kiss her.

"Your laugh," I say.

"You love it?"

"I do."

"It's been here all along," she says.

"I know, sassy mouth. And I've loved it all along too."

I tap her entrance and she sucks in a breath.

"You're teasing me," she says.

"I'm enjoying you," I clarify. "Do you need it fast?"

"I do."

I sink into her and her head falls back.

"*Yes*," she cries.

I move in and out of her, starting out slowly at first, and then gradually building. Her neck flushes, her tits bouncing. She lifts off of the island and balances with her hands, giving me a better angle. My balls slap against her and I watch where I enter her, pressing my thumb on her clit. She sits down on the island and leans back, lifting her legs on my shoulders as I hover over her. She cries out when I go even deeper.

"I'm not gonna last." A groan rumbles in my chest. "I need you to come again."

"So close," she pants.

I piston into her, the sounds the most obscene this kitchen has ever heard, and keep a steady rhythm with my thumb, rubbing circles over her. I see it on her face before I feel the grip from the inside on my cock, and she flies like a rocket.

"*Fuck,*" rasps out of me and I draw her chest to mine, kissing her as I pulse into her.

We kiss for a long time and when I gently pull out of her, she gasps in my mouth.

"You okay?" I ask.

"Yeah. I just miss you already."

"I'm not going anywhere," I promise.

She smiles.

I take care of the condom and carry her to the bedroom. She points to the bathroom, so I walk in there and place her carefully on her feet, still feeling a bit drunk off that orgasm. She's completely naked and I'm naked from the waist down. I tug my shirt over my head and she grins at me in the mirror.

"That's more like it," she says.

She walks to the little room that has the toilet and shuts the door.

"Would you like a shower?" I ask.

"Only if you get in it with me."

"I will never turn that down."

I hear the toilet flush.

She's smiling when she opens the door and moves to the sink to wash her hands. I start the shower and stare at her in the mirror.

"Elle Benton is naked in my bathroom."

She cups her hand around her mouth, whispering, "So is Rhodes Archer."

I grin and watch her step into the shower before I take my turn in the bathroom. She's humming while I wash my hands, and she looks at me over her shoulder when I step inside. She's been more relaxed today than I expected, and I can't even express how relieved that makes me.

She leans her head back into the water and grabs the shampoo, and I take it from there, getting her hair sudsy and rubbing her scalp until she's practically purring. Eventually I rinse her hair until it's black silk against her creamy skin. Her eyes are dazed when she opens them and I lean in and kiss her.

Each time we kiss it's like a shock to the system, a new awakening. I can't get enough.

She takes my body wash and meticulously washes my body. I'm jealous that I didn't get to hers first, but her hands on me feel too good to complain. When she lathers up my dick, I'm already hard and she stares at me, swallowing before meeting my eyes.

She leans up and whispers in my ear, "I've never seen such a spectacular cock."

I bob against her stomach and her cheeks are flushed when she meets my eyes again.

"Do you love it?" I ask.

She nods. "I really, *really* do."

She steps out of the way so one of the showerheads can reach me better and then sits on the bench. She looks up at me and then puts her hands on my ass, pulling me closer to her. My dick is at just the right level to dip into her mouth. She wraps her fist around me and it's pale against my brown skin. Every movement she makes stands out all the more.

When she lowers her pink lips around me, it's almost more than I can take.

"Elle Benton is sucking my dick," I say in awe. Because I *am* a dick and can never be one hundred percent serious for very long. And also because fuck me, *Elle Benton is sucking my dick*.

She hums against me and I groan.

"Fuck."

Her lips pop off of me and she stares up at me, doe-eyed. I nearly lose it once again.

She licks me with a single long stroke, her eyes never leaving mine and my dick taps on her lips in approval. She grins and it's the hottest fucking thing. She licks me from root to tip again, this time topping it with a kiss.

"Show me how you like it. I'm not good at this," she says.

"You're fucking great at this," I tell her. "Open."

She opens her mouth and I slide inside, groaning.

"I like everything you're doing, I promise. Love everything..." I add a moment later.

Her hands wrap around my base, and the magic she creates with her hands and mouth, holy hell. I try to remain still, but when her hands move around to grip my ass and take me even deeper, my head falls back and I rock into her.

When I look at her again, her eyes are on mine and I twitch in her mouth.

"Touch yourself," I tell her. "Let me see you make yourself feel good too."

Her fingers go between her legs and I thrust into her mouth. She swallows and I let out a ragged moan. She gasps and her head bobs over me, the intensity building as she takes her pleasure too.

"You're so fucking good at this," I tell her.

I smooth her hair back, unable to take my eyes off of her. Too many amazing places to look at once, her mouth on me or the way she dips her middle finger inside and presses the heel of her hand to her clit. I'm on overload.

She whimpers and I can tell she's so close.

"Fuck, Elle. I'm gonna come." I tug her hair gently and she doubles down.

And I go to the fucking moon.

CHAPTER TWENTY-EIGHT

FALLOUT

ELLE

Then

I DIDN'T USUALLY GET nervous before seeing Rhodes. Excited jitters maybe, but not nervous. But the past year had been the rockiest stretch we'd ever had. Part of it was not seeing each other as much. After we'd had a rough conversation one night where we'd basically called each other out for a) his inability to be in a relationship, and b) my tendency to be in a serial-relationship, he'd gone out of his way to call more. It had definitely helped, a *lot*, but things had still felt somewhat tentative between us since then. I didn't like it.

I'd seen him on FaceTime at least once a week, but it was the longest we'd ever gone without seeing each other in person. Since that conversation, I'd only seen him for a few hours at a game in Denver. He hadn't even been able to spend the night because his grandma had suddenly passed. We'd gone out to eat after the game and then back to my apartment for a couple of hours when he got the call. I drove him to the airport at three in the morning so he could meet his parents in South Africa.

It had been even longer since I'd seen his parents though. I hoped they would balance out any potential awkwardness between me and Rhodes. How had it come to this? I'd wanted to avoid that more than anything with my best friend, yet here we were.

When I saw his face in baggage claim, holding a huge bouquet of flowers, all my anxieties faded. He rushed toward me and hugged me so hard I couldn't breathe.

"Shit, I'm sorry." He laughed when I squeaked. He rubbed my arms apologetically when he pulled back to smile at me. "Here." He handed me the flowers. "I'm just so happy to see you."

"Thank you. These are beautiful. I'm so happy to see you," I said. I took a better look at him and made a face. "Where are you getting all these muscles? Every time I see you, there are more."

He laughed. "I have to keep up with everyone and maintain my Sexiest Man Alive title."

"Right. Way to go on snagging it yet another year," I said dryly.

"Yeah, you 'congratulated' me already, but I don't think I got near enough props."

He put his arm around me as we walked toward the baggage carousel. A few people recognized him; I saw them elbowing each other as we walked by. It was weird having a famous best friend.

"I gave you plenty of props. Just look at this, hold on." I bent down and dug through my carry-on and pulled out a little black bag.

He lifted his eyebrows, grinning. The guy had always loved a gift.

"What's this?" he asked.

"Open it," I said.

He opened it up and his eyes crinkled as he laughed hard. I think I drooled a little bit, staring up at him. He held up the present—a key chain with a caricature of him...if he was skinny and dorky...with the words Sexiest Man Alive in bold black letters.

"It's so sad that you think I look like this," he said, still laughing.

"You're a *little* better in person."

"You are so good on my ego."

The bags started rolling out.

"Which bag is yours?"

"It's massive and hot pink."

"Of course, it is."

"Oh, over there...that one."

He hauled my bag off and put his hand on the small of my back as we started toward the exit. I shivered but hoped he wouldn't notice.

"Chilly?" he asked.

"A little," I lied.

He put his arm around me to warm me up and I inhaled his spectacular Rhodes' scent.

"My parents cannot wait to see you," he said. "My mom has been cooking for two days and it's been so long since she cooked that she's worried she doesn't remember how."

I laughed. "I'm sure everything she makes will be delicious. It always is. I cannot wait to see *them*. I know I went on about your dad's last movie to you forever on the phone last month, and full disclosure, I'm afraid I might gush over him about it. But I think I deserve a pass because I never have before now."

"Girl, you better not fangirl over my dad. I'll be so jealous. You don't give me that kind of love."

I shoved him playfully. "You've got plenty of love coming in from *all* over."

"Not from the person that matters."

I looked at him and he lifted his shoulder like *what?*

There was a driver waiting outside for us. He opened the door for us and we got in the back seat while the man put my luggage in the trunk.

"Livin' the high life, aren't you?" I teased.

"Always have been." Rhodes grinned and took my hand, threading our fingers together.

It's true, he had always been famous, but I'd never noticed it more than now.

"You've settled into your fame."

His nose scrunched. "That doesn't sound good."

"It isn't a bad thing. When I met you, you were still uncomfortable living under your parents' spotlight. Now you've created your own success and you carry it with confidence. It looks good on you, Rhodes."

He looked at me and grinned, his hazel eyes more green in the California sunshine.

"Thank you. That means a lot coming from you."

"You know I'm proud of you, right? So proud." My voice cracked a little bit.

He lifted my hand and kissed the back of it. "It's what keeps me going, Elle love. I'm proud of you too."

I rolled my eyes, partially to distract myself from the way his kiss made my breathing uneven. "I have some catching up to do. My parents are trying to convince me to move back to Silver Hills. They think it's time I get something more dependable than these writing gigs that hardly pay. I can live at home for a while and save money..."

"Do you want to move back to Silver Hills?"

"I do miss it so much. Honestly, as much as I hate the idea of moving back in with my parents at this age, their house is huge, and I could stand to recoup for a while. And...I do need a job that pays better. They're not wrong about that."

"I wish you'd let me help," he groaned.

If I had a dollar for every time he'd tried to convince me to let him help, I'd be rich. One time, he left a stash of hundreds in my apartment after coming through and I threatened to shave his head if he ever did that again.

I gave him a stern look. "You can help me by being the comic relief I'll need if I do decide to move back."

He squeezed my hand. "You know I can do that."

We grinned at each other.

"How are your parents?" he asked.

"They're good. They're trying really hard to set me up with this guy from their church...Bernard."

He frowned. "What kind of name is Bernard?"

I snorted. "Sounds like a charming grandpa or something."

"Exactly. With a sky blue cardigan. Not for you, Elle baby."

I grinned. "And if my parents are pushing him, that can't be a great sign."

He tilted his head like *you said it, not me.* He looked out of the window for a second and then down at our hands, still clasped. I loved that he still grabbed my hand after all this time. I hoped that never changed.

"Actually, I've met him though, and he isn't bad."

He coughed and dropped my hand when he couldn't stop.

"Are you okay?" I asked when he cracked the window and knocked his chest like he couldn't catch his breath.

He adjusted the vents on his side so they hit him, and he took a deep breath. I put my hand on his shoulder and frowned when I felt how tense he was.

"Your parents have never really liked me, have they?"

My mouth fell open. "Rhodes, they love you!"

"I know they think I'm fun and a good athlete. Your mom laughs her head off at the things I say and your dad is a huge football fan, so I know they're fond of me." His eyes cut over to mine before looking down again. "But they don't *approve* of me."

I sighed. "They might not approve of all that you do... your lifestyle...but they love you."

"Because they know I drink occasionally and am not always at church on a Sunday morning?"

I nudged his shoulder with mine. "I think all the women might have something to do with it too."

"But it's not like I've ever sat down with them and

talked about any women that I've ever slept with. Have you talked with them about the men you've slept with?"

My face heated and my palms started to sweat, just talking about this subject with him. "No. But your life is out there in the news for public consumption."

"And often exaggerated or not true at all," he added.

I lifted my eyebrows and shrugged. "It's a luxury I have, living in Denver and not having reporters following my every move. My relationships are private. My parents have rarely met anyone I've dated and they assume I'm sad and single and just work all the time...which isn't completely wrong." I laughed, but he didn't join in.

"It makes me sad that you can't show exactly who you are to them."

"I could...I just don't want to live with the fallout."

"The fact that there would be a fallout at all is sad." He sighed and looked at me again, his expression apprehensive.

"What is it?" I whispered.

"Promise that you'll only move to Silver Hills because you really want to...and that you won't date this guy Bernard just because your parents are pushing it."

I nodded. "I promise."

His parents had a huge feast prepared by the time we got there and we had such a nice weekend.

But there was a seriousness to Rhodes the whole time. Even his parents kept asking if he was okay and he said he was, but the sadness never lifted. When we said goodbye at the airport, I put my hands on his cheeks.

"Are you really okay?" I asked.

"I'm sorry if I've been a dud. There's a lot on my mind. I'm tired, I don't see you or my parents enough, and when we're together, I'm already thinking about how much I'm going to miss you when you leave."

"I know. I hate that we live so far apart."

"While you're trying to figure out what to do next, you could always come to Miami."

I hugged him, letting his arms around me feel like enough. "I'm glad you love me enough to keep asking."

"It will always be an option."

I pulled back and took the handle of my carry-on from him. "Love you."

"I love you, Elle."

CHAPTER TWENTY-NINE

EIGHTIES HAIR

ELLE

Now

"WHAT IS SO FUNNY IN HERE?" Rhodes asks.

Levi and I are on the floor playing with his trains and look up. Rhodes only has a towel around his waist.

Whoa.

His dimples are out, as well as his exposed chest, complete with droplets of water still dripping down his skin. Damn, he looks good.

And oh, the way he knows how to use his body. Kept me up again all night proving it. I don't have a single regret over the sleep I've missed.

His dimples become sinful when he sees me checking him out.

"Don't you be looking at me like that when I've got this towel situation goin' on—"

I bite the inside of my lip to keep from laughing and turn on innocent eyes, but it's so hard to maintain eye contact when that massive bulge is right there at eye level.

"Mm-hmm. I see what you're doing there with those doe eyes," he says.

I snort and Levi mimics the sound, making us laugh.

"Elle, say his name," Levi says, his little face popping in front of mine.

I hold a train up so Rhodes can see. "Boo Boo." And then another. "Fluff."

Levi throws his head back and cackles. He thinks it is hilarious that I named two of his trains Boo Boo and Fluff. He called the one he was playing with Toot and I just went with it.

"Fitting," Rhodes says, chuckling. "I have an idea I want to run past you."

I point to my chest. "Me?"

"Yes, you." He grins. He motions over his shoulder.

I stand up. "I'll be back in a sec," I tell Levi and follow Rhodes into the hall.

Rhodes' hands land on my waist and he leans in to kiss me.

I'm dazed when he pulls away.

"If you pulled me away from your little boy as an excuse to kiss me..."

"What are you gonna do about it?" His eyes are dancing.

The second I start to worry about what we're doing, the lines we've crossed, I look at him and it disappears. He looks happier than I've ever seen him. *Ever.*

"I'm just kidding," he says, shaking his head. "No, I have an idea. Roll with me here."

"Okay?"

"So yesterday, early, I got this idea and went online and bought a few things. See what you think." He motions for me to follow him and we go through his room and walk into his closet, where he pulls out a bag of clothes and holds them up. There's an outdated sweater and pleated corduroy pants that he holds up to himself and then he hands me bell bottoms and a daisy sweater that are my size.

"This is actually cute." I wave the bell bottoms and sweater. "Okay, you've got me really curious here."

"There's more," he says.

He picks up another bag and pulls out two wigs. He puts one over his head and I laugh so hard.

"Oh my goodness, you look like your *dad*."

"Have you always jonesed on my dad, Elle?" he says it in his dad's British accent and sounds just like him.

"Don't be ridiculous, but you do look like him with that hair. He would never wear that outfit though." I make a face. "The outfit is eighties comedy and the hair is surfer movie star. What was that movie your dad played where he surfed?"

"Maybe this won't work," he says, yanking it off. "No,

wait. I almost forgot—I have glasses too." He pulls them out and I laugh until I cry.

They're huge and brown and hideous.

"I could also do these sunglasses if the glasses show too much of my eyes." He holds them up and they're from the same timeframe.

"What is this about?" I manage to get out.

He holds up a wig with long blonde hair and hands it to me.

"I thought we could wear these disguises and take Levi out to see Santa like we do every year."

I sober and my lips poke out. "Aww." I clutch the wig to my chest and look up at him, about to cry now. "I love that you're trying to figure out a way for me to still do that with you guys. I've been so sad about it this year. We've normally gone by now."

"I know," he says. "Honestly, Levi couldn't care less about seeing Santa, but he loves everything else about the day, and—"

"It's tradition," I finish for him.

"Exactly. What do you think? Can we pull it off?"

"I want to try."

I take the wig and run to the bathroom, trying to fit my hair under the cap as much as I can before sliding the wig on.

Rhodes follows me and watches.

"What do you think?" I ask in the mirror.

"You're still hot as hell, even with huge eighties hair."

"Have you always wanted to be with a blonde?" I move into a sultry pose and then hold up a finger. "Have you always wanted to *fake date* a blonde?"

He gives me a sideways look and I lift a shoulder.

"No, I have never wanted to fake date a blonde. I love your hair just like it is, but if you ever chose to go blonde, I'd probably love it too because it'd still be you in there."

He walks back into the closet, leaving me staring after him with my mouth open.

"Let's try on these clothes and see if they work," he calls. "Maybe we should tell Levi before he sees us this way though."

"We should definitely tell him, or when he sees you, he's gonna think Pop Pop is here for a visit," I say and laugh when he groans.

I know this is one of the crazier things we've done, but I'm having too much fun to not go all in. Rhodes has thought of everything. To cover Levi's curls, Rhodes got him a knitted Christmas elf hat. It has ears and everything. I have to pin up the curls hanging below the hat, but that just makes Levi happier. He dances around the living room pretending to grant wishes.

An hour later, we're pulling onto Jupiter Lane in a truck that Bowie only uses occasionally. Rhodes called to ask if we could borrow it and he came right over. We opened the door and he didn't recognize us until we started talking, so maybe our disguises will work.

Before we left, we told Levi that we were dressing in costumes for the day, all three of us. And he didn't hesitate, he was all in. Now, when we get him out of his car seat and Rhodes sets him on the sidewalk, he is ready for it. He moves between the two of us and takes our hands.

"Swing?" he says, and my heart tumbles over itself.

It's been so long since I've gotten to do this with my boys and I've missed it so much. Rhodes and I take Levi by the hand and swing him out between us. He loves it, wanting us to go higher and higher. The elf ears are hilarious, but he still looks so adorable, I can hardly take it. When it starts getting more crowded as we walk toward the area where Santa is set up, Rhodes tells Levi that we've got to stop swinging. He picks him up and puts his arm around me, holding me close.

I feel like part of a couple...a family...and it feels so real. I can't even let my mind fully dwell on how much I want this. Rhodes smiles down at me and we maneuver our way through the crowd.

Silver Hills is my favorite place to be during the holiday season. It's such a fun combination of whimsical and mystical, with a little bit of the traditional thrown in. Flocked trees are covered in lights and decked with moons and stars, fairies and elves and angels.

We buy hot chocolate from Greer in front of Serendipity and she doesn't recognize us, but she's also swamped with customers.

As we move into the line to see Santa, I get a little nervous. If anyone recognizes us, it will be here. Rhodes is impossible to miss. Whether he's a hot football player or a surfer movie star making poor clothing choices, his height and muscular build demand to be noticed...especially when we are inching forward slowly.

But we make it to the front of the line without anyone saying anything and as we walk up to Santa, I relax. It's a different Santa this year. It's usually Mr. Salvador, but I don't recognize this Santa, and that's probably for the best.

When we walk up, Santa calls out, "Ho, ho, ho, Merry Christmas! What a beautiful family!"

Levi isn't sure what he thinks of Santa. He doesn't want to sit in his lap, but he doesn't mind smiling next to Santa while Rhodes holds him.

We pose and then move around to see how we like the pictures. We end up buying a big package and then go shop for a few presents at the Pixie Pop-Up Market. I can't believe Christmas is not even a week away. It hasn't felt like it this year, but today has definitely helped.

Levi starts getting sleepy, ready for his nap, so we start walking back to the truck. I wouldn't mind a nap myself, before I have to get ready for tonight. But I pause and clutch Rhodes' chest. Lisa Harper is walking toward us with her niece.

"Lisa," I whisper.

"Where?" He shifts us so we're turned away from the sidewalk and we wait until she's passed us.

I can only hope that she didn't recognize us, but it would serve me right if she did.

THE RED GOWN I'm wearing to the Winter Ball is classy, but it's what all of the cheerleaders are wearing tonight, so it's also showing some skin. I've never been to this event before, but I've heard great things about it. Each year a different charity is selected to receive all the proceeds.

Rhodes is just waking up as I step out of the bathroom. He sits up, sliding his hand over his face.

"You look like a dream," he says, his voice raspy. "Come here, let me see you." He takes my hand and I turn around, while he checks me out. "So beautiful." He looks down at my shoes and whistles. "We can have some fun with those." His eyes are light when he meets my eyes again.

"Not right now, we can't." I laugh, skirting out of his reach.

We came home and put Levi to bed and then crawled into bed ourselves. He gave me two orgasms before we fell asleep, driving into me and saying, "Who looks like Pop Pop now?" And then, "Wait, don't answer that. That was weird."

I love that it's as playful with us in bed as it's always been…and I love everything else about us in bed too. My body has never felt so worshipped.

"Are you sure I can't change your mind about driving you into the city?"

"You're sweet for offering. It's too risky though. Enjoy your night with Levi. I'd much rather be spending my night with you guys instead of cheesing it all night with a bunch of strangers."

I lean down and kiss him and back away before his hands convince me to stay a little longer.

I TRY to stay out of Lisa's way at the event and am relieved when she doesn't single me out at any point in the evening. After we do our performance, the other cheerleaders working the event with me spread out and take pictures with anyone who wants to. Security steps in any time people try to touch us, and it's good because some of these old men are handsy. By the time I've taken my last picture, I'm exhausted.

My friends and I huddle together, wishing each other Merry Christmas, and I tell them I'll see them at practice on Monday. Since there's a home game a week from Sunday, we don't have the full week off, just Christmas Eve and Christmas Day. We will be back at it the day after Christmas and the rest of the week.

The weather is gross so it takes me a while to get home. When I walk in the door, there are candles going in the living room and a roaring fire in the fireplace. Rhodes is there, waiting up for me.

He strips me down to nothing but the red heels, and I ride him on the rug in front of the fire.

CHAPTER THIRTY

MORE IMPORTANT THAN THE GAME

RHODES

Now

IT'S SO hard to leave Elle on Saturday.

After I dropped Levi off at Carrie's, I came back to spend a little more time with Elle. I tried my best to engrain myself in her, make it impossible for her to end this with me.

But I still have all the insecurities I've always had with wondering if she'll really believe I'm meant for her.

I think she's in?

I know she's enjoying what we're doing.

But I also see the moments of terror when she stops and thinks about it too much. And that's what I'm afraid will happen when I'm gone for a couple of days. I'll get back late tomorrow night and then we'll be back to work on Monday before being off for a couple of days for the holiday.

Hopefully, the time away will only make her heart grow fonder.

I manage to set up some time with the guys for breakfast on Sunday morning. I saw them on the plane last night, but we weren't able to talk much, and since the topic of Elle is off-limits in most places, we haven't had a chance to fully debrief. Elle and I FaceTimed until late last night and I managed to sleep some, but it sure wasn't the same without her.

I walk up to the table where Bowie and Weston are waiting.

"There you are," Weston says.

"Hey." I look around. "Was Henley able to make it?"

"Yeah, he's coming. Coach flew him in separately and I don't know why Penn isn't here yet."

"Great," I say.

"There's something different about you," Weston says, grinning. "It's like you just can't stop smiling. I also might have heard some things from my fiancée."

"Oh, really." I lean back in my chair, laughing. "Yeah, I ran into Sadie at the bookstore the other night and thought you might catch wind of a few things. I'm surprised my phone hasn't blown up."

"Your phone *was* blowing up. You've just chosen to ignore it," Bowie grumbles.

"Oh yeah, that's right. I haven't been watching my phone because I've been living in my bubble with Elle," I say, grinning from ear to ear. "And it's been so damn good."

They pound me on the back and yell and cheer like we're out on the field. The few people in the hotel restaurant stare at us and I lean in.

"Keep it down, boys. You're gonna get us thrown out of here." I pretend to be worried.

Penn saunters to the table and leans on it like he's exhausted.

"I'm sorry I'm late. I've been on the phone with Sam all morning. He kissed a girl last night."

"No way. The one he liked? What was her name?" Weston asks.

"No. A new girl. She sounds cute, feisty," he says.

"Good Lord, I'm ready for this season to be over so we can get back to our regularly scheduled meetings. I didn't even know Sam was liking someone new," I gripe.

Sam is the kid Penn met through a tutoring program the Mustangs were part of and they've stayed close. Sam's in the foster system and Penn watches out for him. We all feel invested in the boy's life.

"Was it good? Did he do it right?" I ask. "Shit, he's starting young. Isn't he just freshly eleven?"

"Who am I to say if he did a good job or not?" Penn smirks. "He sure seems pleased about it though."

We all laugh.

"I tried to tell him how to kiss before because you know he asks fucking everything, but who knows if he retained it?" He shakes his head. "I tried to only talk about little pecks, but he was like, 'But where does the tongue come in?' I changed the subject so fast. Hopefully he didn't stick his tongue down the girl's throat or anything."

We all laugh.

"Speaking of tongues down throats," Weston says. "Rhodes has some things he needs to share with the class."

"I do have some things I need to share, but they are private and I will keep them to myself," I say, taking a long drink of orange juice.

"Don't you fucking dare," Bowie says, surprising us all. "We are way too invested in this for you to get all discreet on us now."

"He's right," Weston says. "I'm all for respecting Elle's privacy, but come on, give us a little something."

"I'm just going to say that the past few days have been the happiest of my life. I have never been so sexed up and done so right," I'm saying it all quietly, so no one but the ones at this table can hear, and they stare at me, enthralled. "It's just *right* with us," I say. "I don't know another way to put it. I could not be a happier man."

"This is the best news I've ever heard," Bowie says.

"What did I miss?" Henley says as he walks up to the table, slapping The Single Dad Playbook in the center.

"There's that thing. I've been missing it," I say. "It's been way too long since we've gotten together."

"I know this season, with me not being there regularly for the games, is throwing me off. But with the season coming to a close soon, we'll get back on track," Henley says.

"That's what we were saying too. It'll be good to catch up more. Have you noticed it's getting harder now that some of us have significant others?" Weston says.

"Fuck yeah, we've noticed," Penn says. He tilts his head

to Bowie. "Looks like it's just you and me." He looks at Henley. "Oh yeah, you missed Rhodes waxing on about how he's hung up his player ways and gone all domestic with Elle."

I should probably confess something to these guys about that, but now isn't the time.

"I'm really happy for you, man," Henley says.

"Thanks. I'm happy too, but I should clarify that I'm still not fully sure Elle isn't going to bolt at any time. However, it's looking far more promising than it ever has. We still have her job hanging over our heads too, so it's a tentative balance."

"Oh, this is a done deal," Weston says. "Sadie said Elle was glowing."

"So when can we meet again?" Penn asks. He looks at me. "Since I won't have you as my wingman anymore, I'm gonna need more coffee dates scheduled."

"Don't forget we'll have plenty of time together leading up to my wedding," Weston says.

"Yes! Does Sadie have any hot friends I haven't met yet?" Penn asks.

"I wouldn't know," Weston says, dryly.

"Have you decided what you're doing next season?" Bowie asks Henley.

We all turn to look at him. It's been a subject we haven't broached with him lately, but he's seemed better, happier, so it feels like a good time to check in.

"I have," he says. "Well, sort of."

We all look at him in surprise.

"It's possible I'll be the next Monday night commentator. Not as much fun as playing, but I think I'll enjoy it. And I'll get to stay in Silver Hills and help with the team when I'm able. I've also been asked to join a podcast, and it sounds like a fun gig."

We all congratulate him, and even though I miss him out on the field every time we play and know that he'll miss it too, he's not as sad as I thought he'd be. He seems excited about what's ahead. He's had such an amazing run in this sport.

"That's great, man. I'm so happy for you. I'll always miss you out there, but I'm grateful you're doing something you're excited about."

"I do feel good about it," he says. "I knew my time was limited, and the injury just sped that along, but I think this will be a positive change."

"Things are moving and shaking with the Single Dad Players," I say.

Penn snorts. He's always made fun of us for calling ourselves that.

"Henley's got a whole new career ahead, Weston's getting married soon, and I've got Elle in my bed. Nothing could make me fucking happier...except her saying she's gonna stay there forever, and I'm working on that."

I point at Bowie and Penn. "Now we just need to find the loves of your lives too."

"Oh, here we go." Bowie shakes his head. "No one needs to find any loves of their lives, thank you."

"Only if we're talking about many lives that I can love," Penn says. "*That* I could get on board with." He sighs when he looks at me. "You used to at least pretend to feel the same way."

"Yeah, about that," I start.

Weston sneezes and it distracts me. I see The Single Dad Playbook on the table and reach for it, laughing when I see what Weston wrote.

. . .

Kids are the biggest cockblock.
~Weston

I POINT AT THE BOOK. "That is the truth."

They look to see what it says and Henley adamantly agrees.

"Holy shit, we've gotta get ready to go. It's getting late," Penn says.

I pause my reading to look at the clock on the wall and stand up in a hurry.

"We've gotta set up a time. I'm sorry for going off the grid the past few days. Seeing you guys on the field isn't enough, I needed this," I say.

"This has been an important week for you," Henley says. "Despite being nosy bastards, in truth, we all would've clobbered you if you'd missed a second with Elle."

I see Bowie's entry before I close the book and make a face at him.

It says,

Becca's been asking for a sibling a lot lately,
so I need one of you to have a baby soon.
The cousin role will have to be enough for her.
When I brought up Caleb and Levi,
she said they were out of diapers
so they don't count anymore.
Who's it gonna be?
~Bowie

. . .

"NOT IT," I say, touching my nose and backing away.

Everyone else looks and shakes their heads, hurrying to touch their nose.

"Hell, no," Weston says, when he realizes he's the last.

CHAPTER THIRTY-ONE

AUTHOR NERD

ELLE

Now

THE HOUSE FEELS TOO big and too empty with Rhodes and Levi gone.

I had a little trouble falling asleep last night, but being so tired from the past few nights with Rhodes, the exhaustion finally caught up with me.

When I drag myself out of bed Sunday morning, I stumble to the kitchen in need of coffee and stand there in a daze until the caffeine kicks in.

As much as I miss the boys, it's actually good that I have this day to catch up on work. I am so behind on my book and email and all the other things that I can't believe authors have to do every day. I had no idea so much work was required beyond the fun part, writing.

Once I've showered, my head is clearer and I start tackling my to-do list and email. My desktop still needs to be set up, so I read a few emails from my phone and delete a lot of the spam taking up my inbox. I'm one of those people who can't handle seeing a high number waiting for me, so when I see how many I have to go through after neglecting it for a few days, I'm daunted.

I realize I never answered Calista's email to Zoey Archer. *Sorry, bestie.*

HELLO, *Calista!*

Thank you so much for your message. I could feel your love for the characters in every word you wrote, and it meant the world to me. I still can't believe people are reading my stories and loving them.

Your shop and town sounds like an absolute dream. Unfortunately, I am not doing any in-person signings, but thank you so much for the invitation. I would be happy to send signed copies of It Was Always You, as well as my upcoming book, if you'd like.

Sincerely,
Zoey Archer

. . .

I SEND IT OFF, relieved that that's taken care of and laugh to myself. What are the chances my best friend would be obsessed with my book? This career has surpassed my dreams.

Before I do another thing, I decide to get some sort of office set up. If I'm going to stay here for any length of time...which, now that I'm here, I have to admit it's pretty blissful, I'm going to need a place to work. I walk into the room Rhodes put my desk in and see that he has already set up my computer. That guy. He really does take good care of me and always has.

The stack of boxes looms and I don't exactly know what to do with them. Maybe I'll rent a space to keep the books and all the shipping supplies and swag. That's the only solution I can think of, but for now, I finish up with email and get to work writing. The sex scenes come easily now that I have first-hand experience with Rhodes. I lose a few hours in my dream world and then watch the game. My parents had asked me to come watch the game with them, but I'm not quite ready to be jarred out of my dream state yet. I told them I'm catching up after a crazy week and won't be able to come over today. I'll be with them this week...which reminds me that Rhodes and I haven't really talked about what we're doing for Christmas Eve and Christmas yet.

It isn't lost on me that I went from telling Rhodes maybe it was a good thing for us to spend time apart because of my job and what happened before Friendsgiving...to moving into his house and sleeping with him.

God, am I ruining everything? Will this last? What if it doesn't, and I lose him? That's my worst fear. I know he loves me and we're having so much fun, but I'm just not sure if he can be happy settling down with me. He's been out with actresses and models, for crying out loud. And similarly to the way I feel about actors and musicians, being a professional football player isn't the easiest career to sustain a monogamous relationship. My body does an anxious jolt and I try to reel in all the thoughts before I spiral. I've done a fairly good job of not having a meltdown over what I'm really doing here. I'd like to keep it that way.

I set up a wrapping station in front of Rhodes' TV in the living room and wrap a ton of presents while watching the game. The way the guys play and having something to do with my hands helps keep my mounting fears somewhat at bay. The Mustangs are *back*. They're ahead by fourteen toward the end of the fourth quarter and get another touchdown. I yell in the empty house and it's loud.

My phone buzzes and I grab it.

> **CALISTA**
> I need to see you. STAT.

> Are you okay?

> **CALISTA**
> Where are you?

> Okay, you're freaking me out. I'm at Rhodes' house. Are you at the bookstore or home? Should I come over?

> **CALISTA**
> I'm closing up soon. Meet me at the shop?

> I'll be right there.

I listen to the end of the game on the drive to Twinkle Tales, pounding my fist on the steering wheel when they make one last touchdown before it's over. When I park the car, I shoot Rhodes a quick text.

> Best game I've seen in a long time. XO

I tuck my phone into my purse and get out of the car. I want to say so much more to Rhodes.

I miss you. You looked so hot today. I can't wait to see you. Wake me up when you get home.

But I'm still in a bit of panic mode after too much time alone with my thoughts. And I need to get to Calista.

I walk into the bookstore and the look on her face has me rushing toward her. She is not smiling at all. She stares at me as I move in front of her and put my hands on her arms.

"Calista, what happened?"

She reaches over and grabs her phone and sets it on the counter, pointing at the screen.

I move toward it and pick it up. My mouth parts and I gasp. It's the message I sent back earlier. She points at the email address it came from at the top. My personal iCloud email. *Noooo.*

My eyes flick to her and she stands there with her hands on her hips.

"Care to explain why your email address is at the top of this message from Zoey Archer?"

"I—Calista—"

"Are *you* Zoey Archer?"

I swallow hard and feel the blood rush from my face before I nod slowly.

Her eyes narrow. "I want to be mad at you for all the times I gushed over this book. We even talked about the Rhodes and Elle vibes it was giving us and you never said a word! I can't believe you! How could you not tell me?"

"I know and I'm so sorry. I didn't want to keep it from you. I just thought it was the best way to...I never wanted my parents or anyone to find out it was me. You're the only one who knows."

"Girl. I am so fucking proud of you," she yells.

I jump, caught so completely off-guard.

She wraps her arms around me and dances me all over the shop. We're both laughing by the time I stop stumbling and catch up with her. I'm winded when we stop and lean against the counter, catching our breath. She looks at me and every time she starts to say something, she laughs. It happens so much that we laugh until tears are rolling down our faces.

"It was right there in front of me," she wheezes. "Ryder and Eliza."

I wipe my face. "I didn't think anyone would ever read my book and it's just—"

"Exploded," she finishes.

"Yeah. It's been so unbelievable, Calista. I pinch myself every day. But," I look at her, eyes huge, "I had no idea this would happen. Can you imagine if my parents found out?"

She shoots me a look. "No, I cannot. But..." She nudges me with her shoulder. "What if they did? What's the worst that could happen? You're an adult, Elle. You've branched out this year, cheering for the Mustangs when you knew they wouldn't approve. Maybe it's time you step into this and shine."

"I couldn't. For one thing, I don't know if I'd be able to write the same way, knowing they could be reading. Not just them, but all the people at church."

She laughs. "I'm just remembering all the people from church I've seen buying your book. The McDonald twins cannot stop talking about it."

I clasp my heart. "They're *seventeen*." I put my head in my hands and groan. "No. See? I can't do it. This is a small town and I'm already stoking the fire with going out scantily clad and dancing my booty off. My parents would be so ashamed."

"Then let them be ashamed. That's on them, not you. You've written a beautiful book. Your parents should be so proud. *I'm* so proud." She hugs me again. "So, so proud." Then she pokes me in the side and I startle, too ticklish. "I still can't believe you let me go on and on about this book and never said a word."

"I'm so glad you're not mad at me. I was ready to do penance forever after that look on your face."

"Oh, you're still not off the hook, Miss Zoey Archer." She laughs. "You are so talented, Elle. Like, I'm seriously in awe of your words." Her face softens. "And girl, you have got it so bad for Rhodes. I mean, I *knew*, even though you tried to deny it all this time…can we just talk about the way you think you have to hide *anything* from me? Do you not know that I am on your side no matter what? So are Sadie and Tru, for that matter. We *love* you."

My lips tremble and the tears are falling again. "I think I've been conditioned to hide. For a long time there was also the conflict with what do I really believe? But once I got peace about that, there were all of the external concerns. All the rules, all the fear, all the hoping that I don't hurt anyone or disappoint anyone…or send them running. Now, even the things that I don't want to hide are hard to let out."

"It's not easy being a pastor's kid. You've had so much pressure on you your whole life. Growing up, you lived in a fishbowl."

"I want to be honest," I say. "I don't like duping everyone or being anything less than authentic."

"You're the most authentic person I know, even with all your secrets," she adds.

"You and Rhodes know me better than anyone..."

"And we're not going anywhere," she says. She leans in, her hands on my shoulders. "Start by telling Rhodes how you really feel. None of this fake dating bullshit. Tell him about Zoey Archer, so you don't have to carry that alone anymore. And please, please, tell Sadie and Tru...and Stephanie! Their lives will be complete like mine is, knowing it's *you* who wrote our favorite book."

I groan. "I don't know. My life feels like a Jenga game just as everything is about to topple over."

"So get ahead of it. Do like my aunt says and take your life by the horns and drive that ship."

"Ahh, mixing the idioms. I like it."

"You are such a writer nerd. An *author* nerd. I freaking love it." Calista laughs and I'm able to smile back as I wipe the rest of the tears from my face.

"I wish I was a *brave* author nerd and could tell Rhodes I've always been in love with him, but I'm not there yet."

"Well, I'll be here if the blocks start to crumble."

I hug her again and take a deep breath. "I have a feeling I will need to collect on that." I pull back and tell her I love her, just as my phone buzzes.

Calista hands it to me and I hear her laugh and mutter, "You've got it *so* bad," as I read the text.

> RHODES
> I can't wait to get home to you, Elle love.

CHAPTER THIRTY-TWO

CONFESSIONAL BOOTH

RHODES

Then

I WASN'T proud of the man I'd been since the night Elle told me she was, in fact, dating Bernard. I'd seen it coming that weekend in California and could hardly get past it while we were together, already dreading what felt like an oncoming train barreling into me. I'd had a sick feeling that once she moved to Silver Hills, which she did not long after our visit, she'd be sucked into the life her parents wanted for her. One that I had always felt was way too controlling.

And that was exactly what happened.

She probably wouldn't like that I thought that, but it was true.

Elle had so much to be proud of, yet she bent to the way her parents wanted her to live her life far too often. They weren't bad people. They loved their daughter, but they also wanted her to fit in the little box they'd orchestrated. Anytime she did her own thing, she lit up from the inside out, and I wished they knew that side of her like I did.

I hated that something or someone always got in the way of telling her how I felt, or maybe it was just myself getting in the way. I didn't know anymore. I hadn't wanted to be one more person trying to lead her life the way I wanted it to go, I wanted her to *want me*. And I only kept losing her.

I'd drowned in alcohol and tried to escape in any way possible. None of it worked. It had been months now and she was still with him. It was probably time that I accepted that, but my heart didn't want to.

And now I was completely and utterly fucked.

There'd been this woman, Carrie, who had been on me for months. I'd ignored her mostly. She was beautiful, yeah, but there was something about her that put me off. The women I met usually didn't want anything but a good time. It was simple—nothing more, nothing expected. But Carrie, I just didn't trust her. I didn't know why. Maybe because she turned up after every damn game. My teammates and I switched between several bars in town to avoid the jersey chasers, and Carrie always found us. She even showed up at the away games. I'd been drinking too much one night and she cornered me, and I ended up in a hotel room with her.

I'm pretty sure I cried about Elle and then pretended like it was her giving me a blow job.

Definitely a low point.

She had the condoms and when I woke up a couple hours later with her on top of me, I had sex with her.

I could own my weak-ass self, but fuck me, it didn't mean I was proud of it.

I couldn't believe my life was about to change forever.

I pulled into Elle's parents' driveway and sat there for a moment, hands shaking. I felt sick, literally sick.

When Carrie had told me the news, I'd thrown up and then felt ashamed and hoped it never came out in the future that I'd reacted that way.

I got out of the car and went to the door, praying I wouldn't have to see Elle's parents, not today. I didn't think I could stand to see them right now.

I rang the doorbell and Elle's dad answered the door.

"Hey, Rhodes, how are you doing?" He shook my hand and pounded my shoulder.

"Doing all right," I said, trying to force inflection into my tone.

I sounded like a liar.

"Great game last week. You killed it."

"Thanks." I smiled politely.

"Any thoughts about next season?" he asked. "I've been hearing lots of rumors with your contract winding up."

"I'm giving it lots of thought," I said.

At least that wasn't a lie. There were several offers on the table, and I wanted to make the best decision, especially now.

I heard Elle coming down the stairs and looked up, my

insides sailing sideways the way they did every time I saw her, especially when it had been a long time. She grinned at me and then it faltered somewhat. I tried to wipe my expression clear of any sadness. She came over and hugged me hard.

"Hey, it's so good to see you," she said. "I was so excited when you said you were coming through. Come on back."

"Uh, I was wondering if maybe we could go out for a little bit," I said. "It's such a pretty day."

"That sounds good. Let me get my purse." She turned and grabbed her purse off of the hook nearby.

I said bye to her dad and we walked to the car. Elle chatted about the movie we'd both talked about seeing the week before—she'd seen it and I hadn't. I drove us to the park.

"You're awfully quiet," she said.

I parked the car in front of a beautiful lake surrounded by mountains. There was a path here that we hiked whenever I came to visit.

"Sorry." I turned and looked at her. "I'm so glad to see you," I said.

But just looking at her sweet face, my own started to crumble.

"Rhodes," she said, concerned. "What's wrong?" She took my hand.

"Elle," my voice cracked, "I've really fucked up."

"What do you mean?"

"I don't even know how to say this. I've wrecked everything. *Everything*. This is not how I saw my life going." Tears ran down my cheeks and she put her hand on my face.

"Talk to me," she said. "Please. Tell me what's happened."

Her eyes had filled with tears just seeing me cry and the crease between her brows deepened.

"I got a girl pregnant," I said.

It felt like an ax split into the car.

Her face fell and her hand dropped from my face. My life felt fucking over.

She leaned back in her seat and turned to stare straight ahead. When I looked over, I saw the tears falling from her face and I'd never felt so helpless. She lifted her hand up to her mouth, and her hand shook.

"Elle," I whispered, reaching over to touch her shoulder, but before I could, she lifted her hand.

"Just give me a minute," she said.

"Please, look at me."

I needed her to look me in the face and tell me it was going to be okay. I wanted her to tell me it didn't mean the end of us or the hope of maybe one day being more, but I knew that time had already passed. I'd demolished any future for us. She put her head in her hands and I heard her take a deep breath, but I knew she was also crying.

"Elle," I whispered again.

She turned and hugged me, and I could feel her trembling in my arms.

"I'm so sorry," I said.

"Why are you sorry?" Her voice sounded small.

"Because I've ruined everything."

She leaned back and wiped her face and I wiped mine, reaching for a tissue to wipe my nose too.

"You haven't ruined everything. Lots of professional football players are dads and keep their careers too. And you're gonna be an amazing dad, Rhodes. That child will be so lucky to be loved by you."

My career was the last thing I was thinking about right now. My face crumbled again and I lost it.

We sat there and clung to each other in the car until the sun disappeared. Neither of us ever even suggested stepping outside. The car was our confessional booth.

"Do you like this girl?" she eventually asked.

I frowned. "No, I really don't. Not the way I should like the mother of my child."

"You don't?" The shock was clear in her voice. "Shit, Rhodes."

"I know. I used a condom too. I've never not used one. And not that it means anything now, but I avoided this woman for months. She's just always around." I made a face. "And not in a good way. She—" I shuddered. "I'd had too much to drink, but I still knew better. I was in a self-destructive state of mind."

"You were? Are you okay? Why didn't you tell me you were going through a hard time?"

"I—" I swiped my hand down my face and shook my head. "Anything I say sounds like excuses and I'm one hundred percent responsible for this mess. I'm going to try to get along with Carrie...that's her name. I don't really know her. Maybe she's better than I think. Either way, it doesn't matter. We're having a baby and we'll have to find a way to get along."

"Do you think you'll be with her? There must be something about her you liked for you to sleep with her."

I turned to look at her and the light from the streetlamp beaming through the windows cast shadows on her, but her face was bright enough to see clearly.

"I don't think sex means the same thing to me that it means to you, Elle. I love sex and I respect the women I'm with, but I don't sleep with someone if it seems like they'll get attached, because I know my heart's not going to. It's a physical release. So no, I can't imagine being with Carrie, but I probably need to consider it just because we're having a baby together. I've always wanted a child, but this isn't how I envisioned it."

She nodded. "I think you should consider it, and also, you should take a paternity test."

I exhaled. "You're right."

She cleared her throat and looked away from me, out the window. "You've said that about the people you're with before. I think you assume my views on sex are more wholesome than yours. In a way, what I do seems worse. Because I try to get attached and when I don't, whether I sleep with the guy or not, I end up hurting him anyway by not feeling it."

"We're a mess," I said.

"Yep."

"But you like this Bernard guy?" I couldn't help myself, I needed to know.

"He tries really hard," she said. "I do like him. He's smart and works hard. He's helped me a lot with figuring out my finances. I accrued some debt when I was in Denver and I'm getting on my feet now, thanks to him…and my parents for letting me move back in for a while."

"Bernard sounds like a heap of fun."

Her lips lifted slightly. "He's a little more uptight than you, yeah, but he's fun too. He tries really hard," she said again. "And the best part is that he's crazy about me."

"Everyone's crazy about you, Elle. It's if you're crazy about him that matters."

She looked at me and her eyes were distant. "It's possible I'm broken in that area."

I wanted to ask what she meant, but she shivered and I turned on the car.

"I'm terrible. I haven't even fed you. Let's get some food in you," I said.

"Why don't we just grab something quick at Starlight Cafe? It's getting late."

"Are you sure? I have time for somewhere like Rose & Thorn before I have to get to the airport."

I'd come to Silver Hills for one reason only, to tell Elle about the baby in person. She thought I just had an extra-long layover between flights.

"I'm sure. You should start heading to Denver before the traffic picks up."

"Trying to get rid of me already," I tried to tease, but it just sounded sad.

"Never."

We stopped at Starlight Cafe and got a booth in the back. Fortunately, it was a slower night than the other times we'd come here. We were quiet as we ate. Her eyes were puffy and every time I looked at her, my heart broke a little more.

When I took her home and walked her to the front step, I hugged her hard. We both had tears in our eyes as we pulled apart.

"Promise me something?" she said softly.

"Anything."

"Whatever happens with Carrie, let me be part of your life with the baby. I know everything is about to change forever, but I'm still your best friend and I want to help. Don't shut me out, please. It would break my heart too much."

I leaned forward and kissed her forehead. "Don't you

know by now that I can't live without you? I want you there by me every step of the way for the rest of our lives."

She nodded. "I want that too, Rhodes." A tear slipped down her cheek and I caught it with my thumb.

I nodded, the emotion so tight in my throat, I was unable to speak.

She touched my hand on her face and then turned and walked inside.

I cried like a baby on the drive to the airport and then put on my jock/devil-may-care persona, flew home, and tried to figure out what the fuck I was going to do.

CHAPTER THIRTY-THREE

HOME

RHODES

Now

IT'S LATE when I get home. The lights are dim. I walk back to the bedroom, smiling when I see Elle sleeping in my bed.

I've probably thought through a dozen worst-case scenarios since I've been away, all of them involving her not being here when I got back, or even being in her room instead of mine. But the fact that she's here, in my bed, gives me hope.

After I've brushed my teeth and undressed, I crawl in behind her, pulling her back to my chest. She's wearing something short and silky and wakes up enough to say, "You're home," softly.

"I'm home," I tell her, kissing her ear.

"I missed you," she says.

"I missed you too, baby."

She's already fallen back to sleep. And I don't have it in me to wake her up, even though my body's raring to go.

I wake up a little later, feeling her mouth on me, and my eyes open wide.

"Oh," I groan. "You feel so good. What did I do to deserve waking up to this?"

She dips her mouth over my cock and hums before letting me go with a pop. "I tried to stay awake for you."

Her hands slide up my base as she kisses her way up my dick. I enjoy it way too much.

"Can I get inside you?" I ask. "I need to sink inside you and make you feel so good."

"Yes, please," she says.

"Are you ready for me?" I flip her over on her back and slip my fingers between her legs. "Oh, my sweet Elle baby, you're so wet. Does it turn you on, sucking me off?"

"Yes," she says, riding my fingers.

"I love coming home to you in my bed." I hover over her, looking her in the eye. "This means something to me, Elle," I whisper.

My fingers slide in and out of her slowly.

She whimpers from my touch.

"Me too," she says.

And for now, that's enough.

THE NEXT AFTERNOON, on my way to Carrie's to pick up Levi, I think about how far we've come over the years. I was right about her, about nearly every damn thing. I don't trust her. Shit, I've tried. God knows I've tried. I even considered a relationship with her for about a minute, based solely on the fact that we were having a baby together, and then found the condoms that had expired years before. When I asked her if those were from the same box we'd used, she lied but later admitted she'd just really wanted my baby. I'd known I was an idiot for sleeping with her in the first place and a bigger idiot for not using my own protection, but damn, she was also manipulative.

Getting pregnant with my baby was just the beginning.

I never touched her again, although she's tried many times to get me to over the years. There's no way I'd go back to that. She's pretended to be sick many times to get me to spend time with her, pretended to have a crisis in the family for more money, but the surprise was on me when she turned out to be a good mom. I have to say that as manipulative about money and trying to work her own agenda as she's been, when I suggested the move to Silver Hills to raise Levi in this idyllic town, she did the right thing. She agreed. And I will always be grateful to her for that. I bought her a house not far from mine and it's been challenging, but we've made it work.

It's conditional, but she's become more cooperative. That's not to say she isn't still annoying as hell, but she's toned it down. I think she might even be dating someone now, although I'm not sure she'll ever admit it.

She has a beautiful home, gets a shit-ton of money every month, and I've never fought her for full custody of Levi. I think by now she knows that she's got it pretty good. Through an excellent lawyer, an ironclad contract, and a constant striving for patience on my part, we have managed to coexist in the same town as co-parents.

I have the most amazing boy to show for the mess I made.

And I don't regret him for a single second.

I hurry to her door and when she opens it, Levi comes bounding out. I sweep him up, kissing his neck. He laughs and leans into me, loving it.

"We had a really great time this weekend," Carrie says.

"Excellent." I look at Levi. "You ready to go, son?"

"Weady!" Levi says.

"I know it's your turn to have him for Christmas and we've been celebrating all week, but I've got a lot of food left over here if you want to stay for dinner. Same with tomorrow and Christmas Day. You guys can come by anytime."

"We've got plans," I tell her, picking up Levi's bag. "Have a great Christmas, Carrie. I'll drop him off on Saturday."

She takes a step forward and I groan inwardly. "He talked about Elle more than usual. Is she *living* with you?"

She can't say Elle's name without looking like she's swallowed something bad.

"Not your business, Carrie."

"Uh, it *is* my business who my son is around."

"*Our* son has been around Elle his whole life. It's not like she's a new person you need to vet. If she were, we'd have a conversation about her. I'd expect you to give me that same respect with the new people you have around Levi."

Her eyes slide down and it's probably as much confirmation I'm going to get right now that she's seeing someone. I have a feeling that once Carrie finds out I'm sleeping with Elle—and God, I hope more than that—she'll get more vocal about this possible guy. I'd be thrilled if she's found someone to get her mind off of me. I don't think she even really wants me anymore, I've just been one of the few people who doesn't put up with her shit and that makes me appealing.

If there is a mystery man, I hope he's a decent person, for Levi's sake. What she does when Levi *isn't* with her doesn't concern me.

ELLE ISN'T HOME when we get there. She had practice and put in time at the chiropractor's office too, so I know she'll probably be worn out when she gets home. Tomorrow is Christmas Eve, so we both had a lot to do today before being off for the next couple of days. I work on dinner and Levi plays by the tree. When I put the chicken in the oven, I walk over to see what Levi's doing because he's quiet, and he's standing up, whipping his Johnson out near the Christmas tree.

"Whoa, what are you doing?"

He jumps at the intrusion and looks up at me with pure innocence.

"Watewing the twee," he says.

"We do *not* water inside trees. In fact, it's time we stop watering *all* the trees and let the rain and outdoor hoses do that for us. Do you understand?"

"But, Daddy it's dwy. Look!" He points at the needles on the floor under the tree.

"It's dry, but peeing on the tree will not help it. Come on. Let's go potty and then I'll show you how we water a Christmas tree. Forget I ever showed you how to go anywhere but in the toilet." I poke his side and he laughs.

"In the toilet," he says deep like me and laughs.

"It is a good thing you're so cute."

He does his business in the toilet and I go on about what a good boy he is as we wash hands. Elle pokes her head in the door and we all three go full-on cheese smiles.

"There you are," I say.

"Hey," she says.

I lean over and kiss her and Levi does the same. She giggles and nuzzles his nose after and I lean in for a nose nuzzling too.

"Oh, you guys are too much," she says, laughing.

"I went potty on the toilet and not the twee," Levi tells her.

Her eyes go wide and she looks up at me.

"Yeah, it was God's mercy that made me go check on him as he was about to christen the Christmas ornaments."

"I not help it if I pee on it," Levi adds.

"That's right. We've decided we're going to leave the watering of all trees to what?" I look at Levi.

"To the wain and outdoh hoses," Levi recites proudly.

Elle presses her lips together and her face turns pink as she withholds her laugh.

"And I'm about to show him how to *properly* water the Christmas tree." I make a face. "He was right, it *was* dry."

She bursts out laughing and Levi looks at me, as if asking if it's okay to laugh yet, if he's still in trouble.

I laugh too and he grins.

"It's all right, son. Now you know."

We walk into the kitchen, Levi happily chatting about the new presents under the tree.

"I did notice there were a few more under there than when I left," I say, filling the kettle with water.

She smirks. "I noticed a few new ones myself."

I grinned. When I came home tonight and saw more presents, I added mine in there. I'll wait until tomorrow night to fill the stockings and add a few more unwrapped presents under the tree to look like Santa's been here. We take the water to the tree, where I point out where to put it.

"Only good water," I say.

"No tinkle," he says.

"That's right, no tinkle."

Elle chokes back a laugh again and I pretend to give her a stern look.

She takes a deep breath and repeats after us, "No tinkle."

CHAPTER THIRTY-FOUR

YOUR CUES

ELLE

Now

"ARE you sure they're really okay with having us?" Rhodes asks. "Levi and I can stay home while you go to your parents' house."

"They invited you, yes. And if you'd rather stay here, I'll stay here too."

"No, I don't want you to miss being with your parents. I just don't wanna, you know, push this more than you want... the whole fake-dating scenario with your parents," he says.

He put fake dating in quotations, so I do the same, mimicking him.

"Rhodes, even if we weren't fake dating, I'd still want you to come to dinner with my parents on Christmas Eve. Usually your parents are here by now and we're trying to spend as much time together as we can. Why would this year be any different?"

He moves my bra strap over and places a kiss on my shoulder. "I'd say things are a lot different this year. I'm just trying to read your cues, see what you really want me to do."

"I really want you with me," I tell him.

"I'm there," he says, placing a soft kiss on my lips. "And I want to spend tomorrow with you too."

"Perfect."

We smile at each other in the mirror.

"Forever, if you'll have me," he adds softly.

My mouth drops and he nods like he knows he's made me lose my words.

"You heard me right," he says, but he goes on then like he hasn't just floored me. "There's been a loose plan for everyone to come here tomorrow night after they're done with presents, remember?" he asks. "A few weeks ago I thought you wouldn't be here."

"I'll be here," I say, giving him a wobbly smile.

He leans over and kisses my shoulder again. "Nothing could make me happier. You should invite Calista and Javi...they're the only ones I haven't reminded."

"Okay, I will."

We're getting ready in his bathroom in front of the dual sinks. He already pounded into me in the shower earlier, but watching him smooth aftershave onto his cheeks, with nothing but a towel around his waist, I'm ready for another round.

I try to squash down my insatiable need for him. If we're going to make it to my parents' in time, we need to hurry.

"Did you ever hear from your parents?" I ask.

"No, their flight was canceled and it's not looking good," he says. "So many flights were delayed. It's looking like they might not make it for Christmas."

WE HEAD OVER TO MY PARENTS' house. When we walk in, Rhodes is holding Levi and has his fingers threaded through mine. Levi smiles shyly at my parents. He knows them, but not enough to run into their arms right away. By the time we finish eating, he'll be warmed up and ready for that. We sit down at the table and things are a little awkward at first, but my parents are trying and I'm grateful for that.

"Dad and I thought maybe you guys could go to church with us after this," Mom says, piling mashed potatoes on my plate.

"What time does it start? Hasn't it been really late the past few years?"

"We made it earlier this year so everyone can spend time with their families."

"I don't know," I say, looking at Rhodes. "Technically, I'm not supposed to be with Rhodes because of being on the team." I thought I'd told my parents that already, but maybe I haven't.

"Well, that certainly hasn't stopped you," my mom says

sharply. "I think it would be good to go to church if you're serious about being together. What better way to start this than being with family and community in church on Christmas Eve?"

I look at Rhodes and I can tell he's not loving this conversation, but he smiles at me and squeezes my hand.

"I'll do whatever you want to do, Elle love," he says.

My cheeks flush, hearing him call me that in front of my parents, but I kind of love it.

I square my shoulders. "Okay, we'll go. It's not a long service, so we'll still get back in time to have hot chocolate with Levi and get everything ready after he goes to bed."

My dad takes a bite of food and says, "Great. It'll be really nice having you there. Bernard says his aunt is coming in and I know she'd love to see you."

I set my fork down. "I really wish you would stop inserting Bernard into the conversation where I'm concerned. I have no desire to be with Bernard...or hear about him or *talk* to him..."

My dad holds his hand up. "Well, I don't see why you can't still be friendly."

"I'm not going to be hateful to anyone. But I can't be *too* friendly because the two of you...*and* Bernard keep trying to push us together." I glance at Rhodes. "Bernard called on my way home from work asking if we could see each other sometime over the holiday. I said no."

His jaw tightens and he nods slightly.

I look at my parents. "I don't know how to make it any clearer...I don't want to be with Bernard. Ever. Besides the fact that I don't have feelings for him, he has a serious P-O-R-N," I spell out for Levi's sake, "addiction that's keeping him from having a normal S-E-X-U-A-L relationship, and that's just not something I would wish on any woman...not until he's ready to deal with that. But even if he did work on that, I wouldn't want to be with him."

I can feel Rhodes' stunned reaction and my parents both stare at me in shock.

"S-E-X shouldn't have been on the table yet anyway, with the two of you not married, but uh...we...we didn't know that," my mom says.

"Yeah, there's a lot about Bernard you don't know. I haven't wanted to be the one to tell you, but I wish you would just trust me when I say, we're not the right fit. And all of this is a moot point anyway because I'm with Rhodes now. We *do* fit. And most importantly, we're happy."

I smile at Rhodes and he leans over and kisses my cheek.

"Yes, we are," he says.

My mom nods slowly. My dad clears his throat and we eat.

I'm grateful my dad doesn't say anything about me forgiving Bernard. I forgave him a long time ago, not just about the porn and lack of attention when it came to the bedroom, but for the way he tried to control what I wore and how I acted. The way he continuously put me down. He never once asked for my forgiveness. I don't owe him another thing.

"Did you know that Levi knows all the words to 'Rudolph the Red-Nosed Reindeer?'" I ask.

Levi's eyes light up. "I know that song!"

"Oh, I would love to hear that," my mom says.

"How about as soon as we're done eating?" Rhodes says. "That way, the whole table won't also experience Levi's mashed potatoes."

We all laugh and some of the tension eases.

WE WALK into the church just minutes before the service is about to start. We sit a few rows from the back. My mom wanted us to sit up front with her, but I didn't want to be quite that conspicuous. Too bad we couldn't wear the disguises tonight.

The sanctuary is full. The trees are lit with white lights and it's beautiful. A few people wave when they see me and stare at Rhodes in awe. He's been here many times over the years and it's always a big deal when he comes. We sing Christmas songs and a few passages of scripture are read. Levi loves the music. When it's over, we say hello to a few people. I find my mom and we all hug her.

"Thank you for coming," she says.

"We enjoyed it," Rhodes says. "Thanks for dinner too."

"Of course. It was lovely having you and this sweet little boy." She smiles at Levi and then looks at me. "It won't be the same not having you for Christmas Day."

"You should come by the house tomorrow night," Rhodes says.

He looks at me and I nod.

"We'll just be hanging out, eating. Some of my teammates and their girlfriends will be there."

"Maybe we will," my mom says.

It feels like a step in the right direction.

I see Bernard from across the church and turn away. I don't need another confrontation today. I want to get home and spend the rest of Christmas Eve with Rhodes and Levi.

CHAPTER THIRTY-FIVE

NO DOUBTS

RHODES

Now

ELLE and I have hardly been asleep when I hear something. I rub my eyes in time to see Levi doing a superhero run and then diving between Elle and me.

"Mewwy Chwistmas!" he yells.

I try to whisper it back with excitement, but that's

almost impossible to do, try it sometime. I don't want him to wake up Elle, but I also don't want to squash his Christmas joy.

"Merry Christmas, little man," Elle says groggily.

"It's four in the morning," I say. "Are we sure it's really Christmas yet?"

"We did tell him whenever he woke up," Elle says, already sitting up.

"I *awake*," Levi says.

She leans over and hugs him. I love the way she loves my boy.

"All right, let's do this," I say, searching for the candy cane pajama pants Elle gave me last night.

She thinks it's hilarious that the massive candy cane in the front perfectly outlines my dick. It is pretty funny.

"I'll turn the fire on first and then get the camera ready, okay?" I look at Levi. "You hold on tight with Elle, all right?"

"Awight," he agrees, bopping his head.

"Let me get the two of you walking in together," Elle says.

I smile, watching her put on her matching candy cane pajamas without even flashing us once. I'm disappointed I didn't catch a peek, but I know she doesn't want to flash Levi. She has the art down of putting a bra on or taking it off without even showing any skin. It's remarkable.

"I'll be in the pictures plenty. I want to see my favorite people," I tell her, hurrying off to brush my teeth and get this party started.

And oh, what a party it is. Levi is obsessed with the train we set up last night after he went to bed. It's huge and goes around the tree and winds around the living room. He plays with it for hours and barely notices anything else. Elle and I have so much fun playing with him and then take some time to open our presents from each other too. We usually give each other two gifts, one silly and one nice. I try to sneak in more than two presents every year, but it gets me in trouble. I'm wearing my silly gift—an ugly Christmas sweater to go with my candy cane pants—and so is she, a Christmas tree hat that lights up.

The biggest surprises are coming later. I heard from my dad before we went to bed, and they've decided to drive. They should be here by this afternoon, and the present they're bringing with them is one I've been wanting for a long time. I can't wait to see Elle and Levi's reaction.

Elle hands me a small rectangular box. I shake it as I always do, and she rolls her eyes playfully. I hand her a similarly sized box. I've had this gift for a while now and have wondered how she'd receive it. I'm feeling a little more confident now that it'll be okay.

"You go first," I say.

She smiles and opens it without hesitation. It's always so fun to give her gifts.

She gasps when she opens the box. I bought her a Tiffany watch. She loves that Tiffany Blue® and this one is stainless steel with the blue dial and small diamonds surrounding it.

"Rhodes," she whispers and then smiles.

"If it's not the right one, we can pick out one you like better."

She giggles then and I can't tell what's striking her funny.

"I love it," she says. "I love it so much."

"Oh, good."

She surprises me by looking at the back. I thought I'd have to show her the inscription, but she finds it and her head falls back with her laugh. I frown, not sure how to take her laughing so hard at me having *Yours, Rhodes* engraved on the back of her watch.

She wipes her eyes and reaches over to squeeze my hand. "I love it, Rhodes. It's so perfect. *You're* perfect."

She kisses me and it sends my heart into overdrive. I love her mouth and everything about her.

She pulls back. "Here, open yours."

I grin and carefully open it.

"Rip it," she says, laughing.

"But it's so pretty. I don't know how you can get it so pretty. I have to pay to have that done."

She gives me a smug look. "Maybe I'll teach you sometime."

"Mmm, I don't think these giant fingers will ever be able to do this."

"They're just right for other things," she whispers.

I have to adjust my candy cane.

"Keep it up," I tell her, "and this candy cane will be trying to hop out of these pants."

She laughs and I open the box and stare at it in shock.

"Elle, this is…beautiful." I look at her in concern. "You didn't need to spend so much money on me."

She gives me a pointed look. "You did."

I give her a pointed look back. I don't say *but I can afford it*, even though we both know what I'm thinking.

The BVLGARI watch is the *shit*. It's dark green, my favorite color.

She nudges me. "If it's not the right one, we can pick out one you like better…"

I lean over and kiss her. "I love that we got each other the same thing. I'm just…it's…I love it."

She touches the watch. "Keep looking," she says, her lips quirking up.

I pick it up and study it closer and then turn it over. *Yours, Elle* it says. She covers her mouth with her hand, laughing and my eyes well up. Her laugh quietens and she scoots closer.

"*Are* you mine, baby?" I ask her.

Her eyes fill with tears, and she nods. "I am."

"We've always said we love each other, but when I say I love you, I mean that I am bone-achingly in love with you. I have loved you from the first time I saw you, and every minute in between. There will *never* be anyone for me but you. I wish I'd made it clear from the very beginning."

"You've loved me from the beginning? I've loved *you* from the beginning. I'm in love with you too, Rhodes," she says, a tear dripping down her cheek.

I lean in and kiss it, processing her words and reeling with them. "How did we know everything about each other but not this?"

"I know. I can't believe it. I wish I hadn't been so terrified of losing you," she adds. "You were instantly everything to me, and that's still the same today, but we were so young. It didn't feel possible that you could really love me back in that way. You were so confident, so sure of who you were already. I feel like I'm still finding my way, but with you—I've always known how I feel about you. We wouldn't be the same though, if we'd known the feelings were reciprocated. You wouldn't have Levi, and he is the best thing to ever happen to both of us."

I kiss her fingers and cheek and mouth. "I love you for loving him that way."

"He's part of you. Of course I love him."

That makes me reel, her goodness, her love. We sit for a moment, just soaking in these revelations.

"Every time I was about to tell you how I felt, someone new would pop up," I tell her.

"I nearly told you at least a dozen times," she says. "It always backfired."

"Maybe the timing is perfect. We've never been without each other, besides distance, and now we can fully be who we're supposed to be together."

"You're sure?" she asks.

"I have never had any doubts about my feelings for you. I've only ever wondered if I would be able to make you feel the same about me."

She leans her forehead on mine. "I love you so much, Rhodes. And being with you in this *fake relationship that I never wanted to only be fake* has been beyond what I could've imagined."

I can hear the smile in her voice, and I laugh. "I jumped on your fake dating idea so fast…anything to get more time with you."

Her laugh is warm against my skin. "I'm so glad you did. We desperately needed something to force this issue." She frowns. "Levi has been quiet for a minute."

We look at the trains where he's been playing and singing his little heart out, and he's sprawled out, sound asleep.

"That four AM wakeup call has caught up with him." I chuckle as I walk over and pick him up. "I'll be right back."

"Or should we go back to bed?" she asks.

"I love that idea."

I put Levi to bed and when I look in my room, Elle is already there. I crawl into bed and she turns to face me.

"Carrie is going to hate this, you know," she says.

"I know." Carrie's made it no secret how she feels about Elle. "But you don't need to worry about her.."

I lean in and kiss her and she melts into me. My dick swells against her and she grins against my mouth.

"Hello?" The sound comes from downstairs and we freeze.

"Fuck. Is that my mom? They said they were stopping. They must have driven all night."

"They drove?"

We both hustle out of bed, my erection a sad thing of the past, and hurry downstairs.

My parents stand in the living room, and my mom is holding my surprise. Elle gasps and my parents stare at the two of us in shock.

We all start talking at once.

"Hey, guys!"

"You must've driven all night!"

"Merry Christmas!"

"Oh my God, you got a puppy!" Elle rushes to my mom and kisses her cheek before loving on the English bulldog.

"*We* got a puppy," I tell Elle.

"What?" She looks up at me.

I grin at her as we pet the little guy and my mom hands him to me. He's red and white, with the patches over his eyes. He's adorable.

"He is hilarious," Mama says. "I'm already in love with him."

"Hey there, aren't you the cutest thing," I say. I lean into my parents for a side hug to not squish the puppy. "So, we have some news."

My parents stand there beaming.

"Thought you might," Dad says.

Elle's cheeks are pink when I glance at her. I lift my

eyebrows, asking if it's okay that I spill. She laughs and leans into me.

"Tell them," she says.

"We're together. *Elle is in love with me*," I lean my head back to say it loudly, "and we are *together*."

Elle giggles and my parents hug her and me. My mom does a little dance.

"It is about time!" she cries.

"Do you know how hard it was to stay out of it when it was so obvious that you guys were right for each other?" my dad says, laughing. "We knew how Rhodes felt and thought we might know how you felt, Elle, but he made us swear we'd leave it alone. Bloody hell, I thought I might be on my deathbed saying, 'Can I please just say one thing before I go...'"

We all laugh.

"This has made me the happiest mama ever," my mom says. "I have wanted this from the time he called home and said 'I met a girl named Elle.' I wrote your name in my journal that same day, and next to it I said: I think we will be hearing more about her." She reaches out and squeezes Elle's hand. "And when I met you, there were no doubts. I saw the way he looked at you, and that's never changed, not once in all these years. Well, I take that back. What is the word for...the longing..."

"He's been pining for her," my dad helps clarify.

I groan and Elle laughs.

"I've been pining too," she says.

"I wish I'd been clued in to that pining." I roll my eyes, laughing.

"Have you told her just how much you were pining?" my mom asks.

I shoot her a look. "I have been on tenterhooks trying not to scare her off. One thing at a time."

My mom tilts her head like *get after it*. "We're not getting any younger, son."

Elle looks up at me with curious eyes and a bright smile, and I kiss the side of her head.

"Isn't he so cute?" I ask, changing the subject.

My mom snorts, but everyone lets me get away with it for now.

"He's the cutest. Levi is going to freak when he sees him."

"Where is our boy?" Dad asks.

"He got up at four and had the time of his life...before crashing next to the train."

"I'm sad that we missed that," Mama says. "Once we started driving, we just wanted to get here. But now, we need a nap."

"I'm so glad you're here."

I DON'T GET the love fest I wanted with Elle or a nap. We start cooking. My parents lie down for a while and then my mom gets up and helps. Later that evening, when Levi gets up, he meets Bogey, his new puppy, and he's in love. He kisses his nose and can't stop laughing every time he looks at him. Bogey has so much personality. He's clumsy and sweet. I've taken a million pictures already.

Weston, Sadie, and Caleb arrive first and then Bowie and Becca. When Becca sees the dog, she falls in love too.

"He should be ours. His name is like yours, Dad," she says.

Becca has Down Syndrome and you never have to guess what she's thinking. We all adore that about her.

Bowie looks at me. "Yeah, what's with naming your dog Bogey? You have a Bowie in your life, isn't that enough?"

"Never enough. You know you're my favorite, man. But this guy might turn out to be a close second," I tease.

"Great," he says dryly. "And I'm never going to hear the end of this now. First, it was a cat because of Earl."

Tru and Henley have a cat and the kids all love him, but the rest of us haven't succumbed to pets yet. Until now.

"Looks like we're going to be getting a dog," he says when Becca starts singing to Bogey.

Henley, Tru, and the girls come in next, and Penn and Sam are right behind them. Elle's parents weren't able to make it and neither were Calista and Javi, but we talk about doing dinner with them next week.

It's loud and boisterous as we eat, and afterwards, we take dessert into the living room. While the kids are playing in the other room, I take Elle's hand and clear my throat.

"I'd like to say something," I say.

The little side conversations slowly come to a stop and everyone turns to look at me.

"You've been our friends for a long time and some of you have known more recently exactly how I feel about this girl, but I just want to say...it's official. This is *not* a fake dating relationship. This is *not* best friends only."

Everybody laughs and there is whistling and cheering.

"This is my woman. She knows it. And I am her man, and *I* know it. We have *established* it." I hold up my hand to emphasize my words and Elle leans in, laughing at me.

There's a scurry of hugs and cheers as everyone congratulates us. Finally, I clear my throat.

"There's more. I'm going to say something and it probably should just be between me and Elle, but because I tell you guys everything and I have had a reputation of being a player, I want to set some things straight. Penn, you're my man and I have been your wingman since the day we met and realized we could draw in the women."

I look at Elle apologetically. "Sorry, baby. But this face is pretty and we all know it."

She shoves me away, but she's laughing.

"It's my parents' fault," I say, pointing at my parents. They roll their eyes and laugh.

"Don't bring us into this," Mama says.

"Anyway...my parents are also the only ones who know that I haven't slept with another woman since Carrie got pregnant."

Everyone looks at me in shock.

"Sorry, ladies, you didn't ask for this," I say to Sadie and Tru.

"But I am *so* here for it," Tru says and we all crack up.

Elle looks at me, eyes wide. "I am in shock," she says.

"I feel so deceived," Penn says.

We all laugh...even Penn.

"So, the times we were out and you walked a girl out of the bar or wherever we were..." He frowns.

"Once you were out of sight, I would send them home in a cab. I'd also tell them while we were chatting that I only wanted a conversation. Most were fine with that. I wanted you to have fun. I'd learned my lesson after getting Carrie pregnant and thought I had lost my chance with Elle forever." I look at Elle, and her eyes are filling with tears. "The day I told you..." I shook my head, overcome with emotion. "It was the darkest day of my life, knowing I had ruined our chance for good."

She wipes the tears falling down her cheeks.

"Anyway...I just wanted to clear that up because I've let you all think one thing about me and it's not been the case at all. I'm not sorry about Levi, but I wish I had changed my ways a lot sooner. Took me a while, but I got there."

"Wow," Penn says. "So it turns out I'm the only man whore here."

We crack up.

"Well, more like reformed man whores," Weston says, as he laughs and makes a face at Sadie.

"There's no shame," Henley tells Penn.

"When you meet the person for you, you'll be reformed too," Bowie says.

"Well, let's get you situated first," I tell Bowie. "You've never been a player and you deserve to have someone in your life."

"Oh God," Penn says. "Here he goes."

Bowie groans. "I know. Don't start on me. I'm happy. I'm just fine as I am. I have a full life."

"You *are* fine as you are, but you could be even happier," I say.

"Yeah, Dad." Becca walks in and comes straight for the puppy. "You could be happier."

Our phones start dinging and Penn is the first to check his.

"Hey, guys?"

CHAPTER THIRTY-SIX

BIG MOVE

ELLE

Then

I'D FELT like a shell of a person since finding out Rhodes was having a baby. I couldn't even begin to describe the pain I'd felt when he told me he was having a baby with someone else. It was crazy. I had never had any realistic hope that I would have a child with him one day. I mean, he had never given me reason to, but in my heart of hearts, it was what I wanted more than anything.

I had no right to feel any of this, and since I was with Bernard, it really felt wrong that I grieved the news like someone had died.

I was trying so hard to move on from these feelings.

My parents were happier than they'd ever been because Bernard was exactly the kind of man they wanted me to be with. But Bernard had his cracks too.

It was like an extension of how I felt growing up with my parents trying to keep me in line and squashed in a box. And now that I was living back at home, I'd regressed. Bernard underscored everything my parents believed.

He wanted me to dress conservatively. If something was too short, he asked me to change. If I had alcohol, he had something to say about it. Going out dancing was out of the question. But mostly, it was the condescending way he spoke to me. I had tried to break up with him once and he got my parents to talk me into giving him another chance. I should've ended it then, but there were good things about him too. He wanted to help me move out of my parents' house for one, and I was desperate to do so. He'd come up with a plan where I would be able to soon. Unfortunately, it tied me to him more than I wanted since I had trusted him with my finances.

I had a job at the chiropractor's office, a job I absolutely loved. The people were great. It was fast-paced and fun. Then I came home and wrote every night. I started a story about how things could have been if Rhodes and I had ended up together. It was my escape.

WHEN THE BABY CAME, Rhodes called to let me know.

I was genuinely excited when he told me he had a son named Levi. We had talked about that name before, how much we loved it, and knowing that he had, in a way, honored my feelings about the name, was special to me.

"I'm so happy for you," I told him, and I meant it.

"I have news. It's big," he said.

"More news besides a son?" I laughed.

"I took a job with the Mustangs."

I gasped. "No way." My heart started pounding. "You're moving to Denver?"

"Actually, I thought I'd move to Silver Hills. It's beautiful there. I love that it's a small town. I'd like to raise Levi in a place like that. And the best part about it is that you're there. I've talked Carrie into it. What do you think?"

The thought of having to regularly see the woman he had a baby with felt almost unbearable. But I wanted my best friend nearby.

"I'm going to buy a place for Carrie close by," he said.

I sat down. "So you're not going to live together?" I asked.

"No," he laughed, "that would never work."

I sagged with relief.

"Oh, okay. Well, that's incredible, Rhodes. I can't believe we're going to live in the same place again. I'm so excited." I knew he could hear it in my voice now, how much I felt those words. "Knowing I'll get to be part of Levi's life is the best news you could ever give me," I said.

"Thanks, Elle love. It means so much to me that you want to be part of his life. He's perfect, baby. He's *perfect*."

"I bet he is. How soon can I meet him?"

I HADN'T WANTED to take Bernard with me when I met Levi for the first time, but he insisted on it. He wanted to meet the best friend I talked about all the time. He tried to act like he wasn't jealous, but he so was.

"So, he's always been out with a different girl every night but got a girl pregnant...and you expect me to believe nothing has ever happened between the two of you?" he asked on the ride to Rhodes' house.

I'd told Bernard that Rhodes was living the single life. I'd caught him reading things about Rhodes that had also probably shaped what he thought of him.

"Don't believe everything you read about Rhodes. He's very respectful of women and of me," I said.

"Right," Bernard said, laughing under his breath.

"Should we talk about what came up on your desktop after you'd been using it the other night?" I turned to look at him. I'd gone to his house for dinner and he'd left to pick up food.

His cheeks darkened. "Elle—"

"I wasn't checking up on you. I was looking for that address you wanted when I couldn't find my phone. But after I saw the porn, I did do a little history search and... wow. Things make a *lot* of sense after seeing how much you visit those sites."

It was quiet for a second and I sighed.

"It probably wouldn't bother me that you're into porn if we had a normal sex life—"

"I do that so we don't have sex," he said.

"But we've had sex before...just hardly ever," I argued.

"And I felt awful about it. It's not right. We should be married before we're doing that and I just...I—"

"Don't. I don't want to talk about this right now," I said.

We pulled up to Rhodes' gate and were waved through

after we gave our names. Rhodes had flown in to go house hunting and I'd helped him pick out this house, so I wasn't surprised when I saw how impressive it was. But Bernard had something to say about that too.

"Looks like he's trying to overcompensate for something," he said.

"Rhodes doesn't need to overcompensate for anything. He's the real deal and he can afford a big house, so how about we don't judge him for that too?"

Rhodes opened the door with the baby and besides seeing how tired Rhodes looked, that perfect bundle of heaven with light brown skin and the sweetest full cheeks asleep in his arms was all I saw. Rhodes handed him to me.

"Here he is. Can you believe him?" he asked.

"Rhodes, he is perfection." I sighed.

He was only a month old, but he already looked bigger than he had in our video chats. He felt so good in my arms, and he smelled divine.

"I need to feed him," a nasal voice said.

Rhodes shot me an apologetic expression. "Carrie stopped by to bring over some breastmilk."

"Well, since I'm here, I'll just feed him myself and save the rest," Carrie said, holding out her hands for the baby.

She was gorgeous with her long blonde hair and pale skin with a dusting of freckles. The freckles gave her a friendly, soft look, but the way she assessed me left me cold. This wouldn't go well. Her lips curled slightly and I handed Levi to her.

"This really isn't a good time," she said.

"Carrie, I invited Elle here. And next time, call me before you decide to drop by," he told her.

I felt a zing of victory that he was defending me, but it disappeared in the next second because she whipped out her boob and fed Levi right there without trying to cover anything in the slightest.

I loved that women could feed their babies this way and I didn't have any hang-ups about showing skin when they did so, but I knew from the way she went about it that Carrie would *literally* be milking this situation.

Bernard stared at her until Rhodes cleared his throat and held out his hand.

"I'm Rhodes. You must be Bernard."

"Who else would I be?" Bernard said. He laughed, but Rhodes and I just looked at him. "Congratulations. It must be crazy, having a baby. Seems hard to pull off with your career and all."

"My mom will be here for a while, and we'll have a lot of help." He looked at me. "She wants to see you, by the way."

"I can't wait to see her."

"Rhodes, I need a burp cloth," Carrie said.

The diaper bag was within reach of Carrie, with a burp cloth draped over the top, but Rhodes walked across the room and handed it to her. She smiled up at him and it made my stomach curl over and die.

We had the world's most awkward lunch. Rhodes kept trying to talk to me and Carrie kept interrupting.

"Sometimes he smiles when he's sleeping. You'll see it, I'm—"

"Oh my God," Carrie said loudly. "My boobs are crazy hard right now. Oh shit. The milk just dropped again. I swear, I feel like a milk cow. When it first came in, it was intense, right?" She put her hand on Rhodes' hand and he pulled it away. "I sprayed milk all over Rhodes."

Bernard froze and looked shocked.

Rhodes laughed sheepishly. "That's true," he said.

My form of hell.

I spent a couple of hours there, despite being on the verge of tears the entire time.

"Can we go soon?" Bernard whispered.

I wanted to tell him he could go anytime, I hadn't invited him in the first place, but I didn't.

As Rhodes was telling me bye, he leaned in to whisper, "I'll make sure she's not here next time. Please come back. Tonight, tomorrow...all the time. Leave the dud at home."

I laughed in spite of myself.

"What's so funny?" Bernard asked.

"I told her to come back...all the time," Rhodes said.

"Well, she does have a life, you know."

"I know," Rhodes said softly.

"And my life includes you and Levi," I told Rhodes.

He smiled. "I know that too."

He reached out and took my hand. I felt the tension bouncing off of Bernard, but I didn't care. He needed to get used to the way Rhodes and I were with each other.

"Carrie picked her brother to be Levi's godfather, and I'd like you to be his godmother," he said.

The tears I'd been holding back started trickling down my cheeks.

"I'd be honored to be Levi's godmother," I said quietly. And then I frowned. "Is Carrie okay with that?"

"She'll have to be," he said.

CHAPTER THIRTY-SEVEN

SCRATCH THAT ITCH

ELLE

Now

I HAVEN'T LET it ruin my Christmas because I have had the best Christmas ever, but in the hours since we got the group text from Calista saying to check out TikTok, I have spiraled the tiniest bit.

Rhodes managed to distract me in the shower just now, but now that we're drying off, my mind is swirling again.

Those sleuths on TikTok have been compiling pictures of me and Rhodes. Some of them have gone way back to the beginning, pulling up pictures I'd forgotten or never seen, and some are from our Instagram feeds. But there are also photos of him at my condo, at church together at various times, as well as last night's Christmas Eve service, and there is even one person questioning whether it was us out with Levi in disguises.

"Who do you think started this?" I ask. "Someone's sending the latest pictures to these people."

"I don't know," Rhodes says. "It's either paparazzi or just people who know me from football...or you from cheering."

"It doesn't seem like something the locals would really think about much. They've seen us together around here for years, so it's not a big deal. But a lot of people come through here because it's so close to Denver." I make a face. "It could be Brock," I say. "That picture at the condo. Maybe he sent it to them."

He groans. "That bastard."

"Well, I can't be too mad. I sort of asked for this by recklessly following my heart." I laugh when he tugs me to him with a goofy grin on his face.

"It's about time you recklessly loved me," he says.

"Let's go to bed and I'll prove it."

He starts walking backwards, pulling my hand as we walk from the bathroom to his bed. Bogey's head lifts from where he's lying on a little bed and drops back down when he sees it's us. He's worn out from being chased and loved on by Levi.

When Rhodes' legs hit the bed, I loosen his towel and it drops to the floor.

"I'm on the pill," I say softly.

"I've noticed that," he says, tracing soft circles up my chest. "My tests always come back all clear."

"Mine too," I whisper.

"I might be a little too excited about this."

I give his chest a push and he falls back like I've really managed to move his wall of muscle. I let my own towel drop and lean over him. His hands land on my backside, a groan escaping as he kneads my cheeks.

"This ass has starred in every one of my fantasies," he says, leaning up to swirl his tongue around my nipple. "These tits too. I'm *so* glad you don't keep them from me anymore."

I laugh. "They're all yours."

He smiles up at me, and I kiss him, any earlier worry about the speculation of us wiped from my mind. I kiss down his neck and stomach and keep going, my chest hovering over his cock. I lean in and slide him between my breasts and his breath hitches. He leans up to watch, cursing quietly, when I press my breasts closer together, tightening around him. His head falls back as I rub myself against his leg.

"You really went all this time without sex?" I ask.

"Yes." He sounds out of breath.

"I actually haven't had much either."

He lifts his eyebrows.

I kiss his stomach and then shift down so I can get my mouth on him. He hisses when I lick his tip.

"My hand is officially retired," he says. "Thank God."

I grin up at him, and his eyes are dazed as he watches me take him in my mouth. I can't believe he has been celibate this whole time. There's so much I wish I'd known, so much I would do differently. But I can't waste another second thinking about the what-ifs when he's in front of me right now.

I get him right to the edge, pull back, and then start all over again.

"Fuck, love. You're so fucking perfect." He holds my hair back and his jaw clenches when he's trying to hold back.

I love everything about tasting him, the weight of him in my mouth, feeling how out of control he gets, how much he loves it—it feeds me and makes me starved all at once. When he tries to flip me over, I put my hand on his chest and he stills. I turn and straddle him, facing his feet, and lower myself slowly onto him.

"*Oh*," he says. "I didn't think it could be any better than it already was, but skin to skin..."

"*Yes*," I breathe.

I'm so wet, but it still takes a minute to adjust to his size.

We both exhale shakily when I'm fully seated. I lean forward and we both moan.

"You're so deep this way."

"Fuck, Elle. You feel unbelievable. And this view. I want to die just like this."

"Don't you dare." I roll over him, my hips undulating slowly while I slide up and down his length. Leaning forward hits all of my sweet spots and I keep a steady rhythm, unable to fathom how every time with Rhodes feels brand new. And so unbelievably good.

He grips my cheeks and when I turn to look at him over my shoulder, he's watching us with a pained expression on his face.

"It feels too good," he says. "Just watching this ass

bounce on me...taking me in so deep...is going to make me—"

My movements speed up and he breaks into a long groan. I slap against him faster and faster and he grips my hips, thrusting up into me. Pleasure skyrockets between us as we chase that high and when we finally crest, the waves last forever.

THE NEXT MORNING, Lisa leaves a message while I'm in the shower, asking me to meet her in her office in an hour. Practice isn't for another couple of hours, so I rush into Denver with a sense of dread.

Rhodes followed me here and parks in a different area of the parking lot. He's here a little early for practice and will be in the gym working out. He's not going to walk in with me or anything, but he wanted to be sure he was nearby for whatever happens. I get a text from him as I'm grabbing my purse and getting out of the car.

> RHODES
> Let me know how it goes.

> I will.

I walk inside and down the long hallway toward Lisa's office. The door is open when I walk up, and she's at her desk.

"Come in, Elle, and close the door."

I do and she motions for me to sit down.

"I'm sure you have a good idea why you're here this morning," she says. "You have been one of my favorite dancers, and that's not something I throw around lightly.

You're gorgeous, and you have the body and charisma that draws people in." She pauses.

"Thank you so much."

She sighs and lifts her shoulder in a shrug. "When I'm watching the recordings and you're on the screen, I can't look away." She moves a few papers on her desk before leveling me with a piercing look. "So I'm really upset that you completely disrespected me and the team...and everyone else who would've happily taken your place and been content to fulfill their end of the commitment. I communicated the rules of the team very clearly to you, and you blatantly broke every one. You have been seen all over town with Rhodes Archer, multiple times!"

She pauses and when I don't say anything, she continues.

"You're fired. I need you to clear out your locker, turn in your uniform, and leave the premises within the next half hour."

The timeframe is a bit surprising, but everything else is what I expected...except she surprised me with the compliments.

"Thanks for giving me the opportunity. I loved being part of the team, and I'll really miss dancing with the girls. I should've known it would be too hard to stay away from Rhodes. As I told you before, Rhodes' son Levi is my godson, so I should have never joined the team. I just love dancing so much, and I loved being part of this organization. At the time, when I joined, I thought a little space from Rhodes might be what I needed...I was struggling with staying in the friend zone. I'm so sorry for the disrespect. I have nothing but admiration for you and the girls. I actually have you to thank for forcing Rhodes and me to confront our feelings."

Her nod is brisk. "Well, I hope it was worth it." She makes a face like she smells something bad. "You know...I've been around long enough to see the occasional dalliance between players and cheerleaders, but they never last. The sheer volume of women that throw themselves at these players is staggering." She shakes her head. "And like I said, you're gorgeous, but there are a lot of pretty girls out there. You won't always be there to scratch that itch. Rhodes Archer is a hot commodity."

"What we have is more than that. And he's definitely worth it," I say and walk out the door.

CHAPTER THIRTY-EIGHT

MY FAVORITE PART

RHODES

Now

I'VE CHECKED my phone a dozen times before practice begins and there's nothing from Elle. I shoot her a quick text.

> Everything okay?

And then I have to get out on the field before I've heard anything back. It sucks that she's so close and I'm still clueless about what's going on. We practice, I'm distracted as fuck, and Coach calls me out on it.

"Sorry, I'll do better tomorrow," I tell him.

"Just get your head screwed on right before Sunday, is all I ask," he says.

"I will."

When I get back to the locker room, there's a text from her.

> **ELLE**
> I was fired.

I leave the locker room and call her.

"Where are you?" I ask when she answers.

"I'm back home. She only gave me thirty minutes to get my things out and leave. I didn't even get to say goodbye to everyone, and I didn't want to interrupt your practice. I came back and have been hanging out with your parents and Levi...just saw that I'd missed your message."

"I'm so sorry, Elle. This is...I hate this."

"No, it's okay. I knew it was risky—"

"It's not okay. I want to do something about it."

"It's not worth it."

"It is. This was important to you. Let me see if there's anything I can do. I've got to at least try. I don't want you losing something you love because of me."

"It won't do any good," she says. "I willingly broke the rules, and I'd do it again. I told Lisa you're worth it and I meant it."

"You and Levi are my world. I love you."

"I love you too."

We hang up and I go to Coach Evans' office and rap on the door.

"What's up?" he asks.

"Can I talk to you for a minute?"

"Of course. Come in."

I go inside and shut the door.

"I'll just get right to it. I've been best friends for thirteen years with Elle Benton...you've met her at some of our family parties. Well, I'm not sure if you're aware, but she became a Mustangs cheerleader this season."

"Oh," he says.

"Yeah..." I can't hide my grimace. "She loves it and I was so happy for her to be on the team...and then realized what all that truly meant. First, we tried not to see each other, but she's the godmother of my child...and I'm in love with her."

"*Oh*," he says again, chuckling. "I didn't know it was like that, but I should've. She's a great girl. Beautiful too."

"Yeah, it's like that. It's always been like that on my end and we've just realized it has been on hers too. I'm with her, Coach. I'm all in. I'm completely, *madly* in love with her, and she just lost her job over it."

"Damn, Rhodes. I'm sorry to hear that. Happy for you and Elle though. I do remember her. You've needed a good woman to settle you down."

I've needed Elle, period.

"Those rules are put in place for a reason," he adds.

"She's just so good at what she does. And we're not going to cause any drama for the team. It's not like we're just sleeping together for the fun of it...I mean it's *fun*, but this is a forever kind of thing."

He chuckles.

"Is there anything we can do?"

"I don't think so. I can see now why you were so distracted during the practice."

"I'll get it together before Sunday."

"I believe you. I want to keep you happy, Rhodes. I'll talk to Lisa, tell her this isn't just a casual hookup with Elle. But Lisa's pretty firm, and you understand this goes higher up than her. These are rules that have been set in stone for a long time. But we can see if she's open to bringing it up with her superiors."

"Thank you. I'd appreciate it if you try."

I drive home and when I get inside, I don't know why I'm surprised that it sounds like a party.

"Where are all my favorite people?" I call.

"Daddy!" Levi yells, running to wrap his arms around my legs.

He leads me to the kitchen where Elle and my parents are, and I watch them interacting for a moment before they look up and see me. Dad is chopping vegetables. My mom is stirring something on the stove and Elle is working on a dessert.

"Hey, son," Dad says.

I squeeze his shoulder and my mom is right next to him.

"Hey, Mama." I pause to kiss her on the cheek before I reach Elle.

"Welcome home," Mama says.

Elle grins at me over her shoulder. I turn her around to face me before I give her a quick kiss and wrap my arms around her.

"How are you doing?" I ask.

"I'm doing good. *Really*," she says. "Don't worry about me. I'm happier than I've ever been."

"I know you loved being on the team so much. I can't stand that you're out, just like that. It feels wrong."

"You're not on the team anymore?" Mama asks.

"I was fired today," Elle says softly.

"*No*. Because of the two of you? That's so silly..." She shakes her head.

Elle's phone rings and she waves it off, but then it rings again. I move so she can get to it if she wants to, but she doesn't make it in time. After the third time, she hustles to answer.

"Hello?" The color drains from her face.

She holds onto the counter and I move by her and put my hand on her back to let her know I'm here.

"Does it seem like just one person or, like, a lot?" she asks. "Oh, God," she squeaks. "Okay. *Okay*," she says softer as she exhales. She pauses and takes a deep breath. "I'll be okay."

And now I'm really freaking out. What the hell is going on?

"Yeah. I'll let you know. I want to talk to the girls...hopefully before they hear about it from anyone else." She puts her hand on her head and closes her eyes.

"Baby, are you okay?" I whisper, unable to take it any longer.

She looks up at me and I can't read her expression, but she nods.

On the phone, she says, "Okay, I'll call you later. Love you. Bye."

When she gets off, she takes a deep breath and her eyes flicker down to her phone as she seems to try to take calming breaths or something.

"Are you hyperventilating?" I ask.

"I have something to tell you." Her eyes meet mine again.

"Okay." She's scaring me. "Should I sit down?"

"Yes." She takes my hand.

I expect her to lead me into the living room to sit down on the couch, but she takes me up the stairs and down the hall to the room she's using as an office. She's arranged the bookshelves a little, but they're mostly empty. And it looks like she's worked on her desk since I've been in here. Her oversized chair is next to the lamp and shelves and she motions for me to sit there. When I try to tug her onto my lap, she shakes her head.

"I need to pace."

I stare at her with wide eyes, unaccustomed to this side of Elle. She rarely gets this shaken up.

"You can tell me anything. You know that, right?" I say.

I'm not sure she hears me. She makes a pass in front of me once, twice, and on the third time, she turns and moves toward the boxes and grabs a box cutter. Cutting through the tape, she opens it and takes out a book, holding it to her chest. Then she leans against the front of her desk and looks at me.

I wait because it seems like she's struggling with how to get it out and I don't want to rush her.

"I should've told you about this a while ago, and I don't know why I'm so shy to do it now. It's just all rushing at me, what it means for this to be coming out. Know that I wanted to tell you about it from the very beginning, but...there are a couple of huge reasons I didn't."

She turns the book around and holds it up for me to see.

"*It Was Always You*...by Zoey Archer," I say out loud.

I nod and wait. When she still doesn't say anything, my head tilts.

"I've seen that book around..." My eyes narrow. "Was that the book the girls were going on about? I think I bought a copy..."

"Yes," she whispers. She still looks shaken.

"Baby, what is it? Do you—"

"Zoey Archer is *me*," she says.

She clamps her hand over her mouth and hysterical laughter bursts out of her.

"What?" A weird laugh comes out of me too.

I stand up and take the book out of her hands, turning it over like it will tell me more.

"Archer...you wrote a book and used my name and you didn't tell me?" My voice gets louder with each word and her eyes are huge by the time I'm finished.

"Are you mad?" she whispers.

"Am I mad? Are you serious? I'm goddamn elated!"

I hold up the book and put my hand on her waist. She worries her bottom lip with her teeth and I lean in and tug it loose with mine.

"This is your book?" I ask.

She nods.

"My God. I am so fucking proud of you. Tell me everything," I say. I shake my head and laugh so hard. "You wrote a book and put my fucking name on it. God*damn*, Elle baby. Right under my fucking nose!" I laugh until I cry. "It Was Always You..." I laugh harder and she's laughing just as hard.

I flip through the book and see the names Ryder and Eliza and laugh even harder.

"It was right here under my nose all along," I say, clutching my side. "Oh my God. The audiobook I heard. Right?"

She nods.

I can't breathe from laughing.

"Sorry. Get to talking...I'm just in shock over here."

"So, I wrote a book..." she says nonchalantly.

That sends us wheezing for another two minutes.

"And it's about what would have happened if we'd ended up together."

That shuts me up.

"Woman," I say, shaking my head. "You—"

I set the book down and kiss her. It's one of those *swoop her back and kiss her until she's limp as a noodle* kind of kisses. When I lift her upright, she fans her face and dries her eyes.

"I didn't think anyone would read it, but it blew up...practically overnight. It went to number one in the whole Amazon store, and a few months later, it hit the *USA Today* list. I have an agent. Book two is coming out in a couple of months..."

With each new statement she says, I have a physical reaction. My fist is at my mouth, I put my hands on my head, I have to lower them to my knees...I'm a mess.

"Fuck. *Me!*" I yell. "You've become a bestselling author overnight and you haven't told a soul? How do you sleep at night with news like that roaming around in there?"

I wave my hand around her head and she bites her lower lip, grinning so big.

"Wait...so what was that phone call?" I ask.

"I've worked really hard to keep it a secret...obviously. My parents are going to flip, Rhodes. It's one thing to disappoint them with the skimpy cheerleading outfits and sexy dances, but this book...it's where all of my hopes and dreams and pent-up sexual frustration went. I started writing it when Carrie was pregnant with Levi and I'd write every night for weeks and then it would be too hard to deal with reality, so I'd set it aside. Carrie's even in there...as Sabrina." She puts her head in her hands. "She's going to find out," she groans. "The people from church...everyone in town. If they don't already know." She groans again. "So, Calista found out because she'd emailed asking Zoey to do a signing at Twinkle Tales, and when I responded, I did it through my iCloud email from my phone. That was her on the phone, and apparently she wasn't the only one I made the same mistake with that day. I also emailed an influencer who wanted to have me on her podcast and she put two and two together. I'm sure the two of us blowing up online helped because it's all over the place now, and just a matter of time before everyone knows."

"You don't need to worry about what anyone thinks. It's your work and I'd be proud of it no matter what, but for it to be so successful—that's huge, Elle. You should tell the whole world with pride."

"I should've asked permission to use your last name," she says.

"Are you kidding? That's my favorite part."

I back her into the wall and lift her arms over her head. Her tits jut out and I thrust into her, wishing we were naked right now, but her leggings are the next best thing.

"Are you gonna read the book to me now?" I ask, my voice raspy.

"Hell, no," she says.

"Oh, I think you are," I tell her, kissing down her neck. "I think you need to read me every word to make up for the fact that you wrote a goddamn book and became a fucking sensation without letting me know!"

I must have yelled the last part because my parents and Levi come charging into the room just as I'm hiking Elle's leg over my hip.

"What's all the commotion? So much yelling going on! We were too curious," my mom says.

If she's flustered about seeing us making out, she doesn't show it. Amara knows how to keep her cool.

I go to the box of books and open it, taking two out and handing them to my parents.

I nod at Elle like *come on, let it out, baby*.

"I wrote that book," Elle says softly.

My mom does know how to lose her cool after all. "*What?*" she gasps.

When Elle nods, my mom starts dancing around the office and goes over to hug Elle, squealing.

My dad goes over to hug her too. "This is amazing, Elle. Congratulations." He holds it up, studying it proudly, and shakes his head. "Wow. Just incredible."

"I've seen this book all over the place!" Mama says. She points at the last name. "This is what caught my eye." And then it's all smug struts. "Mm-hmm, look at that. That's our girl." She looks at me and points. "And *you* better go ahead and make it official."

"Mama!" I say, laughing.

Elle's cheeks turn bright red, but I just grin.

I'm so ready to marry this girl.

CHAPTER THIRTY-NINE

BREAKING THE INTERNET

ELLE

Now

RHODES and I drive over to Weston and Sadie's place. I'd messaged the girls asking if we could meet up as soon as possible, and Rhodes was already in the middle of a group chat with the guys, so when Sadie invited us over, Weston invited the whole crew. Rhodes' parents were happy to watch Levi. It's nice that it's a holiday week; otherwise, I'm not sure we could've all pulled this off on such short notice.

My inbox on every social media platform is growing by the minute, and I don't know what to say to any of them. My agent calls while we're on the way to Sadie's and tells me to just sit tight until we can come up with a public statement. I'll call her when I get home later.

I'm all nerves as we pull into the driveway. When Rhodes stops the SUV, he reaches over and takes my hand.

"It's going to be okay. All of these people love you and they're going to be so excited. I'll be with you—if you want me—when we talk to your parents too. They'll have to get through me first if they want to say anything negative."

"I'm so glad you know. I would have been *mortified* if you'd found out before we had worked through our feelings, but keeping this from you has been so hard." I grin at him. "And not sharing why I can suddenly pay for things. Last month I made more than I've ever made in all my jobs put together...in one month! Granted, I've never had jobs that paid great, but still!"

He's laughing as he opens the door.

"And here I've been so worried about your finances and frustrated that you never let me help," he says.

Weston opens the door and lets us inside.

Caleb runs over and looks around. "Wheh's Yevi?" he asks.

Levi adores the way Caleb says his name.

"He stayed with his grandparents this time, buddy," Rhodes says. "You'll see him soon though, I promise."

We walk back into the living room, where it's quiet, when suddenly I'm assaulted with colorful silly string spray coming from every direction.

I gasp and try to duck, but they're relentless. The girls

are all aiming their bottles at me and laughing their heads off.

"Zoey Archer," Sadie yells. "How in the world did you keep that from us?"

Tru is bent over, laughing too hard to grab another can fast enough. I run around the room and they chase me with it. Calista and Stephanie are in on it too, and the guys laugh at us from the sidelines.

"Your meetings are more fun than the Single Dad Players," Penn says. "I think I want to join your group."

"Not so fast," Henley says. "You wormed your way into our group. You are not getting out of it that easily."

"Tell us everything," Sadie says, coming over to hug me.

She pulls silly string out of my hair and I pull it out of hers. I hug her and then Tru and Stephanie.

"I saw it on TikTok right before I came," Stephanie says, "and asked Tru if she'd known all along."

"No idea," Tru says, pretending to glare at me.

"I didn't even know until she accidentally emailed me from the wrong account," Calista says.

"I felt so bad for keeping it a secret from you guys, especially when you were talking about how much you loved the book. First of all, I'm still in shock that it's been so well received, so to know that it found its way into your bookstore, Calista, and that you all read it...I still can't get over that! If I could have kept it contained to only you guys knowing forever, I would have."

"Have you talked to your parents yet?" Calista asks.

"No. I just told Rhodes a little while ago. When you let me know that word had gotten out, I told him, and his parents know now too."

"What do you think about having a superstar girlfriend, Rhodes?" Calista asks.

"I am fucking ecstatic," he says, putting his arms around me and pulling me close. "I've wanted her to write ever since the first time I read something of hers. I knew she had a gift back then. The fact that it's such a huge hit is just..." He leans in and kisses the side of my head. "I'm so fucking proud I don't know what to do with myself." He laughs. "Right under our fucking noses."

The guys congratulate me too and Penn says he'll add it to his reading list.

"You have a reading list?" Weston teases, as I'm saying, "Oh, that's okay. You really don't need to read it."

"I want to," he says.

"Are you a reader?" I ask.

"No, but what better way to start reading than to start with yours? I can pull your book out and say I know the author."

He's teased more about it, but my phone vibrating makes everyone look at me.

"I really don't want—" I groan, as my phone buzzes with texts again.

Then it rings. I ignore it. I pick it up and cringe. I don't recognize the number.

"People are messaging like crazy. I haven't even looked at all the videos about me. I'm scared to look."

"It's pretty fun, actually," Calista says. "But now they're putting two and two together and thinking maybe this story is about Rhodes."

I make a face and look at Rhodes, who has a smug, shit-eating grin taking over his entire face.

"So glad we'd worked this out before this news came out," I reiterate, motioning between the two of us. "I need to let my parents know before someone else tells them about it...if that's even possible."

"You're an adult, honey," Stephanie says. "I know you try really hard to do what your parents want. You're a good daughter. They should be proud of how smart you are, how kind and beautiful, and how much you love them and care what they think. But I lived for so long in a house with a husband where I couldn't do anything without wondering how he would take it or how he would verbally beat me up over it. I know your parents aren't doing that exactly, but anyone who shames something you're proud of..." She squeezes my hand. "I don't care if it's your parents, or your children, or friends, or strangers on the internet...you hold your head high and be proud of who you are."

"Thank you, Stephanie," I say, hugging her again. My voice is wobbly as I wipe the tears dripping down my face. "I needed to hear that."

"Well, we're proud enough of you for the whole world, but from what I'm seeing, you've got some serious love going on out there." Calista holds her phone up and waggles it.

"If you need to go and talk to your parents, you can always come back here and keep celebrating with us after, you know, if you need a boost," Sadie says.

"No pressure," Tru adds. "If it's a rough one."

"You guys are the best. I'm the one who begged you to see me in a hurry. I don't want to miss the party."

"Oh, we'll keep partying over this. And now that the word is getting out, we should have a signing at Twinkle Tales," Calista sings.

"Yes," Tru says. "We have to! And Bree would totally want to be there too. I got her to read the book and she's as obsessed as we are."

"You guys are the best. I'm so lucky to have you. Thank you. Thanks for not hating me for keeping it a secret from you. It wasn't because I didn't want to tell you. And I'm really glad you know now. I do think I need to see if my parents are free to talk."

They nod and I hear the guys talking about The Single Dad Playbook stuff. I'd much rather get my greedy hands on that book than message my mom right now. That stuff is gold.

I hear back from my mom right away.

> MOM
> We're home. Come over.

When Rhodes and I say bye to everyone, I let them know I'll keep them posted.

As soon as my mom opens the door, I can tell I'm in trouble. We step inside and no one says a word. She walks us back to the family room, where Bernard is sitting with my parents.

"Why does this not surprise me anymore?" I say when I walk in.

Mom motions for us to sit down and we sit on the loveseat across from my dad and Bernard. It's tight with Rhodes' large frame, but I'd be holding onto him even if we had all the room in the world.

"Don't blame Bernard for this," my dad says. "My phone has rung off the hook for the past half hour. He's dealing with it the same as we are, trying to do damage control."

"How does it involve Bernard when we aren't even together? I'm with Rhodes now, so Bernard doesn't belong here. My business certainly doesn't involve him. And what part of me having this career requires damage control for you?"

My dad gives me an exasperated look. "You've lived in this house, honey. You knew before you did this that it would affect us. It doesn't look good for the pastor of a church to have a daughter writing—such explicit filth. I don't even know what to say..."

"Well, you don't really have to say anything except maybe, 'That's my daughter and what she does doesn't reflect what I believe,'" I say after a long pause. "I'm making a living as an author. It's been even better than my wildest imagination. It's my fault that it's such a shock to you now because I've sheltered you from knowing how I really felt about...a lot of things. From dance to clothes to writing openly about sex, and the list could go on. I respect you and how you raised me, and yet, I don't choose to live the exact same way. I understand if you can't be happy or excited about it, but we don't have to talk about it at all, really. I can keep my work life private—"

He snorts when I say *private* and I grit my teeth, knowing what's coming.

"This isn't private at all. Your life is about to be on display. Apparently, from the passages I saw, there are no holds barred. I didn't even know you knew how to curse so well...and the sex scenes. Well..." He shakes his head. "Do you know what they're going to say about this at church?"

"I have a pretty good idea, but according to Calista, a lot of the people from church also can't wait to know when Zoey Archer's next book is coming out. So maybe you're gonna be all right."

"I really wish you guys would just be proud of her," Rhodes says, gripping my hand. "Elle is the best person there is. She's loving, giving...kind. Even when she does things that you don't agree with, you can still be proud of the person she is. You do things she doesn't agree with, but she's proud of *you*. Love each other, you're all you've got. And if you can't do that, Elle knows she's got me and my family. We'll take care of her and we'll love her the way she deserves."

My dad scowls. "We love our daughter."

"Okay, then, love her. *Truly* love her. Unconditionally. Unconditionally means there is nothing she could do that would keep you from loving her. End of."

Dad's jaw is clenched. "She knows I love her!" He looks at me then. "Of course I love you—I always will and it *is* unconditional. But, that doesn't mean I can't say my piece when you do something I don't approve of!"

I grin. "I think it's safe to say I know what you think about something without you saying it. As you said, I've lived in this house. I've heard your sermons."

"So what you're saying is shut up?"

"No, I'm hoping we can get to a place where we have healthy boundaries. Where we feel safe being who we are with one another and know that it won't be a constant battle when we're together." I take a deep breath. "And a good way to start would be by ensuring that Bernard isn't here when I am."

"Why are you so hostile toward me? We were together for a long time. You must still feel something to have all this anger," Bernard says.

I turn my attention on Bernard only long enough to say, "I assure you I feel absolutely nothing romantically toward you, Bernard. I'm not your business, so stay out of mine."

I look at Rhodes and nod slightly. He stands and holds out his hand for me. "Should we go home?"

"I would love to," I say.

I go over and hug my dad and then my mom. I don't acknowledge Bernard. He doesn't belong in this conversation, so I don't want to give him the satisfaction of even looking at him.

"I love you," I tell my parents.

And we walk out.

I message the group thread.

> Thank you for celebrating with me. 🩶 It didn't go so well with my parents and I think I need to get home and do some damage control with my agent. I love you all SO MUCH.

Carrie is in the driveway when we pull up.

"Are you kidding me?" I say before we get out. "I guess I may as well get it all over with in one night. Word travels fast in a small town, but seriously, this is crazy. I thought I had at least a few days for this to spread."

We get out of the truck and Carrie gets out, leaning against her car.

"What are you doing here, Carrie?" Rhodes says.

"I came to see what's going on here," she says, tilting her head toward me. "It's time you tell me the truth. You guys are together now."

"Yes, we are," he says. "It hasn't been long, and I would have talked to you when we were able to."

"I've known," she says. "And it is so wrong of you to keep this from me when our child is going to be with her all the time. You should have given me the consideration. You made that statement the other day that you would expect me to, and you are so full of shit."

"I meant it," he said, "and planned to talk to you about it as soon as we were able to openly because of the Mustangs situation. But as I said, it's not like you don't know Elle. From the time Levi was born, she's been part of his life."

"You guys have been sneaking around this whole time. You think I don't know that? Coming over here all the time and Rhodes rushing off to your condo..."

"Wait...did those pictures come from you?"

She gives me a smug smile and I want to shake it off of her. "I'm so tired of you and your self-righteous act. You've always thought you were so much better than me." She shrugs. "But I'm not going away. Levi is *mine*, and you're not going to take over now that you're finally in Rhodes' bed." She takes a step closer and points her finger at me. "You are *not* Levi's mother and Rhodes will be bored with you soon anyway."

Rhodes steps between us. "You don't speak for me, Carrie. And not that it's any of your business, but I'll just say it so we're clear. There is not a chance that I will ever be bored with Elle. I'm in love with her and I will spend the rest of my life showing her all the ways. Understand now that you can't ever speak to Elle like this again. You need to go. Go home and stop spying on us," Rhodes says.

"It's easy to do when we're all living here in the same town. I see you coming and going."

"I'll be letting the guards know to not let you through the gate anymore," Rhodes says.

"You can't keep me from my son!"

"You need to be really careful right now," Rhodes says. "You're set up really nicely in your house and paid above what I'm required to pay for child support. You're saying threatening things now? I'll be informing my lawyers about it. I've made this all very easy for you, the lifestyle you have right now, and I can turn it around just as fast."

"How dare you turn all this on me? She's the one trying

to get away with breaking the rules when you're not even supposed to be seen together. Why are you upset with *me*? And this whole thing with the book. You think I don't know I'm in there? I could sue you for talking about me like that." She tries to get around Rhodes and he blocks her.

"Carrie, go home," Rhodes says.

"I'd really hoped we could be friends when I first realized you were going to be in Rhodes' life, but you've made it impossible," I say. "Let's be adults here, Carrie. I'm not trying to take your place with Levi. I'll never do that. But I do have my own place in his life, and I wish you respected me enough to be okay with that. I'm no longer cheering with the Mustangs, so there won't be any more sneaking around." I cross my arms. "You should know by now that I'm not going anywhere. And I'll be taking steps immediately to protect myself, so don't fucking threaten me. How about we each take a step back and not go to this dark place ever again?"

Her defiant stance has dissolved and she looks like all the helium has been let out of her. Deflated.

"You're not welcome here anymore," Rhodes says. "I'll have my lawyer contact you regarding the new arrangements for Levi's drop-off and pickup."

"Rhodes, that's not...please, don't—" she says, starting to cry.

"Until you can prove that you're not going to pull this threatening shit again, that's exactly the way it's going to be."

He motions for his guard and Mitch materializes. He opens her car door and when she gets inside, he closes it. Rhodes puts his arm around me as we wait for her to leave. We wait until she pulls out of the driveway before we go inside.

"There have been times I thought I saw her car outside your gate or near my condo," I say, things becoming a lot clearer now. "That night we kissed, I think she was outside your gate."

He curses under his breath and calls his lawyer.

CHAPTER FORTY

BEFORE FRIENDSGIVING

RHODES

Then

RAP-RAP RAP-RAP-RAP RAP

I opened the door and Elle rushed past me. I frowned and turned, following her into my living room.

"Elle? Are you okay?" I already knew she wasn't. She

hadn't even looked at me yet, but in that brief second that she flashed past, I didn't miss the splotchy cheeks.

Not to mention, we weren't really supposed to be around each other. I'd had to see my best friend only in passing or with our group of friends for months now and even *that* was breaking the rules. I fucking hated it.

"I know it's mid-season right now and we're not drinking, but I could really use a drink," she said.

I avoided alcohol from June to February, and now that she was cheering for the Colorado Mustangs, she did too.

"What's going on?" I asked.

"I've just had the most frustrating night of my life." She paced in front of my bar and then stopped and reached for the vodka. She looked around like she didn't know what to do next and then opened the small beverage refrigerator and grabbed a ginger ale, opening it and the vodka and pouring both into a glass at the same time.

"Okay, so we're doing this. I could've made you something...fancier."

She took a long gulp and shook her head. "Nope, this will do."

"Talk to me, Elle. What happened?"

I pulled down the bottle of Jameson and poured a double. It had been a hard stretch, worrying about Henley's injury. He was getting better, but it didn't seem like he'd be back and that hurt. Losing hurt. After being on the top for so long, it fucking sucked to see it all go down the toilet.

But missing Elle had become a constant ache. Seeing her out on the field looking like perfection was torture, teasing me with how close and yet how far she really was. Watching her talk and laugh with our friends was even more so. I didn't want to share her when I couldn't have any time with her myself. I needed her in front of me, being with *me*, and not just on the phone.

"My day started off with a grueling practice. Lisa was on a tear today. She hated the way Tracy looked on one of her Instagram posts and went on a long tangent about our public persona. I swear, I wish we could just dance and leave out everything else because I really don't like the *everything else*. And then I get to my parents' house and guess who's there? Yep, Bernard."

"What the fuck? When will they stop doing that to you?" It made me fume, the way her parents kept trying to force the issue about Bernard.

"I don't know. I thought I had made it clear to all that I was never going back to Bernard, but he was there and professing his love. Get this." She held up her hand adamantly. "He asked me to marry him in front of my parents. I said no, of course." She lifted her eyebrows and did a mocking bow.

"Hell yes, you said no. What the fuck is his problem?" I said, livid now. "I didn't think the man had balls until now. And now he needs to shove them up his ass and get the fuck out of here."

She laughed. We clinked glasses.

"I will cheers to that," she said.

We both took a hearty drink.

"How are you otherwise?" I asked.

"Good. Everything's good. Life is busy. I just...I really needed this," she said.

"I did too. I miss you so much, Elle."

"I miss you too," she groaned. "I have to stop myself from calling you all the time because now that I'm not seeing you on a regular basis, I think of a million things I've got to tell you and there's no outlet for it. I hate it."

"I hate it too."

We both took another sip and I moved around to the other side of the island so I could lean against it next to her. I bumped her arm with mine.

"It sure is good to see you tonight. I can't even tell you how happy I am that you're here."

She leaned her head on my shoulder. "Thanks for always being there for me. I love you."

"I love you too, Elle baby."

She sighed and I turned so I was facing her. I set my glass down and put my hand on her cheek, looking into her eyes.

"Are you gonna be okay? Is this all too much? Do you want me to have a little talk with Bernard and set him straight?"

"No, I can handle him. It just made me so angry. I wasn't up for it today. But you don't need to do anything about it. Just be you, and be here for me to talk it out, like you always are."

"And I always will be," I said.

She swallowed hard and our gaze held for several long seconds, until it became a weighty, heavy feeling in the air. I glanced down at her mouth and when my eyes flicked up to hers, she was staring at mine. I didn't think about it. I leaned in and kissed her, and it was like heaven touched earth. My heart soared. My brain exploded in fireworks, and when she put her hands in my hair and kissed me back, I thought I could die right then and be a happy man.

But then she pulled back.

"Rhodes. We can't. Wh-what are we doing?" she stammered.

"Doesn't this feel right to you?" I asked.

"Just because it feels good doesn't mean it's right," she said.

"Everything about you and me is right."

"Why now?"

"Because I've been desperate to kiss you for so long and I don't want to wait another second."

She groaned and stood on her tiptoes to kiss me. Her fervor matched mine, letting me know she craved this as much as I did.

My hand fisted her thick hair and my other hand slid up her body, feeling the outline of her breasts as my hand spanned her waist. She gasped into my mouth and I rocked into her. She arched into me and I hitched her leg over my thigh so she could feel me better, and she moaned the sexiest sound I've ever heard.

"You feel so good," I said against her mouth.

She was wearing a cute dress from visiting her parents and I was thrilled she wasn't wearing tights. When she arched into me again, my hand went under her dress so I could touch her silky skin. I teased my way up her thigh and when I reached her core, she clutched my head and kissed me harder.

I felt dizzy with all she was giving me. It had been so long since I'd done this with anyone, but this...*this* was brand new. This was what I'd always wanted.

I rubbed circles over her panties as she whimpered and her head fell back when I pushed her panties aside and touched her skin.

"Rhodes," she cried.

"Does that feel good?"

"Best thing I've ever felt," she whispered.

"I want to make you feel so good, love."

"You are."

My fingers dipped inside of her while my thumb kept swirling the circles. I kept that steady pressure going, stroking her until she was riding my fingers. Her eyes met mine and they looked glazed and drunk with lust. I had never seen anything more beautiful in all my life.

"Yes," I said. "Fuck, Elle, you're so beautiful. I fucking love seeing you like this."

I could feel her getting closer and closer and I didn't let up. Her hand went from my waist to my dick and she palmed me over my sweats. And when she went over the edge, it was so fucking glorious, I went with her.

There was a long suspended moment of peace before her body stiffened and she blinked up at me with more awareness. The lust cloud was gone and her hand dropped.

"Rhodes," she said, her voice cracking.

I adjusted myself and she looked down, eyes widening when she saw the wet spot on my pants. I made a face.

"Felt too good, watching you come, feeling your hand on me," I said. "You felt incredible."

I reached out to touch her face and she stepped away, smoothing her dress down.

"Rhodes...I can't believe...why did you do that?" Her face crumpled and I was horrified to see tears in her eyes.

"You said it was the best thing you've ever felt," I said in confusion.

"It *was*. But it's us. *Rhodes*." A tear dripped down her face. "Sometimes I feel like you're all I have. I know I have other people too, but you...you're everything."

"You're everything to me too—"

"I've gotta go. This can't...we can't. This was a mistake." She shook her head. "I shouldn't have come here tonight. And Rhodes, no one can know about this. I'm sorry."

She left and my heart shattered a little more.

But she'd given me a taste of what we could be, and I couldn't give that up. Not now.

CHAPTER FORTY-ONE

RINGING IN THE NEW YEAR

RHODES

Now

IT'S the day before our game, and I'm about to take off for the hotel when I hear Elle on the phone.

"I appreciate your call, but...no, thank you. You don't need to change the rules for me. I broke the rules and I deserve to live with the consequences. It would have been fun to be with everyone in this last home game, but I will be on the sidelines cheering my man on, front and center. No more hiding for me," she says and laughs.

My man, she said.

Damn, am I ever glad I didn't give up on us after that crazy night we first kissed. She almost had me convinced we'd never be together like that again, but here we are.

When she hangs up a few minutes later, I come up behind her and kiss her on the cheek.

"Cheering your man on, huh? Is that me?"

"No, it's Bowie. He's hot and isn't always demanding attention." She jumps when I tickle her side. "Of course, it's you," she yelps. "It's always been you, remember? There's no one else for me."

"That's more like it," I say, dipping her back and kissing her.

I'm so grateful I didn't stop hoping for this with her one day. It's better than I could've imagined.

When I lift her back up, she pokes my side and laughs when I jerk to the side.

"That was Lisa. She called and said I could dance with the team tomorrow. She didn't *realize* I already had such a big career going on the side and that they were lucky to have me on the team. She hoped there were no hard feelings and said an exception could be made for this game. She also said she hoped I'd do a charity event as Zoey Archer with them in the future. I said I'd be happy to consider any charity events when the time comes."

"Look at that, her groveling with you and you turning her down."

"Yeah, it just felt manipulative after all was said and done. I'm tired of doing my own part in the manipulating and tired of putting up with it from anyone else. I'm ready for things to just be out in the open."

"You won't get any complaints from me there," I tell her, kissing her.

THE GAME GOES WELL. We win. One more game unless we make the playoffs as a wild card. But when I see Elle after we win, not too far from the field, I run over and motion for her to come down the rest of the way. She does, jogging down the steps until she's at the bar separating us. I lift her over the bar and she laughs, wrapping her legs around my waist as I kiss her lips off. It's everything.

"You look so fucking good in my jersey."

"Way better than my cheer uniform any day."

"Mmm. I will miss that uniform."

When we pull away, we realize we're on the jumbotron and that the crowd is going nuts for us.

She leans her forehead on mine and laughs. "Guess the secret's fully out now."

"Thank. God."

THE NEXT FEW days are spent around the house, hanging out with the family. We have a great time with my parents and when Elle is out of the room, they help me work on a plan for New Year's Eve.

Bogey is getting better each day. So far, the little guy is a pro with potty training and he's only chewed one thing but stopped once we gave him toys he was interested in. The only complaint I have about the little dude is that now, when Elle and I start to fool around, he whines at the bed like he should be able to come up and be part of things. Thankfully he's still too short to try to watch us.

No sir, I don't think so. I'm not into sharing.

Elle thinks it's hilarious. The poor guy's in love with her about as much as I am and follows her around like she's his favorite person. I get it, I really do.

Carrie apologized for how atrocious she acted the other night. I told her she needed to apologize to Elle too, but she hasn't, so I don't buy into her apology. I wanted to call the sheriff about the pictures, but Elle said not to because she wanted to just forget about everything Carrie had done and move on. I had a call with my lawyers just in case Carrie does anything else to jeopardize our custody arrangement. I've remained firm on the drop-offs and pickups happening elsewhere, and so far, she hasn't fought it. I hope she won't stir up any more trouble, but I'm not counting on it.

I work on this New Year's Eve plan and have a restaurant reserved for the evening. The guys are all in; each one has a job. Weston is in charge of inviting everyone. Penn is in charge of getting the menu in order. Bowie is in charge of getting security lined up. I don't think Carrie or anyone else will cause any trouble, but I want to be on the safe side. Brock hasn't been a problem, but again, security knows to keep an eye out for him. Henley is in charge of the flowers and decorations—well, Tru and Bree are actually working on that more, but he's helping deliver all of it. My parents are bringing Levi and watching him for the night so we can stay out late.

I invited Elle's parents too, but I haven't heard back from them yet.

Earlier in the afternoon on New Year's Eve, I tell Elle I'm going to run an errand and I go to her parents' house. I had called earlier to set this up and knew that unless they were busy, they were too courteous to say no.

Once I get to the house, I'm greeted warmly and it already feels better than the last time. I'm glad fucking Bernard isn't around.

"Thanks for calling," Doug says. He looks around and his shoulders drop a little. "Oh, Elle's not with you."

"No, sir, she's not. I wanted to speak with you and Louisa alone."

"I was hoping she would be. I'd like to talk to her. I've thought a lot about what you said last week, and you're right. How can I preach love and forgiveness if I'm not loving my own daughter the way I should? And I forgive her for doing—well, you know in my eyes, what she's doing is a sin, and I forgive her for that."

"But she's not sinning against you. If what she's doing is a sin at all, she's sinning against God, not you, so it's really between her and God."

He points at me. "Maybe you should be the preacher," he says, laughing sheepishly. "You make a good point."

"I'll let you keep to the sermons," I tell him, laughing.

We walk back to his study and Louisa pokes her head in the door to say hello.

"Hi, Louisa. I'd really like to talk to you both about Elle and me," I pause and take a deep breath.

I really don't want to botch this.

Louisa comes in and sits down and both of them look at me, waiting.

"I love Elle. Completely. I'm *in* love with her…and have been since the day I met her, and that's never stopped. I've made mistakes. I should have let her know right away how I felt, but we had this pact going where we would not cross that line of friendship because it meant so much to us. I tried to hold to that and didn't do such a good job in my agony of not being with her the way I wanted to be. I should've just held on and waited for her." I lean forward. "And then Carrie got pregnant, and I knew I couldn't mess around like that again. I wasn't sure Elle and I would ever be on the same page, but there's no one else I want."

I take another deep breath and can't tell from their expressions how they're taking this.

"Come to find out, she loves me back. She has all along too, which is just fu—flipping fantastic. And now that we're finally here, I don't want to waste any time...I want to marry her." Another deep breath. "But I would love your blessing. I know that it means something to Elle to have your blessing, and therefore, it means something to me too. I hope you'll give it and maybe even be happy for us when we get married...if she'll have me." I wipe my forehead because I'm suddenly sweating like I'm in a goddamn sauna. "I kind of think she'll say yes," I finish quietly.

No one says anything at first. And then I hear Louisa sniffling. She reaches over to grab a tissue and wipes her face. Doug comes around to the other side of his desk and leans on it in front of me.

"I appreciate you coming and talking to us," he says. "You guys are old enough to not need our permission by any means, but it means a lot that you want our blessing, and I'm giving it to you now." He looks at his wife and she nods. "We're giving it to you. I know we've pushed another agenda on Elle and it's time that we stopped doing that. If she says yes to you, we will support it one hundred percent."

"Thank you, sir. That means so much." I stand up and shake his hand and then move toward Louisa.

She stands up and hugs me. "Thank you, Rhodes," she

says. "I'm sorry things have been strained between us. We want to be part of your life with Elle."

"Thank you. You're invited to Rose & Thorn tonight. I've rented out the place and I'm asking her to marry me there with our family and friends present. I would love for you to be part of it."

"We'll be there," Doug says.

I hang around a little longer, talking football with Doug. When I head home, relief and adrenaline courses through me.

I'm ready.

AND I'M STILL ready when we pull into the parking lot of Rose & Thorn. According to the group thread, everyone's already here as planned. Elle looks too gorgeous for words in her little black dress, as I help her out of the SUV.

But I get hit with a case of extreme nerves.

I didn't think I was capable of this feeling anymore, but when it comes to Elle, I just always want to get it right.

"Oh my goodness, everyone's here!" Elle says as we walk inside.

She hugs the girls and when she realizes her parents are here too, she stops and turns to look at me, eyes wide.

"Did you know everyone was coming? You didn't say it was a New Year's Eve *party*!"

I cough and try to make it sound like a chuckle. "Yeah, I knew everyone was coming."

The restaurant has a few tables cleared out, and our friends and family are either sitting already or standing around talking. There are flowers everywhere.

"Everything looks so pretty. How fun!" She does a

double take when she sees my face. "Are you okay?" She studies me closer when I don't say anything.

I have trouble swallowing all of a sudden.

"Rhodes? Are you sick? You don't look so good. I mean, you look *so* handsome tonight, but...are you okay?"

I swallow again and pick up a menu specially made for this event and fan my face. She pauses to look at it.

Rhodes and Elle's Menu, it says.

Her eyes are wide.

"It's our party?" she says, looking around nervously.

"It's our party," I say, nodding.

Her eyes light up and she smiles, leaning over to kiss me. I lead her to the table in the middle before I lose my nerve. I sure hope she likes this surprise. She's been talking about everything being out in the open, but this might've been going too far.

She hugs Greer and Wyndham from Serendipity on the way and waves at Calista across the room.

There's an elaborate flower arrangement from The Enchanted Florist on the table and Elle leans in to smell it before sitting down.

"Everything looks so beautiful, Rhodes."

"You do most of all."

Her cheeks flush and I feel a surge of energy, my nerves falling away.

I sit down and there's a microphone next to my place setting. I lift it, making sure it's on, and stand up.

"Hello, everyone. Thank you for coming! I promise I'm not gonna do much talking tonight, except to let you know a little bit about why you're here, and then we'll just have fun for as long as we want. Thanks to the staff at Rose & Thorn for opening up your place to us tonight. You've been so accommodating and we're grateful. And thanks again to all of you for coming to spend New Year's Eve with us."

I look at Elle and she's smiling up at me with such love in her eyes, it nearly takes me out.

I take a deep breath and look around the room, my eyes landing on the table next to ours. Levi is sitting between my parents, and Elle's parents are across from them. My dad gives me a slight nod, encouraging me.

"I think any of you who have spent any significant amount of time around me knows how much I love Elle Benton."

The room erupts into cheers, mostly coming from Penn, but Henley, Bowie, and Weston are doing their share too, as well as the other guys from the team.

"For over thirteen years now, we've been best friends. And it's only been recently that we have crossed over into much, much more."

Again, with the whistles.

I laugh and Elle does too. She looks so happy and it emboldens me to keep going.

"I, for one, could not be happier about the much, much more. We had to keep it on the down-low for various reasons, so a lot of you have not even seen us together as a couple yet, but I wanted to let you know that I am *so in love with this woman!*"

The room explodes again, and I hold up my hand, shushing everyone.

And then I get down on my knee and there's a holy hush, the only sound being Elle's gasp. When I take the ring out of my pocket, her eyes are already filling with tears. She holds onto my hand and I can feel hers trembling.

"Rhodes," she whispers.

"Is this okay, love?" I ask.

"It is so okay," she says, her laugh shaky too.

"I love you with all my heart," I tell her.

"Say it in the mic," someone says.

We laugh and Penn rushes over to hold the mic for me.

"Do you wanna be heard?" he asks quietly.

"I want the whole world to hear this, but it's only important if you do," I tell Elle.

"Let us in on it," Penn says.

Elle laughs and nods happily. "May as well, since we're all here."

"Now you're talking." Penn holds the mic close to both of us.

"Being with you has made me the happiest moth—man alive," I say, rushing to clean up my language with the kids that are here. "Every day with you has always been enough, but now, every day, knowing that you love me back, holding your hand and living by your side...there isn't even a word for how happy and content you've made me."

There are lots of *Awws* over that.

"But the one thing that would make me the happiest is if you'd be my wife. What do you think? Will you marry me, Elle Benton, and be mine forever?"

"Yes," she says, crying. "Yes!"

I glance over at Levi and he's ready. He runs over with a flower and lifts it up to Elle.

"Be mine foh-evah too?" he asks.

She leans down and puts her forehead against his. "Forever and ever."

He beams and I think there are a dozen sniffles going around the room, mine included. We all share a hug and when Levi goes back to sit down, Elle pulls my face to hers and kisses me.

Everybody claps as we kiss and kiss and kiss, until someone says, "Get a room!"

We break apart, laughing, and I hold up the five-carat princess-cut diamond ring. She stretches out her hand and I slide it on.

"Oh, it's so pretty, Rhodes," she whispers. "I love it. I love you."

I kiss her again, and then I stand up, leaning over her chair, until she lifts onto her feet and stands flush against me, returning my kiss. The girls throw flower petals on us.

That was their idea, not mine. But I have to admit, it's a festive touch.

We spend the rest of the night with our family and friends. The tables are cleared out and Rose & Thorn turns into a makeshift club. We dance with Levi for a long time and then my parents take him home to put him to bed.

When the countdown begins, I yell, "There's no one I'd rather be bringing in the new year with than all of you!"

In Elle's ear, I add, "But as long as you're with me, I have all I need."

My lips are on hers when the clock strikes midnight.

And then I take her home and ring in the new year in the best way—making love to her all night long.

Life is just getting started.

CHAPTER FORTY-TWO

READER FRIENDS

ELLE

Now

A COUPLE WEEKS LATER, I am sitting in the back of Twinkle Tales trying to calm down my jitters over the signing about to take place. Rhodes has sent me a video of the long line that's outside the store and all the way down the street...which isn't helping to calm me down.

Calista comes in with a bottle of champagne. She opens it and pours me a glass with a flourish before pouring her own glass. We tap them together.

"Thank you so much for doing this," she says. "I know you wanted to stay hidden forever and you could have, even after the word got out. But I'm really, really glad you're doing this for me."

"You're doing this for *me*," I say. "Thank you for being such an advocate of my book and for selling it, even before you knew it was mine."

"Girl, your book sold itself," she says, laughing. "I'm just so glad I found it and that the rest of the world did too. And so, so glad you're my best friend."

"Me too." I hug her and fan my face, feeling myself getting emotional.

"You ready for this?"

"I think so."

Rhodes knocks on the door and comes in, looking like a kid. We celebrated his birthday a few days ago and had so much fun, but you'd think today was his birthday for how excited he is. Levi pokes his head around Rhodes' leg and runs in when he sees me. I hug them both. Rhodes kisses my cheek.

"You look beautiful. Don't be nervous. You're going to do great," he says.

"Oh, that's easy for you to say," I whisper.

"Do we have time for a quick surprise?" he asks.

"How quick?"

He pokes his head out the door and motions for someone to come. Tru and Henley pop inside.

"I snuck them in," Rhodes says.

"Aw, hi guys!" I hug them and then pull back, eyes crinkling. "Okay, what's going on here? You look extra glowy."

Tru holds up her hand and I'm blinded by a gorgeous sparkly diamond. "We're getting married!"

"Ahhh," I yell. "This is the best news!" I hug both of them. "Oh my goodness, you guys. I'm so happy for you both."

"The hundredth time I asked her finally worked," Henley says, kissing Tru's hand. "She said yes last night and we were waiting to tell everyone in person. But the guys got it out of me when we got here." He laughs.

"And I knew you'd want to know right away," Rhodes tells me.

"Absolutely." I hug Tru again. "So, so happy."

She can't stop smiling and she nods. "Me too. Sadie was there when Henley told the guys, so I just need to find Calista now and tell her the news!" She looks at the clock. "Oh yikes, I think the doors will be opening soon."

After more words of encouragement and hugs, they go get a seat. Calista leans in long enough to say she's going to open the doors. I pace back and forth until she calls me out there, and I'm surprised to see all the chairs filled, plus people lined up on either side and as far back as they can fit. There's a rush of applause when I walk out and Calista starts the event, asking a few crowd-warmer questions. I see people from church and my former co-workers from the chiropractor's office. Yesterday was my last day working there. Almost all of the cheer team is here, despite the football players in attendance, but Lisa isn't here, so maybe they'll be okay. There are a lot of people I don't recognize too, and based on Calista's questions, it sounds like many drove here from all over Colorado. One came from New Mexico, which is just shocking. The signing was only announced a week and a half ago.

I expect the Q&A to be a little awkward, but Calista

makes it easy, and the readers are so nice. The time goes by fast and it's mostly questions about the storyline and characters...until the very end.

"So, is it true that this story is based on your life?" It's a girl who looks too young to be reading my books, and my cheeks burn with the thought of her reading the spicy scenes.

"Uh...well, it's the story I *wished* was happening in my life," I say.

There are a few laughs and I look at Rhodes.

"And then the story that really happened after writing my book is even better."

That gets applause, and Rhodes sends me a look that makes me excited to get back home. Once the signing starts, I'm not nervous at all. I sign books for hours, smiling till my face hurts and posing for so many pictures. But it's one of the most fun nights I've had, especially for any kind of work event. If this is what work feels like, it's exhausting, but so fun. Rhodes keeps coming over to check on me throughout the evening. The guys are here to keep him company and to show their support. They're so cute standing in line to get their signed copy.

At the end of the night, the crowd thins out and we reach the end of the line.

Becca comes up and says, "Hi, Elle! This is my new friend, Poppy. You can sign her book. You wrote it!"

"Hi, Becca. Poppy! So good to see you again!"

I grin at Poppy briefly before smiling at Becca again. Bowie tried to get her to call me Zoey for the day, but it didn't take...and I don't mind one bit.

"Any friend of yours is a friend of mine, Becca, but turns out, Poppy and I have already met."

Becca's eyes get big. "You know my friend Poppy too?"

I nod, turning my attention to Poppy. She is *gorgeous*, with long blonde hair and pale blue eyes, but what strikes me most is how sweetly she smiles at Becca. Becca is one of my favorite people in the world. She's so lovable, and it seems like Poppy has immediately recognized that.

"But I didn't know I was meeting Zoey when I met you!" Poppy says, laughing.

"Surprise!" I hold up my hands and Becca mimics me. She's the cutest.

"Thanks for introducing us again, Becca," Poppy says, smiling at Becca.

I was charmed by Poppy the first night we met, but now I really am.

"I loved this book." Poppy clutches the book to her chest, closing her eyes and smiling for a second.

Becca laughs and picks up an extra copy and mimics Poppy. We both laugh.

"Well, thank you so much. I sound like a broken record, but I still can't believe people are reading it."

"I will read whatever you write," Poppy promises.

"Me too, Elle. I read what you write too," Becca says.

"When your dad says you're old enough to read these, I'll give you your own books, okay?"

"Dad, Elle will give me books when I am old enough," she yells.

Bowie rushes over.

"That's excellent. Inside voice, please, Becca," Bowie says quietly.

"Dad, this is Poppy, my best friend, and Elle loves her too. Elle loves me and Poppy."

I watch as Poppy's cheeks flush when she looks up at Bowie, but she surprises us both by holding out her hand for Bowie to shake.

"Poppy Keane. It's really nice to meet you."

"Bowie Fox," he says curtly. "Nice to meet you too."

"Your daughter is delightful," she says. "And I'm a huge Mustangs fan. Great win last week."

I stand watching this exchange, enjoying every second. The way Bowie is so stiff and awkward and Poppy is so bubbly and animated with maybe a teensy bit of flirtation laced in there...it's everything my little romance writer heart adores.

"You are de-lightful," Becca says loudly, as if she's trying out a new favorite word. "Sorry," she whisper-shouts, "you are de-lightful."

Bowie is not indulgent with his smiles unless it's directed at his daughter or one of the other kids in the Single Dad Players group. He hands them out freely to them, the rest of us have to earn them. He's the sweetest man I know, but open and bubbly, he is not. He smiles at Becca now and then is stern by the time he looks at Poppy again.

"I want Poppy to come over for dinner," Becca says.

Poppy's cheeks flush again.

"We can't ask strangers over for dinner, Becca."

"Not a stranger!" Becca's voice is rising again. "She is my *best* friend."

"That's very kind of you to invite me for dinner," Poppy tells Becca. "I've already had dinner, but I'm really glad I got to meet you."

Poppy reaches into her purse and takes out a card, handing it to Bowie. "Maybe Becca would enjoy coming to one of our activities sometime," she says.

Bowie barely glances at the card. "She's very busy."

Poppy laughs. "It sounds like it. She was telling me about her schedule. Whew!"

"I have time, Dad."

This time I laugh along with Poppy. Rhodes walks over and puts his arms around my waist.

"What did I miss?" he asks.

"This is Poppy."

"Nice to meet you," Rhodes says.

"You too," Poppy says, smiling at us.

"Poppy and Becca are trying to talk Bowie into some kind of activity," I say, enjoying the look Bowie shoots my way.

"Oh, what kind of activity?" Rhodes asks.

"I'm an Adaptive Recreation coach for kids at Briar Hill," she says. "And there are just so many fun things that we do…swimming, track and field, gymnastics, volleyball… flag football."

"That sounds *perfect* for Becca," Rhodes tells Bowie.

"Perfect!" Becca nods. She pats Poppy's arm. "I like Poppy."

"I like you too, Becca," Poppy says, smiling back. She looks at Bowie. "There's no pressure at all. But it could be fun. One of the first things Becca said when she introduced herself to me over there," she points toward the front of the store, "was that she can run faster than you."

Rhodes cracks up. "She's got you there. You're fast, but Becca can *run*."

Becca smiles at Rhodes proudly.

Poppy shrugs. "There you go. Meant to be." She looks at Becca. "I'm so happy I got to meet you today." She glances at Bowie and away quickly, the flush on her cheeks deepening. "And your dad."

Bowie's expression doesn't change, but is that a slight flush to his cheeks that I'm seeing as well?

"Hug!" Becca says.

Bowie's eyes widen, and Rhodes and I look at each other in surprise. Becca's incredibly social, but she's as choosy with her hugs as Bowie is with his smiles.

"I would love a hug," Poppy says.

They hug and after she walks away, we all stand there watching her go.

"I like her," I say.

"Me too. I like Poppy," Becca says.

"And she liked you..." Rhodes tells her. Lower he says, "And did you detect that flirting she was doing there, my man?"

Bowie scoffs. "She was not flirting."

"Was she flirting, Elle?" Rhodes asks.

"She was definitely flirting."

CHAPTER FORTY-THREE

IDEAL

RHODES

Now

WELL, our season is done. It's sad to think that we didn't make it to the Super Bowl after we had that winning streak for so long, but honestly, I'm so happy to be spending my days with Elle and Levi that I'm not too broken up about it.

While Elle is writing each day, I teach Bogey tricks.

He's so damn cute and he's freaking smart too. When Levi's home, he helps with Bogey and loves giving him treats. So far Bogey can sit, stay, roll over, shake, fetch...and there's a new trick that I'm working on in secret.

Bogey's reward is these beef chews that he would do anything for, and my reward is the way Elle laughs in delight when we've shown her the latest trick he can do. It's the greatest motivation.

When she pops out of the office, her hair on top of her head and dragging toward me like she's almost sleepwalking, I put my arms around her and lead her to the kitchen where I've made her a healthy dinner. The more bites she takes, the more energy returns and midway through dinner, she bounces back and gets chattier.

"What's your ideal wedding scenario?" she asks.

"You, standing in front of me, saying 'I do.'"

Her eyes turn melty. "Well, yes, but...I'm a given. What else?"

"Our family and friends there? Although I'd marry you if it were just the two of us in the middle of nowhere. What about you? What do you want?"

"I know what I don't want...I don't want a long, drawn-out engagement or a big wedding. I don't care where we are. I'd like Levi and our parents and close friends to be there. Nothing else matters. I mean, except you."

"Well, yeah," I say. "I'm a given."

We grin the same sappy grins at each other.

"Do you want to get married in your dad's church?"

She shakes her head. "No, but I would love for my dad to marry us. I'd rather get married by the water or on a pretty mountain...or surrounded by both. Your yard is gorgeous...out by the little waterfall."

"Your yard too," I remind her.

She's put her condo on the market and I love that she's never going back there. And not just because of Brock. I love that she's officially moved in with me for keeps.

"But it's cold out there right now," I remind her.

"True...which pushes us back a few months at least," she says.

"I loved it when you said no long, drawn-out engagements."

She giggles. "You did, huh?"

"I thought it was a brilliant statement and I wholeheartedly agreed with it."

"Okay, well, we'll either have to get lots of heaters and dress warm or look for a destination spot where everyone wouldn't mind traveling."

I snap and point at her. "I love the way you think."

She laughs as she takes her plate to the sink. "Okay, cornball. Thanks for dinner. Thanks for feeding me." She kisses me and my hands land on her amazing ass. I thank God for it daily.

"It's the least I could do after keeping you up all night. Were you able to get the words you needed?"

"I need to finish this chapter and then I'll be done for the night."

"Okay, I'll be here."

She goes back to her office and I search for beautiful locations for weddings. When I start looking at pictures online, it hits me and I don't know why I didn't think of it before.

I wait until she comes back out of the office and have a plate of fruit cut up for her. When she's in the zone, my girl forgets to eat.

"Shut me down if you don't love it, but I've got an idea for our wedding."

"What?" she asks, popping a grape in her mouth.

"My parents' place in California..."

Her eyes widen. "Rhodes! It's perfect. I've always loved that house. The view. The beach is right there. Do you think they would be okay with it?"

"Are you kidding? I don't even need to mention it unless we think we want to do it, because they'll both jump all over it."

"Let's do it. I love this idea."

When we FaceTime to talk to them about it, they're ecstatic, as I knew they would be, but when I say we want to do it as soon as possible, two things happen.

"Are we having a baby?" My mom claps her hands.

"No, Mom, just excited to start our life together as husband and wife." I laugh. I glance at Elle and lift an eyebrow. "You don't have anything you want to tell me, do you?"

"Not yet," she says, laughing. "But you'll be the first to know."

My mom immediately goes into super planner mode with all these amazing ideas that sound daunting, until I stop her and say, "We don't want a production. Right?" I look at Elle and she nods. "I think we'd both be happy eloping if it meant all of you would be there...but being home on the beach sounds even better."

"Exactly," Elle said. "We're thinking simple and elegant. Out on the beach for the ceremony, and then for the reception, we could add another long table by the one already out there and everyone would fit."

"You don't want something a little...fancier?" Mom asks.

"Flowers, good food, and the scenery...with all of you. That's all I need," Elle says.

"That's easy," Dad says, beaming. "Let's do this!"

WE WOULD'VE NEVER BEEN able to pull this off during football season, but since it's not, two weeks later, we're all heading to L.A. in a private plane for the wedding. Bogey is a hit with the flight crew. When the flight attendants go on over how cute he is, I open his carrier and have him shake their hands.

The little dude is a showstopper.

The whole crew is on this plane—my guys and their girls and kids, Elle's parents—all of us.

I wasn't sure how Weston and Sadie would feel about doing this so close to their wedding since it's only a month off. They're going for more of a traditional wedding than we are, so I thought it could be a stressful time to try to leave. Elle and I went to them first and asked them to tell us honestly if the thought of going to California for the weekend stressed them out too much. Sadie's pretty chill about the wedding stuff and Weston just wants to make her happy, and they both said they were so ready to get away and put all the wedding planning on hold for a few days. They also said they were so excited for us to finally be together that even if it did stress them out, they wouldn't miss this for the world. Elle and I promised to work our asses off doing whatever they needed for their wedding and it was all settled.

With our wedding at the end of January and Weston and Sadie's the end of February, we'll have time to go on our honeymoons and still be back to enjoy plenty of home life before next season begins.

There's very little to do when we arrive. My parents have worked hard and have hired people to help, so we have the time of our lives relaxing and hanging out together. The night before the wedding, I follow Elle up the stairs to our bedroom. I have a hard time keeping my hands off her ass anytime I'm behind her, so I get grabby and she laughs, jogging up the stairs faster. But when she reaches the door, she turns and puts her hand against my chest.

"Huh-uh," she says, shaking her head. "You've gotta sleep somewhere else tonight."

I look at her incredulously. "There is no vacancy in this house tonight. We are filled to capacity." I put my hands on her waist. "And I'm dying to fill *you* to capacity."

She smirks but doesn't budge.

"You're really saying you can sleep a night without me?" I pout.

She makes a face. "Well, I'm not saying it sounds *ideal*, but we both need our rest and it's a tradition..."

"Of all times for you to get traditional..."

"I know." She grins, her hands winding around my neck. "Just put up with me, and tomorrow and the rest of our lives, we will sleep in the same bed as much as we're able to. Think of this as a night before the big game where you have to go get your rest so you're all prepared to win."

"I just want to touch down with you right now. I want to bring in our wedding day the right way."

She laughs. "You are so ridiculous."

"And you love me for it."

"Yeah, I do." She squirms when I nuzzle into her neck.

"Okay, how about I just make it real quick?"

"How quick are we talking?"

"Long enough to make you come twice instead of five times."

"I guess that would be okay," she says, pulling me inside the door.

I start by closing it behind her and getting on my knees.

When she's yanking my hair and biting her fist to keep from crying out, I let her ride her orgasm out before picking her up and tossing her onto the bed.

"Is this fast enough for you?" I tease.

"Well, you haven't made me come twice yet, so we'll see."

"Oh, *you*..." I tickle her stomach and she cackles and then covers her face with the pillow.

She peeks out at me. "Get after it, mister."

"Yes, ma'am."

I bury myself inside her with one long stroke and she trembles around me.

"Rhodes," she whispers. "How does it always feel so *unbelievably* good?"

"I don't know, Elle. I think you and I were made to do this."

"Think of all that time we wasted," she says.

"We're not wasting time anymore," I tell her.

And then I make her come again.

I WAKE up next to Penn on my wedding day. It was either crash Penn's bed or Bowie's, and Bowie was too sprawled out to make that work. Penn glances up groggily when I get out of bed.

"Was it good for you?" he croaks.

I laugh. Dude's got jokes even half asleep.

"I've had better," I say. "*Much* better."

"Ouch."

I actually slept and feel pretty damn great.

Today's my wedding day, and I'm gonna marry my best friend, the woman I love.

After getting my shower, I have breakfast with my dad and the guys, and eventually, we go upstairs to Henley's room. He's in the biggest room besides my parents' and Elle's, and we all get ready in there. Elle and the girls are getting ready in our room.

"Are we ready for this?" Henley asks.

"I'm so ready," I tell him.

He hands me The Single Dad Playbook and I smile when I see it.

"I just wrote a little something in there for you. I know we don't have much time, but when you get a minute, you can take a look."

"Thanks, man, I can't wait to see what you wrote."

"I might have added something in there before that," Weston says.

"Well, someone should have given me the memo," Penn says.

"Same," Bowie grumbles, but they're both smiling.

I open it and see Weston's entry first.

> *When I told Caleb we were going to*
> *see Uncle Rhodes get married,*
> *he said, "He mawwied Elle."*
> *I said, "Yes, he's marrying Elle this weekend.*
> *We get to go to the wedding."*
> *And he said, "No, he mawwied Elle."*
> *Apparently, he's thought all this time that*
> *Rhodes and Elle have been married all along.*
> *It makes me think maybe his intuition*
> *will take him places.*
> *~Weston*

I SMILE AT WESTON. "I love that kid. If he would've just told me this months ago, it would've saved me quite a bit of agony."

Everyone laughs.

"Where are Caleb and Levi?" Penn asks.

"My mom is playing with them for a bit. She'll bring them up in a few."

I look back at the book to read Henley's entry.

When you realize the woman you love is having your baby, there's nothing like it. Every experience I've had before has been great. I loved Bree, but it was different. The love I feel for Tru is transcendental and she's having my baby.
~Henley

"WHAT?" I yell. "Are you saying what—oh my goodness! When? How long?"

The guys grab the book and we all start yelling at once.

"Congratulations, man." I hug him hard.

"Thank you. I know it's not the typical Playbook entry, but it felt fitting today to say it. When you and Elle start your family, it's just gonna complete everything you've already built together. Levi will be amazing with a baby brother or sister, and you'll have the experience you missed out on before. My situation is a little different because what I had wasn't bad with Bree," he says, "but this pregnancy is so much more, because Tru and I are meant to be together. I can't wait to see you become a dad again."

"Let's get him married first," Bowie says. "Then they can work on that."

Laughter fills the room and I don't think I can take much more happiness than this.

But then I see Elle walking toward me on the beach. Her hair is down and her white dress is beautiful, but it's her face that enraptures me. Her smile is radiant. I'm not ashamed to say that I ugly cry.

Her dad officiates the ceremony and I honestly don't even comprehend what he's saying because *Elle is standing in front of me.* She's looking at me with so much love, so much trust, and I see all the versions of her I've loved throughout our life together. The girl in college with baggy clothes who would drop anything to hang out with me. The first time I saw what she'd been hiding under all those baggy things. The tears over hurts and stresses and when we'd see each other after a long time had passed. The excitement that lit her eyes every single time I walked into a room. The devastation when I told her I'd gotten another woman pregnant. The first time I kissed her, made love to her...all of it whirls at me and I grip her hand tightly, wanting to remember all of it, but to be right here, feeling this moment now most of all.

When Doug turns to me to say my vows, I can only hope that I'll be able to speak without losing it.

"*Elle.*" We smile at each other. "When you entrusted me with your friendship so many years ago, you gave me the greatest gift I've ever known. It was so great that I did whatever I could to protect it, sometimes failing miserably, and often at the cost of experiencing what we've found here today. Your friendship will always be what carries me, what fills me with joy, but it's your love that sustains me and fills the void that was always missing. It feels like we've already lived a couple of lifetimes in this relationship, but I'm most excited for this next one we're starting together. I promise to love you, honor you, and cherish you through every single step of us. I promise to make you happy, do whatever it takes to make it right when you're not, and to always keep you fed."

She laughs through her tears at that last one.

"You're forever for me. I've waited a long time to say that you're mine and I'm going to be grateful until the day that I die that I can say it now. And I'm yours. Always have been. Always will be."

She dabs her face with a pretty handkerchief and clears her throat. Her voice is shaky when she starts.

"Rhodes, it was always you." She gives me a wobbly smile. "I have always been in love with your smiling eyes, your generous heart, the way you can make me laugh so hard, and how everyone is comfortable around you. Don't get me started on the dimples..."

Everyone laughs and her smile brightens as her eyes never leave mine.

"We said we were *just friends* a lot, but it's never fully been true because the word *just* will always be too limiting when it comes to you. You are larger than life, unfairly beautiful," she pauses when everyone laughs again, "and have the biggest heart I know. And you have always, always loved me so well. I will love you with everything in me for as long as I live. I will honor who you are with pride, and I will cherish this life we have been given. I promise to never keep another secret from you again, I'll always put you and Levi first, and I will be present so I don't miss a single moment. I'm yours, forever. Always have been. Always will be."

I wipe the tears from my face and bring her hand to my lips to kiss her fingers.

"I love you," I whisper.

"I love *you*."

"Do you have rings to seal these vows?" her dad asks.

I grin and look back toward the house. Bogey's there, sitting like a good boy. I had one of my cousins watching to make sure he stayed in place. We put a wooden runner down the beach so Elle's dress wouldn't get dirty walking down the aisle, and when I whistle, Bogey displays the trick we've been diligently working on. He hops up on a skateboard and that short little leg bobs out to get him started. He rolls toward us to the delight of everyone, especially Levi and Elle, and stops when he reaches me. I bend down and take the ring that's tied around his bowtie and give him a treat from my pocket.

"Good boy," I tell him. "You are a fine specimen and an exemplary ring bearer, dear sir."

Elle leans down to pet him, still laughing. "And the cutest thing I've ever seen."

I turn the skateboard around and he skates back to where he started.

"Amazing," Elle says, cracking up again.

She beams up at me and I hold onto my heart because she steals it every time with that smile.

We exchange rings and when we're pronounced husband and wife, I don't wait for her dad to tell me I can kiss her. I tilt her back and kiss her as if I've got all the time in the world to do it.

Because I do.

EPILOGUE
MILESTONES

RHODES

Now

WE CELEBRATED Levi's birthday when we were on our honeymoon, but two weeks later when we're back, we have everyone over to celebrate again. Levi's having the time of his life, running around the house with all his friends, and the guys and I take a few minutes to catch up on the deck. I have the fireplace on and the outdoor heaters, so it's perfect out here.

"Look at you, looking all vacationed and loved up," Henley says, nodding at me.

"It's a good look on you," Weston adds.

"Now that I know what you look like after having sex all the time, I can't believe I ever believed you were keeping up with me," Penn says.

We all laugh.

"You're a fool," I say, still laughing as I hug him.

"Welcome back," Bowie says.

I pat his cheek. "Did you miss me?"

He holds his fingers together a tiny bit and makes a face.

"A lot then, is what you're saying," I say, nodding. I point at him. "Have you taken Becca to visit Poppy yet?"

He frowns. "No, and I'm not going to." He sits across from me and sighs. "But she's driving me crazy about it."

"What's it about? Who's Poppy?" Weston asks.

"A woman who really liked what she saw when she looked at Bowie," I say.

He groans. "Not true. Let's move on. How was your honeymoon?"

"It was incredible. I took Elle to meet my family in Cape Town. We stayed there for five days at The Silo Hotel, which was incredible. My parents watched Levi, and we saw him a little bit those first few days but still had time to ourselves. Then my parents kept Levi at my mom's cousin's, while Elle and I escaped by ourselves. It was perfect."

"Sounds like it. And if that smile is anything to go on..." Henley grins.

"How's Tru feeling?" I ask.

"She's doing pretty well so far. She says she's getting a little pouch, but it's so barely there." He laughs.

"You look so happy, man. It's really great to see," I say.

"So do you," Weston says.

I point at him. "And your wedding...I'm back now. Put me to work. I will be at your beck and call."

"There's really not that much to do until a few days before the wedding," he says.

"I'm in for all of it."

Bowie sets The Single Dad Playbook on the table and I'm the first to grab it.

"I've got a thing or two to get off my chest." I look at Bowie and Penn. "Did you write in it after the wedding?"

"We did," Bowie says.

I go to their entries and laugh when I see Penn's.

I thought I was jealous of Rhodes
because of his player status.
(Later confirmed that I shouldn't have been.)
And because he has such a gorgeous best friend
when I'm stuck with you guys.
(Just kidding. You're all hot as fuck.)
And because he has the cutest, funniest
four-year-old I've ever seen.
(This is still completely true.)
But then I saw the trick
he taught Bogey the freaking Bulldog
for the wedding and realized
I have things to be jealous of
that I didn't even know about.
Where can I get a dog
and do you think I can teach it how to count cards?

~Penn

I LAUGH MY ASS OFF. "Get a dog and I'll teach it whatever you want it to know."

"How did we not know you're a dog whisperer?" Weston says, cracking up.

"I never saw that coming," Bowie says.

"It's all Bogey, man. He's a genius." I shrug. "I also have some tricks I can pull out when the time comes to get you started," I assure Penn.

I look at the book and turn to what Bowie has written.

*Sometimes I think I'm not capable
of raising Becca by myself.
Not because she's a girl
or because she has a disability
or because I'm exhausted enough as it is...
or maybe it's for all those reasons put together.
But I think it's simply because
it's such a monumental responsibility
we've been given
to raise a child
and we hope that we don't do anything
to mess up their future.
And then Becca will hug me and say,
"I love you, Dad."
Or I'll read these entries...
And I know that I'm not alone at all.
~Bowie*

"FUCK," my voice cracks. "You got me, Bow. I thought I got all my crying out at the wedding."

The guys start laughing.

"Cried like a *baby*," Penn says.

"Every time I looked at you, you looked like this." Henley curls his face up and we all laugh.

I toss a napkin at him.

"Best day of my goddamn life," I say. "And it's only looking up from here."

There's an entry from Weston too and I shake my head as I start reading.

> *Caleb and I have been practicing*
> *our wedding day faces every day...*
> *Because only one of the Mustangs can do*
> *the ugly cry at their wedding,*
> *and that was Rhodes.*
> *~Weston*

"FUCK YOU VERY MUCH," I say, laughing my ass off.

"It was a beautiful sight," Weston says, wiping his eyes.

Once the laughter has died down, I grab a pen and write a few lines I've been thinking about.

> *Levi's birthday has always been hard for me.*
> *Sometimes I blink and can hardly remember*
> *how I felt when he was a baby.*
> *The fatigue was always taking over*
> *a lot of what should be memories now.*
> *Each phase has been so fun and so challenging,*
> *and just when I think I've gotten used*
> *to this parenting thing,*
> *we enter a new phase.*

*But I've decided to enjoy all the growing pains,
mine included.*
~*Rhodes*

ELLE POKES HER HEAD OUTSIDE. "Did Levi find you yet?"

"No, last I saw him, he and Caleb were playing that fishing game he's loving. I told him I'd be out here, but I haven't seen him."

"He's ready for the cake."

I nod. "I'll be right in."

We stand up and go inside and Levi runs up to me, wrapping his arms around my legs.

"Cake, Daddy. Elle says theh's cake!"

"There sure is," I say, bending down to swipe him up in my arms and kiss his neck until he's cackling.

I put him up on my shoulders and bounce him to the cake. Elle lights the candles and Levi claps his hands in excitement. I place him carefully on the stool in front of the cake and everyone gathers around to sing. He looks around, listening to us, and his little cheeks probably ache from how hard he's smiled all day. My sweet boy.

"Thank you," he says when we're done singing, and that's it, I'm done.

I wipe my eyes, and Elle comes over to lean into me after he blows out the candles.

"How's my softie husband doing?" she asks.

"I'm a mess."

"And I love you for it," she says.

I cut the cake and Elle passes the pieces around to everyone. Calista jumps in and helps her. When I've got my piece, Levi wants to clank our forks together. I don't have the heart to tell him it's probably not the best sanitary practice to clank forks. I'll wait to tell him another day.

There's plenty of time for that later.

For now, I've got a wife and a son to enjoy.

They're everything I could ever want.

Want more Rhodes and Elle? Click here!

https://bookhip.com/NQCQBKA

For Bowie's story
pre order Wicked Love Here!
https://geni.us/Wickedlove

WICKED LOVE COMING SOON!

**Chapter 1
Our Story**

BOWIE

I follow my daughter into the house, feeling like I'm letting her down with each step. She's tearing through the kitchen with her new present in her hands, rushing to showcase it in her bedroom.

"Look, Dad," she calls.

I follow her up the stairs, stopping when I reach her room. She turns to see if I'm there and when she beams up at me, I smile back and move closer to her.

"Look, Daddy, I put it next to my favorites," Becca says.

She places the "present"—a picture frame of a woman and a young girl next to the others. This one has a woman with long blonde hair, and the young girl's hair is like Becca's, light brown. We can only see them from the back.

They're walking by a lake with lots of fall leaves on the ground. All the other pictures have young girls with light brown hair, but the women's looks vary. The common thread is that all the pictures look like a loving mom with her daughter.

I've tried to talk Becca into filling these frames with pictures of her with friends or of the two of us. There are pictures of us together, and one of Becca with my parents, but the dozen or so frames of moms and daughters are her "collection" and she refuses to replace the stock photos.

"Where is my mom?" she asks quietly, almost to herself.

"I don't know, sweetheart."

It kills me every time she asks, which is often. Once her mom, Adriane, decided to leave, she made a clean break. I don't get check-in calls or updates on what she's doing with her life, she just disappeared.

She taps the picture. "This looks like Poppy and me."

I press the bridge of my nose between my fingers. Ever since Becca met Poppy Keane at our local bookstore, Twinkle Tales, a couple weeks ago, she hasn't stopped talking about her. Poppy didn't help matters by suggesting Becca come to Briar Hill where she works as an Adaptive Recreation coach. Since Becca has Down Syndrome, I'm already familiar with Briar Hill. They have an excellent reputation for all they do for kids with disabilities, but I'm hesitant to take my daughter, even knowing she'd love the activities they offer. Because of Poppy Keane.

Even though it's fairly typical of kids with Down Syndrome to accept and be friendly with new people, it still concerns me how quickly she attached to Poppy.

The frame with a lookalike Poppy and Becca is just another case in point.

She looks up at me. "We see Poppy again?"

I'm saved by my phone buzzing. I wave it. "This is Weston. I need to answer this. Can you be ready to leave for his house in five minutes?"

"Set the timer!" She hurries to hand me the timer we keep in her room and I set it for five minutes. I hand it back to her as I answer the phone.

"Hey," I say to Weston, giving Becca a thumbs up. "Everything okay?"

"Will you guys be hungry? We haven't eaten yet, so I was going to order some takeout."

"Becca and I ate at Starlight Cafe just a little while ago, but go ahead. We can come later if you want."

"No, come on over. We'll just do leftovers for us then since you've already eaten."

"Yeah, man, we're good. We'll be over there shortly."

I hang up and Becca holds up the timer.

"It's almost time," she says. "Time to see my pretty dress again."

It's wedding season for my best friends, who also happen to be my teammates.

"Tell me our story...about our framily," Becca says on the drive over.

She loves our friends with a passion and loves to hear me talk about our friends. We call them framily around our house. I'm fortunate to have friends who have welcomed us into their lives. We're closer to them than our biological relatives.

It's both sweet and heartbreaking that my girl craves family more than anything.

I take a deep breath, about to use most of my words for the day. I'm the quiet one in our friend group and everywhere else, but there's very little quiet time when Becca and I are together. She likes to discuss all the things.

"Okay, here's the rundown," I begin, same as I always do. "As you know..." I glance over at her and she's looking at me with her bright eyes. She has the sweetest smile. "I'm a linebacker for the Colorado Mustangs, and Weston Shaw is our quarterback."

"I love Weston, and Sadie is the *best*," she says.

"Yes, they're great. Weston and Sadie are getting married in a couple of weeks, and Caleb is two years old and adorable."

"Yes, he is," she says emphatically.

"Our tight end, Rhodes Archer, just got married a couple of days ago and is on his honeymoon right now."

"Oh, I love Rhodes! And Elle is the *best*."

I chuckle. "I think you could tell our story better than I could. His son Levi is four and also one of the cutest kids I've ever seen."

"Levi is cute," she agrees. "He has curly hair. He opens doors for me."

"Levi's a little gentleman, isn't he? And even Henley Ward, our wide receiver—well, *former* wide receiver now, after a serious ACL injury—is engaged now."

"I am sad Henley's hurt," she says. "I love him and Tru is the *best*."

I laugh again. She thinks all the women are the best. She's not wrong; they are incredible people.

"Henley and his ex-wife Bree have three daughters, Cassidy, Audrey, and Gracie, that we love dearly."

"So dearly," she adds.

If I don't say that every time, she's sure to add it.

"They're thirteen, nine, and six," I say.

"I'm nine soon," she says. "Me and Audrey."

The girls dote on Becca, and Caleb and Levi adore her

too. She's treated like a princess every time she enters the room and I fucking love it.

"That's right. All of you are growing up too fast."

"And you bonded..." she starts then pauses for me to continue.

"The guys and I originally bonded over football and the fact that we were all dads raising our kids by ourselves, but we can't exactly call ourselves the *Single* Dad Players anymore now that some of the guys are getting married."

"You're not married," she says, her lips puckering out.

"No, I'm not. We meet on the regular to talk about all things kids, life, football...and lately, a helluva lot about the women in *their* lives." I emphasize *their* because I need her to understand there will not be a woman in my life.

Her smile is long gone now and I focus on the road in front of me to avoid her scowl.

"You need a woman to talk about a helluva lot...on the reg'lar."

I clear my throat and charge forward, trying both not to laugh and to distract her from the topic of women.

"We have a book that we write in all the time, The Single Dad Playbook, where we exchange advice and stories when we're not together in person."

"And Penn too!" she says.

"I haven't forgotten Penn Hudson, our running back. He isn't a dad, but even he has developed a fatherly bond with Sam, a kid that he mentors. It started through a tutoring program, but Sam has become like family to all of us by now, right?"

"Right. Sam is eleven and so pretty," she breathes. "But Penn is the prettiest."

I roll my eyes and she sees it in the rearview mirror. Her loud laugh fills the car.

"Neither one of them are *that* pretty," I grumble.

"You call Penn pretty boy, Dad!" she argues.

"Oh yeah, that's right."

She leans back in her seat, satisfied.

Besides me, Penn is the only other single one at this point.

He sees a lot more action than I do though.

I'll be living and dying on the single dad hill.

"You're pretty too, Dad," she adds.

"Thanks, Tater Tot."

She giggles. She loves it when I call her that.

From the backseat, I hear, "I love you, Dad."

"I love you too, Tator Tot."

Damn near melts my heart every time, and she says Dad a lot, so basically I'm mush when my daughter's around. Have been since day one.

She's the only one capable of eliciting that in me. She proves I *am* human after all, I guess.

"I call you Daddy too," she says.

"Yes, my literal girl, and I love when you call me Daddy just as much."

When we pull into Weston's driveway, Becca claps when she sees Henley and Penn's cars.

"Our friends are here," she says happily. "Look, Daddy!"

I smile over at her. "Yep. And you, Cassidy, Audrey, and Gracie are going to be the prettiest flower girls who ever lived."

"We are pretty a lot," she says. "Levi and Caleb too."

I know she's thinking about Rhodes' and Elle's wedding now.

"You were *beautiful*, but you always are. I wasn't in any

weddings as a kid. Do you like being in all these weddings?" I ask.

"I like it lots." Her lisp is extra pronounced when she's excited and she's practically bouncing in her seat. "Sadie says we blow bubbles, but we wait until they say *I do*." She holds out her hands and bounces them with *I do*.

"That'll be fun."

We get out and walk to the door. I let Becca ring the doorbell.

Henley opens the door, holding Caleb. Caleb loves all of us, but "Unca Hen" is his favorite.

"Unca Bowie!" Caleb says happily.

I hold my fist up and he bumps it with his.

"Hey, you two, how's it going?" Henley asks.

"Great," Becca says. "Right, Dad?"

"Right." I nod, smiling at her when she looks back at me.

"Excellent." Henley grins and tilts his head to the side. "The girls just went into the family room, Becca. They're waiting on you to try on the dresses."

"I try on my dress now," she says, rushing off to the family room. She's moving so fast, she nearly collides with Weston. "Oh! Sorry, Weston! I want to be a princess."

He laughs and holds his hands out toward the family room. "Right this way, Princess Becca."

He walks with her the rest of the way, and Penn sticks his head out of the living room as Henley and I walk back with Caleb.

"There you are. Dude, preparing you now. Sadie's not giving up on this date business. Have you found a date for the wedding yet?" Penn puts his hand on my shoulder and squeezes.

"Not happening," I say.

Weston walks in then. "What's not happening?" he asks.

"A date for your wedding," I say.

"Oh man." He laughs. "Sadie really thinks you need to bring a date."

"Even if it wouldn't be fun for me?" I ask.

He grins. "She seems to think we could make it fun."

"I don't know where she's getting her information," I grumble. "I don't have a date and I have not planned to find one between now and then. Your wedding is just around the corner."

"Man, it can't come soon enough for me," he says, grinning. "I can't wait to marry that woman."

"I can't wait for you to marry her either...so you can get off our backs about a date," Penn says. "Women get weird around weddings. It's more of a time to get acquainted with a stranger in a hidden nook in the church rather than be all formal and make things seem more serious than they are..."

"Gross," Henley says, laughing.

"I'm kidding. I'm not that bad," Penn says. "Unless she's really beautiful..."

I roll my eyes.

When the girls come out later, they're hyper from getting the final measurements on their dresses. As they're making popcorn, Sadie corners me.

"So..." she starts.

I shake my head.

She pouts. "But I want you to have someone to dance with."

"I'll dance with whoever wants to dance...but I don't want to have to try to make awkward conversation during dinner. I want to actually enjoy your wedding."

Her face breaks out into a smile. "As long as you're

dancing, I'm good." She hugs me and then goes off to help the girls.

Weston smirks at me and I swipe my hand down my face.

"She's really hard to say no to," I admit.

"Don't I know it." He looks at Sadie with such reverent love in his eyes, it makes my heart ache.

I was in love once.

I don't intend on making that mistake again.

For Bowie's story
pre order Wicked Love Here!
https://geni.us/Wickedlove

ACKNOWLEDGMENTS

So grateful for all of you who read my books and send messages and make collages and write reviews...it makes my LIFE!

Special thanks to those who helped this book come together in the way that it did.

Christine Estevez, I have countless things to thank you for. With this series, especially, I have relied heavily on you, and I just love you so much.

Georgie Grinstead, thanks for a MILLION things. I love you beyond.

Katie Friend, your comments give me life.

Kalie Phillips, thank you for being an awesome sensitivity reader and reader of my books, period. Love you!

Natalie Burtner, you are the best and I love you. Thanks for keeping things running smoothly...and so much more.

Kelly Yates, thank you so much for going above and beyond as a sensitivity reader!

To my husband and kids, Nate, Greyley, Indigo, and Kira, I love you more than I can say. Your joy for me throughout all of this is the sweetest and I'm grateful for every day with you. Kira Sabin, the special edition artwork...it's amazing, just like you.

Kess Fennell, thank you for bringing my ideas to life with your artwork. You really belong up there in the family category. ^^

Emily Wittig, I adore you, and working with you is so much fun.

Laura Pavlov and Catherine Cowles, I'm so lucky to be doing this career with you, love chain! My favorite cheerleaders and fellow sprinters, thanks for being more excited for me than I am for myself. LOL

To the VPR team, I'm so grateful for you! Nina, Kim, Valentine, Charlie, Christine, Sarah, Josette, Meagan, Kelley, Ratula, Amy, Jill and Megan, thank you for EVERYTHING!

To the Lyric team, Kim Gilmour and Katie Robinson, it's been so fun!

Sean Crisden and Angelina Rocca, thank you for bringing these characters to life in audio!

And just because I love you and you put up with me in one way or another and have for so long and are my favorites...Christine Bowden, Tosha Khoury, Courtney Nunness, Gracelyn Szynal, Steve & Jill Erickson, Savita Naik, Claire Contreras, Tarryn Fisher, Winston, Troi Atkinson, Phyllis Atkinson, David Atkinson, Destini Simmons, Terrijo Montgomery, Jesse Nava...THANK YOU FOR LOVING ME BACK!

ALSO BY WILLOW ASTER

The Single Dad Playbook Series

Mad Love

Secret Love

Reckless Love

Wicked Love

Crazy Love

Landmark Mountain Series

Unforgettable

Someday

Irresistible

Falling

Stay

Standalones with Interconnected Characters

Summertime

Autumn Nights

Kingdoms of Sin Series

Downfall

Exposed

Ruin

Pride

Standalones

True Love Story

Fade to Red

In the Fields

Maybe Maby (also available on all retailer sites)

Lilith (also available on all retailer sites)

Miles Apart (also available on all retailer sites)

Falling in Eden

The G.D. Taylors Series with Laura Pavlov

Wanted Wed or Alive

The Bold and the Bullheaded

Another Motherfaker

Don't Cry Over Spilled MILF

Friends with Benefactors

The End of Men Series with Tarryn Fisher

Folsom

Jackal

FOLLOW ME

JOIN MY MASTER LIST...
https://bit.ly/3CMKz5y

Website willowaster.com
Facebook @willowasterauthor
Instagram @willowaster
Amazon @willowaster
Bookbub @willow-aster
TikTok @willowaster1
Goodreads @willow_aster
Asters group @Astersgroup
Pinterest @willowaster

Made in the USA
Monee, IL
18 April 2025